Escape
Book One of the Unchained Trilogy

By Maria McKenzie

Dedication
For Richard

Acknowledgements

To Lisa McKenzie – The best writing teacher ever! Thank you for your amazing insight and for stretching me as a writer! Thanks also for your superb editing.

To all of the incredible writers in my writers group: Elaine Olund, Melissa Booth, Miguel Trejo, Andrea Rotterman and Maria Ramos. This book could not exist without you!

To Paula McKenzie Nahm – My awesome mother-in-law! Thanks so much for the use of your sharp eye in the final proofreading!

Special thanks to Renae Denbow for another beautiful cover, to Earl Hughes for his wonderful feedback, to my mom for her valuable input, and to my husband for inspiring, as well as enriching the story!

Introduction
The Story of The Unchained Trilogy

Fade to white...Just who do you think you are? Steven Jordan thought he knew, until his grandmother, Selina Manning, threw a grenade that put his identity in question. She reveals a secret: her grandmother was a black woman, born a slave. Yet Selina has lived her entire life as white.

Will Steven ever accept this root hidden beneath his family tree, or choose to leave it buried? Uncertain of what he'll find, he delves into the past to learn where the secret began.

The Unchained Trilogy is an explosive three book series of love, deceit, emotional destruction and in the end, forgiveness. It spans a time period of one hundred and forty-two years, with Escape (Book One) opening the series in 1856, and Revelation (Book Three), closing it in 1998. Time does move fast in this family saga, and since there are several years to cover, some purposeful time gaps do exist to move along the narrative. For a brief overview of the entire trilogy, here's what to expect in every story:

Book I, *Escape*: The year is 1856. Lori is a black woman, born a slave, but Daniel Taylor, a young abolitionist from a wealthy merchant's family, falls in love with her, and risks his life to help her in a daring escape.

After overcoming torturous trials and challenges, Daniel and Lori have a family. However, their youngest daughter, the beautiful and treacherous Lavinia, chooses to pass as white. But will she ever find true happiness while hiding behind a mask?

Book II, *Masquerade*: Lavinia runs away from home at age seventeen to pursue a life of decadence as an actress. Married to a powerful showman in New York, Lavinia weaves one lie after another, doing whatever it takes to keep the truth about her "Negro" mother a secret.

Selina Standish, born during her mother Lavinia's second marriage, learns the truth about her ancestry as a young girl. But Selina is convinced by Lavinia never to acknowledge her "Negro blood." However, Selina finds this difficult after meeting her "Negro" relatives, whom she comes to love. Eventually, Selina makes a choice that binds her heart and troubles her future.

Book III, *Revelation*: In 1998, one hundred-year old Selina Standish Manning reveals a secret that she's carried for nine decades like a painful chain bound around her heart. Now, near death, Selina tells her family the truth about her black ancestry.

Her relatives are surprised by this revelation, and her grandson, Steven, struggles to accept that black blood courses through his veins. One moment he's an average white guy of European descent, and now this! Despite Steven's initial misgivings regarding the secret, he and the rest of his family are eager to hear what Selina has to say, and their lives are forever changed as the past is revealed...

Author's Note

Unchained was conceived in 1998 as I thought about how sad it would have been if my husband and I had known each other 150 years earlier. Then, being an interracial couple, we couldn't have gotten married. The rest of the story snowballed from there, and eventually swelled to over 700 pages! I worked on it off and on until finally completing it in 2008.

After seeing the movie *Titanic*, I decided to use flashbacks. I originally opened the story in 1998 with Steven learning the secret at the very beginning. Then the narrative moved back in time through flashbacks.

However, after letting it sit in my drawer for while, thinking it was too long to do anything with, I decided to turn it into a trilogy. Now flashbacks will only occur in part three (which does open in 1998). I hope you'll enjoy this ride through time and see how one family faded from black to white!

Maria McKenzie

Chapter 1
Wilmington, North Carolina
July, 1856

I can do this...I can do this...Lori repeated the words to herself as if willing them to be true. Under a brightly shining moon, she stood on the back porch of Rebecca Taylor's home and slipped the strap of a filled canteen around her neck. Lori tucked it to one side, then reached for the worn leather satchel at her feet and did the same. The cornbread and salt pork wrapped inside would last for about three days.

Miss Rebecca was dead now, leaving Lori with no alternative but to run.

You'd be a fool to try! Don't even think about setting off on your own, you'll never make it! Lori forced Daniel's protests from her mind, instead hearing the cicadas and crickets chirp around her. Daniel couldn't stop her because she refused to be dragged off to Dancing Oaks!

This was her one chance at freedom. *Don't go...you can't...*Again, Daniel's words played through her head—and this time, also her heart. For a moment, Lori hesitated. Her feelings for Daniel were silly.

He was Miss Rebecca's son, yet why had he been so adamant about her not trying to escape? He'd tried to convince his uncle to free her — but that hadn't worked, so now Lori was taking matters into her own hands.

I can do this, she told herself once more, and I won't get caught, I *can* do this. Seeing the glimmer of fireflies, Lori wondered, could she really? She was terrified. However, was she more terrified of trying to escape, or of being forced to work on a plantation?

Lori started slowly down the steps. It would take about three hours on foot to reach Laid Low Farm. She knew the way. Miss Rebecca and her family were abolitionists, and Daniel had taken Lori with him several times to Laid Low to give food to the runaways. Of course, they'd always traveled by wagon, but Miss Rebecca disapproved of Lori going at all. She'd said it was no place for a lady.

Laid Low Farm was where the fugitive slaves hid. There was a whole community of them living near its swamp land. Lori figured she could hide there for a short while, then head off to Canada.

She trembled. As Lori stepped from the last porch stair to the grass, her eyes watered. Why did Miss Rebecca have to die? Lori thought angrily. She was supposed to take care of me.

After inhaling deeply, taking in the scent of magnolia blossoms and the ever present odor of the manure muddled through the streets, Lori began to run. This was no time for tears. Holding the canteen and satchel close to her sides to keep them quiet, she pushed herself through the thick humid air. Perspiration began seeping through her kerchief and calico dress as she darted behind the large houses lining Walnut Street.

Once beyond the houses, she'd come to the woods, from there she could travel safely to Laid Low. Lori felt the warm night breeze press against her face. If Miss Rebecca hadn't died, she wouldn't be in this predicament, but Lori would manage to get herself out of it and live in freedom. That's what kept her going, built her determination and infused her with confidence.

Wearing brown brogans on her feet, Lori ran swiftly, feeling magnolia branches and azalea shrubs brush against her arms. But at the sound of a barking dog, she stopped abruptly. Afraid and deflated, Lori realized she'd only made it past the third house down from Miss Rebecca's. There were two more before she'd reach the woods.

Hearing the ground grinding of wagon wheels and the plodding of a horse's hooves, Lori knew it was the patrollers. Her heart began racing even more rapidly than it already was.

Paid weekly by some in the community, patrollers drove slowly and carefully each night, surveying the area for runaway slaves. Lori found a large azalea shrub in a clearing between the houses and crouched behind it.

For three nights she'd stayed up late listening for the patrollers. They usually made rounds about one a.m. But now it was past two. From behind the houses, she could hear male voices over the jingling of reins as they came closer down the dirt road out front.

"Why'd Elmer bark?" She heard one of them say. "It's quiet and I ain't seen nothin'."

"Maybe we'd best get out and take a look," another man said.

Lori's trembling turned to shaking.

"Maybe not. He ain't barkin' no more. Besides, he ain't all riled up like usual when there's a nigger runnin' loose."

"The dog was barkin' at somethin'."

"Well, there usually ain't no problems 'round these here parts."

"There's always a first time for problems. Niggers is always itchin' to run, even if they's treated good."

Lori heard what sounded like two large feet hit the ground. One of the men must have jumped from the wagon.

"I'm gonna take Elmer and have me a look around!"

"Git back up here, Travis," the other man yelled. "We already got a late start! There ain't no niggers runnin' loose here, but we just might find us some near the O'Reilly place. His niggers is always running off on account a how much he beats 'em."

"But I just got me a feelin'."

"Last time you had you a damn feelin' it was the clap!"

"Shut up! I'm gonna have me a look anyway!"

"Then go alone, but don't take the dog!"

"*I'm* takin' Elmer!"

"But there ain't nothin' out there, and the damn dog's just gonna waste time pissin' on everything!"

"Fine — I'll go alone!"

Lori could see the bright flame of the patroller's torch as he moved from the front of the street, on through the clearing between the houses. Lori sat still and quiet, holding her breath. But she prayed a strong silent prayer for God's angels to protect her.

For a moment the man hesitated, lifting the torch higher. Lori could see his hat brimmed silhouette clearly through the shrub. Slowly, he began walking toward it, crushing grass beneath each heavy footstep. When he reached the shrub he stopped. Lori began to feel the warmth of the flame as he leaned down.

"Travis!" The other man yelled. Travis turned toward his partner's voice. "If you ain't seen nothin' yet, there ain't nothing back there to see!"

The man, Travis, then walked away from the shrub cursing. "I'm comin'!"

As the man walked away, Lori exhaled. The canteen slipped a little. Lori clutched it quickly to stop it from making noise. But her slight movement rustled the shrub, creating enough of a sound to send the man back running.

"I knew it!" He yelled. "I got me one!"

Lori had no time to flee. In only seconds the man was behind the shrub. He still held the torch in one hand, and with the other, yanked Lori so hard, she felt as if her arm was pulled from its socket. But the pain didn't faze her. She was too frightened, although not too scared to fight.

"Let me go!" Lori tried to disentangle herself from the patroller's grasp. With her free arm she clawed at his chest, and then kicked his shins. He was skinny, not too tall, and reeked of moonshine. Determined to get away, she kept fighting.

"If you don't stop squirmin' around," the patroller said lowering the flame toward her skirt, "I'm gonna take this here torch and light your dress." Lori stopped struggling at the thought of being burned alive.

By this time the other man approached, dragging along a lazy looking bloodhound. The man smiled upon seeing Lori, the flame reflected blackened teeth. He dropped the dog's leash. "We can have us some fun with this one," the man said as the dog relieved himself near a tree.

"You first, I wanna watch." The torch man pushed Lori to the other patroller who immediately grabbed her around the waist and lifted her from the ground.

Lori kicked, screaming, "Get off me—you filthy, drunken trash!" This man was skinny too, but stronger, and the smell of alcohol on him more pungent.

The man laughed as he put a large calloused hand over Lori's mouth. "Got us an uppity nigger here!" Lori continued screaming, despite the rough smelly hand on her face. "The more noise you make," the man said over her protests, "the uglier this is gon' get 'fore we haul you off to the jailhouse!"

A gunshot rang through the air. The dog yelped and ran away. The man holding Lori put her down, but didn't release her. Another shot fired. This time the bullet kicked up dirt by the torch-bearer's foot. "Sheeit!" It was so close he jumped.

"What are you doing with my slave?" An angry voice called from the darkness.

"Just doin' our job, mister!" said the man with the torch.

"We done caught your nigger before she run away!" The other patroller still held Lori, but she'd ceased struggling, relieved to be rescued.

The torch reflected Daniel's face, angrily creased by the sight of the patrollers mishandling her. He carried a lantern in one hand. Shoving the pistol in the back of his trousers, Daniel said, "Let her go." The man holding Lori roughly pushed her in Daniel's direction. She ran quickly to him, but stopped just short of throwing her arms around him. "I'll handle things from here—gentlemen."

Daniel grasped Lori's arm brusquely and led her away. He didn't say anything as he dragged her back to his mother's house.

"Daniel, I—"

"Shh...don't say anything," Daniel whispered. "You've already created enough commotion for one night. We're lucky Uncle Elijah sleeps so soundly. When I left the house, I could hear his snoring all the way from the second floor. And hopefully, if the neighbors heard anything, they only thought it was the patrollers—doing what they're paid to do."

Once at Miss Rebecca's back porch, Daniel finally dropped Lori's arm, then placed the lantern on the steps. He looked at her for a long time, but said nothing.

"I'm sorry—" Lori began softly.

Daniel crossed his arms. "And I'm glad that's *all* you are!"

Lori's eyes widened and she put a finger to her lips. "Not so loud," she reminded him, then rubbed her aching arm, realizing how painful it felt.

"They hurt you!"

"I'm fine."

"You could've been raped, imprisoned — or even murdered by those drunken fools!" Daniel said in a loud whisper. "So I'm glad you're just sorry."

Lori looked down. "I *am* sorry."

"What were you thinking, Lori! You promised me you wouldn't try to run away!"

"I was desperate — your uncle's never going to let me go! This was my last chance!" Tears welled in her eyes. "I didn't tell you — because I knew you would've tried to stop me — or maybe even insisted on coming with me, half cocked as you are sometimes!"

"You're right. And if you're determined to do this — I'm going with you to protect you."

"No! They'll kill you!"

"Lori, you only got three houses away before the patrollers found you. An escape takes a lot more planning than this. You have to promise me you won't try something this harebrained again."

"Harebrained? How *dare* you insult me."

"I don't mean to insult you, I just want to keep you alive. Lori, I don't want anything to happen to you. Just be patient with me and —"

"Patient! Master Elijah's been here since last week to help close up your mother's estate but he hasn't changed his mind about me!"

"Lori! I'm trying—you have to believe me! I'm doing everything I can!" Daniel reached for Lori's hands and held them tight. "I promise you'll be free one day—just promise me you won't try to escape on your own again. Lori—I couldn't live if—just promise me, okay?"

Lori held Daniel's gaze for a long moment. She knew in her heart she could never live without ever seeing him again—and for that reason, Lori promised she wouldn't try to escape again.

Chapter 2

The next morning, Lori tiptoed to the drawing room where Daniel spoke with Master Elijah, Miss Rebecca's brother. In only a short while, Lori would be leaving Miss Rebecca's for good, along with Daniel and Master Elijah for Dancing Oaks, Elijah's rice plantation.

Lori reflected that Miss Rebecca had passed away only three weeks earlier. She'd been fine that morning, but then something terrible happened. "Lori," Miss Rebecca had called, "I need you!" Lori ran quickly from the other room, shocked to see Miss Rebecca clutching her head. "My head — it feels like it's about to explode!" Lori stood frozen as Miss Rebecca cried, "I feel like I'm not here!" Then she'd fallen to the floor.

It took Lori a few moments to gather her wits and find Daniel. But when he saw his mother — he knew she was dead. She was pale; her eyes were open, but rolled back in her head. And when Daniel placed a small mirror under her nose, it didn't fog up.

Daniel cried. Lori had never seen him cry, and it unnerved her. For a while she'd watched him silently, as he knelt next to his mother weeping. Lori didn't know what to do. But after a few moments, she stood behind him and placed a hand on his shoulder. He immediately turned to her, still on his knees, and grabbed her around the waist. Then he'd wept into her skirts. For a long time, Lori just remained there, stroking his hair.

The full impact of Miss Rebecca's death hadn't really hit Lori until the next day. Now, as she approached the drawing room, Lori said to herself, if only Miss Rebecca hadn't died before — but she stopped that thought, ashamed by the resentment she'd felt since Miss Rebecca had abandoned her by dying. She didn't *mean* to die, Lori reminded herself for the umpteenth time as she inched closer to the entrance of the drawing room.

Peeking inside Lori saw the large space, now devoid of furniture. Elijah stood in the middle of the room with his back toward her. He faced his nephew, who was standing in front of the white marble mantle holding a small velvet pouch.

Lori's heart pounded strongly as she looked at Daniel. His black hair was thick and wavy, and his eyes a deep set brown.

Lean and muscled, he was well over six feet tall, and his chiseled face was perfect, like the statues of Greek and Roman gods she'd seen in Europe.

"Uncle Elijah, I appreciate the locket," Daniel said, "but I still believe Annabelle should have it. She's your daughter and she's getting married soon, so since it's —"

"I know it's supposed to be handed down as a wedding heirloom," Elijah interrupted, "but Annabelle's got more jewels than a crown empress. Your sister said she can't pass it down to her children, because she doesn't think she'll ever have any. And I think she's right. She and James have been married for a long while with no babies, so it looks like Sarah *is* barren.

"She gave the locket to me for Annabelle, thinking it would be fitting because of her upcoming nuptials, but my Annabelle's a spoiled girl. When Sarah got married, your mother handed it down to her, and now, since Sarah's ready to pass it on, I'd rather you have it than Annabelle."

Daniel opened the pouch and took out the heart shaped locket. It was gold, encrusted with diamonds and rubies. While he gazed at it, Elijah said, "That locket was my grandmother's. Annabelle wouldn't appreciate it. So you just keep it, and give it to the fine young lady you'll be sure to marry one day."

For years, Lori had seen Miss Rebecca wear the trinket around her neck before she'd given it to her daughter. Now Lori imagined how painful it must be for Daniel to think of his mother wearing it, knowing he'd never see her again. But Lori's mind quickly flitted from Daniel's pain to her own, as she wondered when he'd bring up the topic of her freedom again.

Daniel placed the locket back in the pouch, then put it in his pocket. Elijah smiled. "So, no more arguing about that?"

"No, Uncle Elijah...not about that. But Lori's well being is another matter."

"For the last time," Elijah said, raking a hand through his graying curls, "I want to make it clear how things are gonna be for her at Dancing Oaks. I know you're concerned, but—"

"I *am* concerned because she wasn't treated like a slave here!"

Elijah hesitated. "Your mother was lenient on the girl, wasn't she? Treated her like one of her paid servants."

"Lori was treated even better than that. She was more like..." Daniel trailed off, as though unsure if he should finish his sentence.

"Like what?"

"Like—like family."

Elijah said nothing for a moment as he drew in a long breath.

"Now, Daniel," he began slowly, "we all have

servants that we're close to. They can seem like family, but they know never to cross that line between black and white. God knows we're supposed to keep separate—and we all know our places in life."

As Lori hovered near the door frame with her face partially obscured, she continued to gaze at Daniel. He couldn't see her, but that was just as well. He wouldn't want her to know that he still hadn't made any headway regarding her freedom. Lori eased away from the drawing room, no longer able to see inside, but she continued to listen.

"Uncle Elijah, I'll give you five thousand dollars for Lori!" Daniel said.

"Boy, money's not the issue here and—"

"I'll double it then! Ten thousand dollars for her freedom. You're a businessman, Uncle Elijah. Just think of all the investments you could make."

Lori was amazed at her worth to Daniel. Her heart beat so hard she thought it would burst, even though the thought of being sold like a prized cow was rather humiliating.

Miss Rebecca had died a very wealthy woman from the family inheritance she'd received, plus her husband's success as a merchant. After his death a year earlier, she'd made the shrewd decision to sell his business, increasing her already sizable fortune.

"The answer's still no!" Elijah said firmly.

"You're only eighteen and talking like a fool! You don't need to be squandering off your inheritance over some darkie."

"But Uncle Elijah—can you at least give me a reason *why* you won't sell her to me?"

Lori peeked in the room again, just long enough to see Elijah adjust his trousers over his girth. "There's no need for me to justify moving *my* property to *my* plantation. She'll have food, a place to sleep, be with people she knows—"

"Be in bondage! My mother wouldn't want things this way for Lori!"

"Dern it, boy! I'm sorry Lucinda ever gave your mother permission to bring that little darkie here in the first place! After her mother died—all that pickaniny did was cry! Only time she seemed happy was when your mother visited."

"You should have sold her to Mother then!"

"Boy—don't be telling me what I should have done! Lori wasn't supposed to stay here long as she has. It was only supposed to be for a short while; long enough for her to get over her mother's passing. And she's stayed *way* past that time—a good ten years! So you ought to at least be thankful for that!"

"I *am* thankful, Uncle Elijah! But Mother wouldn't approve of what you're doing! She'd be appalled, and she wouldn't—"

"Your mother knew Lori wouldn't stay here

forever! Now," Elijah sighed exasperatedly, "she'll be treated just fine at Dancing Oaks. She won't be living in the cabins, she's gonna be inside working as a housemaid. And she'll share an attic room with one of the other girls. Those surroundings won't be strange to her. Before she came here, she used to live up there with her mother."

Lori remembered her cramped attic room. Even as a child, it had seemed small to her. The heat was stifling in summer and the cold near freezing in winter.

"She'll be fine," Elijah continued, "and she couldn't ask for more."

"Except her freedom!" Daniel exclaimed.

Lori had heard enough. Slowly, she walked up the three flights of stairs from the foyer, then wandered down the hall to her old room, a safe haven of lavender walls. Miss Rebecca had loved Lori like her own child. She'd even given Lori her deceased daughter's bedroom. Miss Rebecca had said, "perhaps God gave you to me to help ease the pain of losing my little Mary."

From Miss Rebecca, Lori had learned to speak properly, and to dress and act as a lady. Although Master Elijah and his wife, the wretched Miss Lucinda, were under the impression that Lori worked as a housemaid, alongside Miss Rebecca's paid servants, they were mistaken.

Being treated more like a sister to Rebecca's other children, Lori had even traveled abroad with Miss Rebecca's family. And in Europe, she'd been treated no differently than anyone else.

But to keep in place the charade of Lori "working as a maid," Miss Rebecca had Lori serve tea whenever her brother's family visited. And to prevent any suspicions regarding her upbringing, Miss Rebecca had privately instructed Lori to discreetly disappear for the remainder of her relatives' social calls. However, Lori was convinced that those brief glimpses of her by Lucinda, had caused the woman to hate her.

Lori never wore a servant's uniform, but instead dressed in beautiful clothes. She carried herself as if she were no less than a princess. "A lady," Miss Rebecca had said, "imagines herself as a princess." Gazing down at her pink cotton dress, Lori smoothed the thick, unruly waves of hair she'd managed to style into gently padded rolls puffed over her ears with a chignon swirled in back.

She was a year younger than Daniel. Lori knew this, because Miss Rebecca remembered the year she was born. Miss Rebecca had liked Lori's mother, who'd been a housemaid for Miss Lucinda, and she'd remembered when Lori's mother had given birth.

Since Lori was close to Daniel's age, Miss Rebecca had seen to it that the school instruction Daniel received from a tutor was given to Lori, as well. Miss Rebecca had instilled in Lori the importance of an education. She'd even encouraged her to become a teacher. But now a future as a teacher seemed impossible, Lori thought, because she was doomed to live as Dancing Oaks chattel.

Miss Rebecca had promised Lori her freedom, but it had to be in the form of an escape, since Master Elijah refused to free her. But Miss Rebecca hadn't planned the escape yet. It wasn't to happen until next year, and it was to be carefully orchestrated and safe. That's when Miss Rebecca had arranged for Lori to attend Oberlin College. College was an unimaginable dream for a slave like Lori. But now it was a dream that would never happen, because Master Elijah was here to collect his property.

Daniel and his sister, Sarah, had decided to sell the house, and whatever items not sold at auction were to be given to Uncle Elijah. When Daniel had told him that he'd planned on moving to Ohio to live with his sister, and that Lori would go as well, provided Elijah free her, his uncle had objected.

Putting down his beefy, black booted foot, Elijah had said, "Now don't you go forgettin', boy—freein' her isn't somethin' I plan on doin'!"

Then he'd eyed Lori condescendingly, his lips sneering beneath a thick graying moustache. She could tell he didn't approve of her familiarity with Daniel. "Miss Lucinda's got plans for you," he said.

Lori didn't like the sound of that. And later, when Daniel wasn't around, his uncle had swaggered up to her, with his large protruding belly bursting from under his vest. "Look here, Missy," he'd said, spittle flying from his mouth, "don't you even think about runnin' away."

That memory brought Lori back to the present, yet she wiped her chin thinking about Master Elijah's spit landing there. Feeling listless, she drifted to a small round window near the corner of her room. She peered out from it for the last time into the hot hazy air suspended on Walnut Street. Soon she'd be leaving for the Cape Fear River to catch the steamer for Winnabow, where Dancing Oaks awaited her.

From the window, Lori studied the live oaks draped in Spanish moss. But at the sound of Daniel's boots on the heart pine floorboards, her breathing ceased. His steps were slow and steady.

When he stopped at her door, Lori took in a deep breath and turned to face him. He was handsome like a prince, and she wished they could run away together.

To Mexico, to Europe, to Canada—to any place the color of her skin wouldn't matter, and to any place she couldn't be owned as property.

****

"Lori," Daniel said softly, "we have to go." Tears glistened on her dark brown skin. At one time she'd loved to smile, and she'd smiled at him often with her brown, almond shaped eyes. She'd loved to laugh, too, but since his mother's death, Lori hadn't smiled much and she'd hardly laughed at all.

"I know." Lori dropped her head and began to cry. "Daniel, what's going to happen to me?" He quickly walked to her and put his arms around her. "You promised me," Lori wailed, "you said I'd be free! But now I'm going to Dancing Oaks—and it's all your fault!"

"Lori, I'm sorry—I'll make everything all right." His embrace grew stronger. "I'll do everything I can to set you free, but you'll have to trust me."

Lori pushed him away slightly to look up into his eyes. He towered over her tiny frame. "Trust you? When I'm supposed to be hauled off to your uncle's plantation as property?"

Daniel felt the hot burn of tears, but managed to hold them back. Despite this, Lori must have seen his eyes well.

"Daniel, I'm sorry. I know I can trust you. You're the only person I *can* trust. Forgive me. I'm—I'm not in my right mind."

"It's all right, Lori," Daniel said quietly. His brother had been murdered a little over a year ago, right before his father died from consumption. Now his mother was dead and he'd failed Lori.

"It's *not* all right. With all you've been through—I'm ashamed of what I said."

"Don't be ashamed. I know you're afraid."

"Oh, Daniel, I *am* afraid—I'm trapped! My life is at stake and I have no rights. What if— what if they do sell me—but not to you?"

Daniel pulled her close once more. "I *won't* let that happen."

"But you can't stop them. I'm their property. They can do whatever they want with me!" She cried.

Daniel continued holding her, and said softly, "I promise, Lori, I won't let them sell you. You're going to be free—somehow. But I can't figure out, for the life of me, why Uncle Elijah's being so stubborn about this."

Lori closed her eyes and nestled her head in Daniel's chest. "I wish I could stay right here...forever," she murmured quietly. After a few moments, Lori said, "Daniel—I think the only reason your uncle won't free me is because of your Aunt Lucinda. She hates me—I know she does. I can feel it—whenever she looks at me."

"But, Lori," Daniel began, but she cut him off.

"When I was a little girl—I was afraid of her. After my mother died, I cried a lot. She used to—slap me—to make me stop." Daniel stroked Lori's cheek, as she looked into his eyes again. "Miss Lucinda's bitter—and I think your uncle will do anything to make her happy. She's probably the one who's insisted on keeping me a slave."

"Lori, Aunt Lucinda doesn't like anybody! She's an old sour puss—that's just how she is!"

"But Daniel—I think she resents the way I carry myself—the way I speak—the way I dress. I think—that if it weren't for her, your uncle would've freed me a long time ago."

Daniel didn't respond right away. "Maybe so," he said. "But no matter what, Lori, we're going to get through this—as long as we have faith—and hope."

"Daniel!" Elijah's booming voice called up the stairs. "It's time to catch that boat!"

Daniel caressed Lori's shoulders. "Don't worry, Lori, things will be fine," he assured her. "Uncle Elijah said you'd be treated well, and I'll make sure of that.

"Daniel—the slaves at Dancing Oaks—they call your aunt—Cap'n Cindy. I don't want to *live* on her property or *be* her property any longer than I have to. No telling how she'll treat me—or what she'll do to me."

Daniel's grasp tightened on her shoulders, as he said, "Lori, I don't know how long you'll have to stay there. I've let Uncle Elijah believe he's talked me into living at Dancing Oaks for a year before I go off to college in Ohio. I have a feeling he wants me to forget about leaving North Carolina at all, so he can teach me how to run a plantation, then manage another one he wants to buy. Of course, that'll be after he convinces me that slavery isn't all that bad if you treat your people right," Daniel added sarcastically.

"But, Lori, the only reason I've agreed to live at Dancing Oaks is to protect you, and I have no intention of either of us staying there for a year. I don't know how long it'll take for me to get you out of there, but right now we're just going have to make the best of it."

When Lori looked down, Daniel put his fingertips under her chin, then lifted her pretty heart shaped face to his. "But I do know this — if I can't come to some kind of amicable agreement with Uncle Elijah, I'll steal you away from that blasted plantation myself!"

This brought a slight smile to Lori's face. "You'd do that — for me?"

"Lori, I'd do anything for you." They held each other's gaze, then leaned close as if to kiss.

"Daniel!" Elijah bellowed once more, breaking the intensity between them.

"We — I'm coming, Uncle Elijah!"

"And just where's that girl!" Elijah yelled, his tone suspicious.

Daniel paused, then shouted back, "I'll find her!" He lowered his voice, then took her hand. "Lori, we'd best get going."

"Lord help us," she murmured quietly.

"He will," Daniel said, as he led her from the room.

Chapter 3
Near Winnabow, North Carolina
Dancing Oaks Plantation, One Month Later

Annabelle sat bolt upright in bed. Moonlight shone brightly through her bedside window, illuminating the darkness with a silvery glow. Annabelle wiped perspiration from her forehead with the sleeve of her nightdress. She'd awakened in a cold sweat.

A nightmare roused her from a peaceful sleep. In it, a Negro had been elected governor. Annabelle wouldn't dare mention this to a soul for fear of being labeled a lunatic. What could have possessed her to have such a horrible dream? Probably Daniel's abolitionist influence.

She couldn't bear the thought of him living in her house for a whole year, before going off to that appalling Yankee institution, Oberlin College in Ohio. His behavior was already shameful enough. He treated the darkies just like whites!

Annabelle resigned herself to Daniel's unfortunate existence under the same roof, but she wouldn't let that deprive her of any beauty rest.

After adjusting her nightcap, she grabbed her feather pillow and fluffed it. Before settling back to sleep, Annabelle glanced out her window. She saw the moving light of a lantern. Someone carried it to light his steps. But then she realized not one person walked, but two, and they held hands. Gasping, Annabelle felt her heart catch in her throat. It was Daniel—and that wench!

Shocked, she sprang quickly from bed. What Daniel was doing was inexcusable and wouldn't be tolerated at Dancing Oaks. The shame, the disgrace! The hardwood floors creaked noisily beneath her bare feet as she moved rapidly through the dark hallway, feeling her way with outstretched hands.

Her parents' bedroom door was closed. Elijah snored heavily, so Annabelle didn't bother to knock. Instead, she opened the door and rushed quickly to her mother's side of the bed.

"Mother." Annabelle shook her mother's bony shoulder.

"Huh? Annabelle? What in the daylights is wrong with you?" Lucinda whispered loudly over Elijah's snoring. "It's the middle of the night."

"Mother, it's Daniel," Annabelle hissed. Her tone, combined with the subject matter, was enough to move her mother quickly from bed.

Lucinda lit the candle on her nightstand. "I don't want to talk over your father's snoring."

Carrying the candlestick by the brass ring of its holder, she clutched Annabelle's arm, and then steered her eagerly to the hall.

After Lucinda closed her bedroom door, she said, "So, what's your cousin done now? For you to wake me up, it must be something terrible."

"It is, Mother. I just saw him from my window — with the wench from Aunt Rebecca's! They walked off together, hand in hand!"

Lucinda's mouth fell open, but then, setting her jaw tight, she narrowed her eyes. "Oh — I knew it!" Lucinda said harshly. "I knew there was something wrong about the two of them! He was always looking for her, and interfering with how many chores she had to do. I told him he'd better stop prying into the affairs of my household and keep his distance from that girl, or I'd send her to the fields!"

Lucinda started anxiously for her daughter's room. "What they're doing," she declared, as Annabelle followed her, "is an abomination, a sin against nature. I can't even bear to think about it, it's too disgraceful!" After setting the candle on Annabelle's nightstand, Lucinda climbed onto her daughter's bed. "Just when did you see them?" She asked, leaning on the window sill, peering sharply from the window like a hawk.

"Only moments ago," Annabelle replied.

"Well," Lucinda said, gazing into the darkness, "I don't see any sign of them now, but what he's doing won't be stood for around here! The last thing we need is a yellow baby, white darkie bastard!" Lucinda sighed, pushing herself away from the window, then sat on the bed. "Thank goodness for you, Annabelle, you're like a second set of eyes and ears."

"Mother," Annabelle sat next to Lucinda, "I think that wench should be—"

"Oh," Lucinda laughed almost wickedly, "you let *me* think about what should be done with her! Then we'll talk about it in the morning, *after* breakfast, when your father's gone for the day. I don't want him interfering with any punishment I decide to dole out!" Putting a hand on her forehead, Lucinda blew out a deep breath. "Oh, the things I have to deal with!"

****

The next morning, Daniel drove from the stables to the slave cabins on a sturdy dappled gray horse. Dancing Oaks was located in the northern end of the Carolina low country, and Uncle Elijah was the third generation of his family to enjoy its prosperity.

Although the bright sunshine remained the same, the plantation's beauty and magnolia fragrance diminished the closer Daniel came to the slave quarters.

Manicured gardens and flowering trees and shrubs gave way to sand, dirt and red clay, near the wooded edge of evergreens and oaks. Here, the malodorous smell of human waste wafted through the air.

A plantation, Daniel imagined, was like a fetid French whore. Pleasing to the eye, but hiding the stench of disease beneath fine silk skirts.

As he approached the row of small cabins, he saw an old Negro woman watching a group of slave children. The woman's skin was very dark. Although she wore a red calico bandana wrapped around her head, Daniel could see short gray hair peeking from beneath it. She sat on a low wooden stool, holding a long stick, as about a dozen children, bare foot and dressed in ragged cotton shirts to their knees, ran about playing in the dirt. None appeared older than four. By five they'd be put to work.

The woman's expression appeared dazed, and almost sad, but upon seeing Daniel, an invisible mask subtly transformed her countenance into one of pleasant good cheer. Daniel had seen this all too often since living at the plantation. Wearing a dirty gray blouse and skirt, the old woman immediately stood up, leaning heavily on the stick she apparently used as a cane.

The woman's gnarled hands and swollen knuckles prevented her from holding the stick too tightly. "Morning, Massa." She smiled. All of her teeth were missing.

"Good morning. And there's no need for you to stand," Daniel said as he dismounted. "Please sit down."

"Thank you, sir."

"I'm Daniel Taylor."

"Yes sir, Massa Daniel. You's Miss Rebecca's boy."

"That's right. And please call me Daniel." The old woman didn't respond. She only stared dumbfounded. "And your name?

"Opal."

"So, Opal," he looked toward the tiny cabin behind her, "is this where you live?"

"Yes, sir."

Daniel glanced down the entire row of cabins and counted them. There were fifteen. "How many live with you?"

"My son, his wife and child, and my daughter and her two children."

"Do you mind if I look inside?" A piece of wood, thrown by one of the children, landed near Daniel's foot.

Opal swallowed hard as the little boy ran to hide behind her dress. He looked to be about four. "I's sorry, Massa," Opal said, "the child didn't—"

"It's all right. He meant no harm." Daniel picked up the wood and approached the child, still hiding behind his caretaker's skirt. Dirt streaked the boy's clothes, face and all visible parts of his limbs. Dried mucous was crusted in the space between his nose and upper lip.

As Daniel reached to pat the boy's head, the child began to cry and held tightly to Opal. Daniel immediately pulled his hand away. Crouching next to the child, he smiled saying, "Don't be afraid. You don't have to cry." He gently eased the wood toward the boy. "Here's your toy." The boy stopped crying, then hesitantly took the wood and ran off.

After this, Opal said Daniel could look in her cabin. Upon pushing open the door, he saw one room. Flat pallets lined the dirt floor; corn husks protruded from them as stuffing. There was a small fireplace and only one window with a rickety shutter. Daniel walked to the window. When he pushed open the shutter, he saw that there was no glass. The window was used only for fresh air, not light, he determined.

As soon as Daniel stepped from the cabin, he saw his Uncle Elijah galloping toward him on a powerfully built chestnut, its silky brown mane flying in the wind. It stood about sixteen hands high.

Opal pulled herself up again.

"Daniel, just what in the world are you doing out here?" Elijah said incredulously, looking down from his horse. "You said you were going riding."

"I have been."

"You checking on how my people live?" Elijah asked with suspicion. "They live well, I told you so! They've all got a place to sleep and decent food. Most people only get one set of clothes a year, but mine get two!"

While Opal stood unsteadily on her dry cracked feet, almost wobbling back and forth, Elijah acted as though she didn't exist.

"You don't mind if Opal sits down, do you?" Daniel said.

For the first time, Elijah looked in the old woman's direction. "Of course she can sit down."

"Thank you, Massa."

"Son, you get back on your horse. Come with me while I make my morning rounds 'fore I go into town. I'll show you the real beauty of this place. You don't want to be over in here. There's nothing worth seeing."

Daniel said nothing. He only looked at Elijah, feeling ashamed of his uncle's callousness toward the old woman.

Daniel then nodded to her. "Opal, it was a pleasure to have met you."

"Thank you, sir." Her red eyes watered.

Daniel remounted and rode alongside his uncle. Upon approaching the splendid surroundings away from the quarters, Elijah inhaled deeply, savoring the fresh smell of the early morning air. Sunlight shone on his graying curls, turning them to silver, and his jovial face split into a broad smile as he took in the wealth of his land.

"No doubt about it, son, this plantation is a beautiful and productive piece of property. Your mother ever tell you how this place came to be in the family?"

Daniel hesitated as the steady steps of the horses' hooves filled the silence between them. "No. She never talked much about it, other than its use of…"

"I know," Elijah said, "slave labor."

Elijah rode silently, taking in the landscape of his estate. Daniel gazed at the hanging leaves of cypress trees that swayed in the gentle breeze like billowy green curtains. Majestic long leaf pines stood tall with their branches reaching high into the sky, while the stout live oaks proudly spread their abundant foliage.

It was the leathery leaved magnolias, with velvety white blossoms, that filled the air with a sweet and pungent fragrance. And off in the distance, Daniel could see the rippling water of the Cape Fear River while hearing its soft, soothing flow.

"The place was purchased around 1800 by our grandfather as a business investment," Elijah said. "When our grandmother first saw the big house, she fell in love with it. Greek revival style, that's what it's called, white brick with those big old columns. And she thought the drive to the mansion, lined up with all those live oaks, was the prettiest sight she'd ever seen. That's how the place got its name. She said the trees looked like they were dancing."

Elijah exhaled. "We've got about five hundred acres and over a hundred slaves. Since rice is the main commodity, about a hundred and fifty acres are dedicated to that. But we've also got wheat fields to the west and —"

"Uncle Elijah," Daniel interrupted, "I counted only fifteen slave cabins, but you have over a hundred slaves."

"You don't need to be giving me an abolitionist lecture, boy! The cabins are sufficient to meet the needs of the people," Elijah said harshly. "And not all of them live out there. Quite a few live on the third floor of the big house."

Uncle Elijah didn't elaborate further, but Daniel burned, thinking of the injustice of it all. While the slaves labored and bled for this plantation, never receiving a cent, those in the big house enjoyed the rewards of the land.

They'd ridden a good while when they came

to a clearing Daniel could see a short distance ahead. Acres and acres of flat, square rice fields stretched before them. They appeared inundated with water.

"Rice cultivation is complicated," Elijah said, as they rode toward the fields for a closer look. "That's why I plan on buying a cotton plantation; the money's good and it's a crop that's a lot easier to grow."

For the number of slaves at Dancing Oaks, Daniel noticed that the amount working here seemed relatively sparse. Several women were scattered in the flooded fields working up to their knees in mud.

"Right now the women are plucking weeds."

The work appeared tedious, tiring and hot as the women swatted at mosquitoes. Bent over, they struggled to move through the muck in heavy dresses weighted down by muddy water. He couldn't imagine Lori being subjected to this.

One girl looked about Lori's age, and the curve of her neck reminded him of her. But there was no softness in this girl's face, only a hard, cold hopelessness.

Lines creased her forehead, as though painfully etched into it. This couldn't be Lori's fate, and Daniel wouldn't let her be reduced to this.

Despite the August heat, the thought of Lori up to her knees in mud and mosquitoes sent a chill through his bones.

Daniel had devised a plan for her escape. Although dangerous for both of them, her freedom was worth it. He now believed Lori's suspicions regarding his aunt. Lucinda had already threatened to send Lori to the fields, and now he feared she might make good on that threat for the least little offense.

"Last month, we had the harvest flow," Elijah said, interrupting Daniel's thoughts. "And next month, the harvest will begin."

While he spoke, overseer Luther Jenkins rode toward them. His sleek and shiny horse was solid black. "Morning, Mr. Calhoun, Mr. Taylor." Jenkins said. A humorless Yankee from Indiana, the man rarely smiled. Tall and skinny, he wore only a white cotton shirt with his blue pants and leather boots. The fabric under his arms was already saturated and his pockmarked face glistened with oily sweat.

After exchanging greetings, Daniel noticed the lash, coiled like a rattlesnake, visibly attached to Jenkins's worn leather saddlebag. And upon closer inspection, he saw faint stains on Jenkins's shirt that looked like splattered blood.

"No problems here, Mr. Calhoun," Jenkins remarked, a little defensively. His horse snorted loudly, as though in agreement.

"Didn't think there were, Jenkins. Just showing my nephew some of this beautiful land."

"Then if you'll excuse me, sir, I'll be moving on."

"I know you've got a million things to do. Don't let us hold you up."

After Jenkins rode off, Daniel asked, "How often does he use that lash?"

"Jenkins is a good overseer!" Elijah sounded exasperated by Daniel's question. "He mainly carries the lash for show. Just seeing it is incentive enough to keep my people working like they should. Now, if it were up to me, I wouldn't use it at all. But your Aunt Lucinda insists on it for two reasons: running and reading."

"Punishment for God given rights," Daniel muttered bitterly.

"Don't you be sassin' me boy! Since it's against the law for a slave to read, we're just *enforcing* the law."

Daniel felt his chest tighten. No one at Dancing Oaks knew Lori could read, and that would have to remain a closely guarded secret.

"And besides," Elijah continued, "a man's gotta do what's necessary to keep things running smoothly on a plantation. Now, when your Aunt Lucinda was growing up, there were some rough times at her father's place, so she's more partial to the lash than I am."

Daniel was silent for several moments as he thought about Lori's escape. It wouldn't be immediate. Correspondence was required.

"You have something else on your mind?" Elijah asked.

Lori was the main thing on Daniel's mind, keeping her safe, out of the fields, and ensuring her freedom. "No," he replied quietly.

Chapter 4

Lucinda sat ramrod straight at her slant top desk in the library. She exhaled deeply, tugging at the high collar of her gray cotton dress. It buttoned stiffly at her throat. With dull brown hair netted in a chignon, her furrowed brow and down turned mouth did little to enhance her ordinary appearance. Steely gray eyes sat perched atop a small beak-like nose, and thin lips appeared barely visible above a receding chin.

While waiting for Annabelle, who primped upstairs for a carriage ride with her intended, Lucinda dipped her steel pen in the inkwell to compose a journal entry.

August 25, 1856
It seems Rebecca's passing continues to bring even greater turmoil upon my household. While alive, she tried to bring about our financial ruin by feeding our slaves foolishness about freedom and equality. Some, so spurned on by her rhetoric, actually ran away. How Rebecca could selflessly impose such monetary losses to her brother's family still appalls me!

Now her son, with his abolitionist beliefs, lives within these walls. He is doing something so unspeakable that I refuse to even write about it! But it shall be dealt with today. As I burned his copy of that disreputable book, Uncle Tom's Cabin, so I shall end his illicit and sullied activity.

Rebecca's death has further caused me undue stress by bringing relatives here who long ago outwore their welcomes. I detest the

"Mama Cindy!" A cheerful voice called before Lucinda could finish writing her sentence.

Lucinda put down her pen and shut her eyes for a moment. After closing her journal, she forced a small smile, the biggest she could muster, and gazed toward the doorway. There stood Priscilla, her son Jesse's wife. Bright red hair cascaded in untamed curls about her shoulders and an abundance of freckles spotted her face and arms. She wore a pink striped dress that almost matched her pinkish skin.

"So, dear," Lucinda said, "are you all packed and ready for Mocksville?"

Priscilla had inherited a tobacco plantation from a bachelor uncle who had died a few years earlier.

She and Jesse would be leaving today to go back. After Rebecca's passing, they'd come to Dancing Oaks and stayed for several weeks. But Lucinda had been ready for them to leave after one.

Priscilla smiled broadly, exposing the spaces between her teeth, as she walked into the library. "We are! But I bet you'll be glad to see us go!" She laughed in a loud cackle. "I know it's been hard havin' all your kinfolk around! But I just want to thank you again for all your gracious hospitality!"

"You're quite welcome," Lucinda replied stiffly. "And it's been no trouble at all." At least with the two of them gone, there'd be some semblance of peace in the house. Priscilla had the annoying habit of adding a "y" or an "ie" to everyone's name, and she chattered away incessantly. And as for chattering, Jesse was almost as bad.

"We've certainly enjoyed our stay," Priscilla said. "It's just a shame it couldn't have been under happier circumstances." She pulled a handkerchief from her bosom. "Just thinking about Aunt Becky's unfortunate demise — makes me want to start crying all over again. A life — snuffed out much, *much* too soon." She sniffed.

Oh no, Lucinda thought, the only thing worse than Priscilla's cackling laugh was her uncontrolled wailing. Lucinda, now convinced that the crying was contrived, had grown tired of it a long time ago. And Priscilla had shed enough tears for the entire family before, during and after the funeral. And if she'd said it once, she'd said it a thousand times that there —

"There was never a sweeter soul to live than Aunt Becky," Priscilla said, wiping her eyes.

"Dear—you must cheer up. After all, our Rebecca is in a much better place."

Priscilla smiled through her tears. "I suppose you're right, Mama Cindy. And now she knows the truth—up there in heaven."

Lucinda's downturned lips pulled down a tad further. "Just what truth are you referring to?"

"Well, all Aunt Becky's talk 'bout ablishnism just got me to thinkin'."

"Why would you do that, dear?"

"Aunt Becky said the coloreds have souls."

Lucinda sat speechless for a moment, but tried to remain calm. "Why, that's utter nonsense." So as not to scream, she picked up the pencil next to her financial ledger and held it tightly with both fists.

"But, Mama Cindy, what if it's not? My family's always been kind to our people—but you get one that's strong willed—that upsets everything! You can't control that kind without being cruel. Sometimes Jesse and I just want to wash our hands of the whole business—free our darkies and sell off the place."

Lucinda snapped the pencil in two. "That's ridiculous!"

"Oh, Mama Cindy, your pencil!"

"Never you mind about my pencil, Priscilla!" Lucinda took a deep breath. "You'd lose a fortune. Don't let Rebecca's words blur your judgment. Now," again she forced a smile, "just when will you be leaving for the steamer?"

"Not for a few more hours, so I have plenty of time to visit with you!" Priscilla smiled delightedly, as she spread her dress and settled on the settee across from Lucinda's desk. Just then, Annabelle appeared in the doorway. "Annie!" Priscilla waved enthusiastically. "I was just gettin' ready to set a spell with your mama."

"How nice." Annabelle smiled tightly.

"Plenty of room right here." Priscilla patted the yellow satin cushion beside her.

"As much as I'd like to — visit," Lucinda said, "I — I can't, not right now." She grabbed a fan and began waving it rapidly. "Annabelle and I need to discuss an urgent matter. Perhaps, afterwards, we can — set for a while."

"Oh, that'll be fine, Mama Cindy." Priscilla smiled and stood up. "Bet you'll be talking 'bout Annie's wedding plans." She laughed. "And speaking of weddings, I have a couple cousins who're looking for husbands. Handsome as he is, Danny'd be a good catch! Not to mention that he's smart as the daylights.

"But anyway, I just can't decide which one he'd like more. Them being twins and all, they look just alike! Oh," she waved her hands, "let me stop runnin' my mouth and leave ya'll to your urgent matter!" Priscilla grabbed her skirts and swirled around to leave.

Annabelle quickly closed the door as soon as Priscilla left the room. "So, Mother, what's your decision—regarding the problem?" As Annabelle walked toward Lucinda, the twelve yards of blue fabric covering her hoop skirt moved swiftly, as though blown by a strong, cold wind.

Fair, with frosty white hair, Annabelle's glacial beauty was delicate and refined. Lucinda had no false perceptions about her own looks. Although plain in appearance, she was strong in spirit. That's what Elijah loved about her.

"That Daniel—just him living here's a problem that I can't do anything about!" Lucinda said. "I wasn't too enthusiastic about your father extending him an invitation to stay for such a long time. But that was the proper thing to do. Even though the boy's an abolitionist, he *is* family." She sighed exasperatedly. "At least he's not white trash!"

Annabelle sat on the settee. Ice blue eyes boring into her mother's she asked, "But what about the wench?"

Lucinda pursed her lips. "She's going to the fields. I never should have let Rebecca keep that girl as long as she did. Being exposed to all those abolitionist ways couldn't have been healthy in cultivating a slave mind. With all those airs she puts on, she's probably never worked hard a day in her life!

"The fields will teach her what it's like to be a slave! And the more distance we put between her and your cousin, the better. Elijah didn't want her working out there since his sister liked her so much, but he didn't know she was doing the unspeakable with Rebecca's boy!"

"Aunt Rebecca would be appalled if she were alive. And Sarah—"

"Don't mention this to Sarah. You know how she is. She'll be leaving in a couple days, and I'd rather her go peaceably than with her feathers all ruffled over this. And if she finds out about what her brother's been doing, she might want to stay longer and talk some sense into him.

"I've been counting down the days 'til she and that Yankee husband of hers go back to that no-account darkie town!"

Sarah and her husband, James Cartwright, had come down from Ohio after Rebecca's death, and they'd stayed at Dancing Oaks since the sale of Rebecca's estate.

"But what I'm going to do won't require any talking of sense," Lucinda said. "It ought to straighten up Daniel's behavior in no time, at least 'til he goes up there with Sarah next year to that radical, self-righteous Oberlin College! It's bad enough the women attending there right along with the men, but throwing darkies in the mix, too? The whole place will probably go to hell in a hand basket!

"Rebecca thought she'd raised such a decent, upstanding young man," Lucinda said with self-serving satisfaction. "At least he's defiling that wench instead of an innocent white girl. But I won't have *that* going on around here.

"I've *never* liked the way that Lori behaves herself! Traipsin' around like the Queen of Sheba when she's nothin' but a nig—" Elijah disliked referring to the blacks as niggers, but when angry, Lucinda tended to slip, "...nothin' but a darkie—a darkie that's Dancing Oaks chattel, now."

"But, Mother, why can't you just sell her?"

"Your father doesn't want that. He promised Daniel she'd be treated well since Rebecca liked her so much. Of course, he didn't know what they were up to. But if that keeps on even after she's in the fields, then selling her South will be the only option!"

Chapter 5

Fanny, one of Lucinda's housemaids, stood outside the closed library door with her ear firmly pressed against it. Negroes knew all the gossip. That's what the white folks said, Fanny thought, and this was one way to hear it first hand.

Master Elijah was a decent soul, but everyone knew Cap'n Cindy ran things at Dancing Oaks. Fanny's round, pleasant exterior hid her pain. Over Master Elijah's objections, her husband, Zeke, had been sold because Miss Lucinda had found out that he could read. At least Master Elijah had convinced her not to have him whipped first.

Now in her middle years, Fanny had been a servant at Dancing Oaks as long as she could remember. She knew Miss Lucinda and Miss Annabelle well. The daughter was just as black hearted as the mother.

But it was a pleasure having Master Daniel in the house. He was a godly soul and just as sweet as pie. Never a cruel word crossed his lips.

Miss Rebecca had raised him right, because Daniel lived as the good Lord commanded: "Thou shalt love thy neighbor as thyself." That was Scripture the slaves never heard preached at Dancing Oaks. But Miss Rebecca had quoted it, and Fanny's husband had read it himself from the good Lord's Word.

Cap'n Cindy brought in a preacher once a month, and every one of his sermons was the same—obey your master and don't steal from him.

Daniel had asked Fanny to keep an eye on Lori to make sure she wasn't mistreated. Touched by his concern, Fanny willingly agreed. "She's a precious child," Fanny had said, and to this, Daniel replied, "She's precious to me. I've known her since what seems like forever and more..." he'd stopped, but then turned beet-red. Next thing Fanny knew, more words spilled out of him like a bucket of fresh, warm milk. "More than anything," Daniel had said, "I want Lori's freedom." Then he'd surprised Fanny by saying he *cared* for Lori, really cared for her. Fanny looked at him like he'd turned idiot. "Fanny, I'm telling the truth. But promise you won't mention what I've said to anyone," he'd pleaded.

Fanny assured him she wouldn't, since she liked him so much and didn't want to see him hauled off to a lunatic asylum.

"You crazy?" she'd asked. "Crazy to care for her like I do? Maybe so," was all he'd said. Then Fanny had asked if Lori felt the same and cared for him. "I think so…I hope so…I don't know Fanny, but even if she doesn't, I still want to see her freed."

Because of Daniel's feelings for Lori, and the fact that he'd been raised right by Miss Rebecca, Fanny knew he wouldn't do anything dishonorable. But him sneaking off with her, no matter how innocently, would no doubt arouse suspicion. Fanny didn't know where Daniel was, or when she'd see him again, but she'd have to tell Lori as soon as possible about Cap'n Cindy's plans for her.

Miss Annabelle's fiancé and his aunt had just arrived to fetch Miss Annabelle. While they sat in the parlor, Fanny debated knocking for Miss Annabelle or running off to find Lori first. She'd better not keep the white folks waiting and risk getting in trouble, so she knocked.

"Come in," Miss Lucinda called. "Yes?" Cap'n Cindy looked rather annoyed upon seeing Fanny.

"Pardon me, ladies, but Mr. Nathaniel and Miss Emma are here for Miss Annabelle.

"Tell them I'll be right there, Fanny," Miss Annabelle said.

"Yes, ma'am." After telling the guests Miss Annabelle was coming directly, Fanny rushed off to find Lori.

****

Lucinda mopped the sweat from her brow with a handkerchief, as her daughter stood to leave.

"Mother," Annabelle said, "I'll die of shame if Nathaniel's family ever finds out what Daniel is doing. It's disgraceful."

"They won't find out, because it won't go on any longer. Now you run along. Don't give your cousin a second thought," she said disgustedly. Lucinda rose from her chair, but her head throbbed wildly. She sat back down, placing a hand on her forehead to calm the pounding.

"Mother, what's wrong?"

"I have a sick headache. Feels like a drum's beating in my head — all because of your cousin's latest adventure." Lucinda sighed and picked up her fan. "Make my apologies to Nathaniel and Emma. I can't muster the strength to speak to them right now."

"I'll have Violet bring you some water."

"That would be nice." Lucinda fanned herself with broad strokes. "While you're gone, I'll rest a while. When you come back I'll be as good as new. Then we can discuss some details about the wedding."

"All right, Mother." Annabelle turned to go, then looked back at Lucinda. "I can't wait to be Mrs. Nathaniel Applegate, Mistress of Appledown Plantation." A small smile brought a hint of rosiness to Annabelle's cheeks.

"His mother's good and ready to pass on that responsibility to you, being a widow and all." Lucinda exhaled. "Nathaniel's a fine man, but the life of a plantation mistress isn't all that easy. You have to rise before dawn with the darkies to make sure they do their work, and you have to give orders almost every minute of the day."

There was also the pain of childbirth and the possible loss of children to sickness. Lucinda had lost two, but she didn't bother to bring this up now. Annabelle would face enough difficulties as a young wife running a plantation.

"Mother, I know all those things. But I love Nathaniel, so it won't matter." After saying goodbye, Annabelle turned to go.

Thankfully, Lucinda reflected, as she watched her daughter leave, the Applegate family, like the Calhouns, didn't tolerate the familiarity of young female slaves with the men in the household. All the Applegate female house servants were old and ugly.

But there were countless white men that found physical pleasure among the slave women by force, or promises of freedom, food or pretty clothes.

However, there were those slave whores who gave willingly. This was one aspect of plantation life Annabelle would be spared. Lucinda hadn't had to live with it either, yet her mother hadn't been so lucky.

After Lucinda was born, her mother, Magnolia, a sick and weakly woman, was warned that another pregnancy would kill her. For her "protection and well being," her husband, Samuel, established separate sleeping quarters for them. Then shortly afterwards, before Magnolia's very eyes, her wifely duty was usurped by Maisy, a kitchen house servant.

By her teen years, Lucinda finally realized why Maisy was seen coming and going from her father's bedroom so often, and why, as servants, Maisy and her two girls—Samuel's children— were treated so nicely. Lucinda hated Maisy, and she hated her white nigger brats. Both were more beautiful than Lucinda, and in addition, well pampered by her father.

When Samuel died from poisoning, Maisy, in charge of food preparation, was arrested and hanged. She'd pleaded innocence, but her pleas had fallen upon deaf ears.

After Samuel's death and Maisy's hanging, Magnolia attempted to sell Samuel's bastards to a slave trader, but both of them ran away. Although slave catchers found them, neither girl survived the attack by the bull mastiffs after the bloodhounds had tracked them down.

Lucinda would never forget her mother's reaction to her father's death. Magnolia had only glanced off into the distance, then said, "Fancy that."

Lucinda suspected her mother responsible for the poisoning. It was clear to see that she'd been driven to the edge of insanity by Samuel's behavior.

There was nothing wrong with Lucinda's mind. But she'd been sorry she hadn't thought of poisoning her father years before to save her mother from the humiliation and indignity she'd suffered for so many years.

Maisy had ruined her mother's life. Lucinda wouldn't sit by and watch Lori destroy a white woman's life and marriage as Daniel's concubine. Hard work in the fields was just what that wench needed so she'd know her place in the world.

Lucinda looked up just as Violet walked in with a glass of water. "Your water, Miss Lucinda, ma'am. Miss Annabelle said you was feelin' a might sick."

"Thank you, Violet."

Although Violet was a product of miscegenation, it was by no fault of the Calhoun men. Elijah looked down on such shameful behavior. But acquiring this girl was done as a favor for a friend.

Violet's father was Caleb Thorne, a neighboring planter and childhood friend of Elijah's. Violet's slave mother revealed the identity of the child's father, and as punishment, Caleb took her baby.

But rather than sell her off to strangers, he asked Elijah to take her. He knew she wouldn't be mistreated at Dancing Oaks as long as she didn't read or run.

At first, Lucinda had opposed the child coming to Dancing Oaks. She didn't know how many slave children Caleb had fathered, but two of his house servants looked enough like his own children to be mistaken for them.

Caleb's wife, Clarissa, turned a blind eye to the situation, and carried on as though life were completely normal. Because of Clarissa, Lucinda had agreed to bring Violet to Dancing Oaks.

If she hadn't, chances were that Caleb would have relented about the baby, and placed it into his own home as a house servant.

Then Violet would have been one more reminder to Clarissa of her husband's infidelity. As the girl matured, Lucinda was relieved that, other than eye color, she bore no resemblance to Caleb or Caleb's other children.

Violet had been a fine and obedient playmate for Annabelle. The two had grown up together, and now Violet displayed the qualities of a most faithful and loyal servant.

Sipping her water Lucinda thought, if only all of my servants could be like that.

"You be needin' anything else, Miss Lucinda?"

"No, Violet. You may go."

"Yes, ma'am." She turned to leave, but Lucinda called to her.

"Oh, Violet."

"Yes'm."

"You won't be sharing your room with Lori anymore. She'll be going off to the fields in the morning. I know you've admired her clothes. They're yours now."

Violet gasped with delight. "Thank you, Miss Lucinda. Is that all ma'am?"

"Yes, you may go."

****

"It's a shame Miss Lucinda's sending poor Lori out there. She won't know what to do," Fanny fretted, as she worked with Violet setting the table for supper.

"I don't see what you worried 'bout, Fanny," Violet said, putting her hands on her hips. "That girl thinks she's better than all of us, with her highfalutin self. If Cap'n Cindy says put her in the fields, that's fine with me, especially since I got *me* some mighty fine clothes because of it!" She laughed.

"You hush up, Violet!" Fanny snapped. "Lori's a sweet child. She don't deserve to be thrown into the fields. She's never done any work like that."

Violet clicked her tongue. "Well, it's 'bout time she learns with that dark skin and nappy, wild hair. Humph, the fields is right where she belongs, anyway."

Violet took pride in her light brown skin and straight hair that fell to her waist when not in a turban.

"Miss Rebecca did her share of dotin' on her and givin' her nice things," Fanny said, "but Lori, she's always been kind. And she's been willing to work hard around here without complaining."

"That Daniel done complained for her! Sayin' she had too much to do." Violet chuckled. "Cap'n Cindy put a stop to that right quick, tellin' him he didn't run things around here, and for all she cared Lori could be a field hand tomorrow!" Violet paused as she finished placing the glasses around the table. "I ain't heard him say anything 'bout her work for a while, so why's she goin' to the fields?"

"I couldn't say."

Violet grabbed a handful of knives. "I never liked her. Talked like *she* was the plantation mistress." When Violet finished putting the flatware on the table, she asked, "You think Miss Rebecca did any book learnin' on her?"

"I don't know. But I do know she means an awful lot to Master Daniel."

"They were playmates, but that don't mean anything. When white children and niggers are growed up, the white children know they're the master."

"Well, they seem close."

Violet eyed Fanny suspiciously. "How do you mean close? And just why you so worried 'bout her goin' to the fields in the first place?"

"Honey," Fanny said, suddenly realizing she'd said too much to Violet, whose greatest possession was a vindictive streak, "stop makin' somethin' out of nothin' and get back to work."

Chapter 6

Lori walked down the backstairs of the big house. It was well past midnight. She'd seen Daniel waiting as she looked from her cramped attic window moments earlier. Lori had debated about whether or not to come out. But she had nothing to lose. She'd be sent to the fields tomorrow as punishment for having already been seen with him.

Even though angry with Daniel, being with him was where Lori wanted to be. Every night since they'd arrived at Dancing Oaks, Daniel had secretly met with her outside. It was their only uninterrupted time together, and he'd read poetry to her.

Lori left the big house through the back door, then trudged toward the front, wearing only a gray cotton dress with no petticoat. Her hair tumbled freely past her shoulders in a mass of waves and curls.

"Lori," Daniel whispered upon seeing her. "I've been waiting a while. I almost thought you weren't coming out."

Lori stalked past him without stopping.

Daniel's sleeves were rolled up and his white shirt untucked, hanging over his trousers. He walked quickly to catch up with her. "What's wrong?" He held the lantern high to see her face. "You look upset."

She stopped. "That's because I *am*!"

Daniel tried to hold Lori's hand, but she pulled it away and started off again. The warm, sticky air smelled syrupy sweet and crickets chirped loudly as Daniel and Lori walked barefoot through the damp grass.

"Lori, what is it?" Daniel asked, as they approached a moonlit pond far away from the big house. Frogs croaked and the water shimmered while cattails surrounded it like a wreath.

Lori plopped down by the water's edge. "You don't know, do you?"

"Know what?" Daniel sat next to her, placing the lamp gently on the ground.

Lori crossed her arms tightly. "Just read me something."

"Well, I didn't bring any poetry books tonight. But I wrote something. No matter how bad our circumstances are —"

"*Your* circumstances haven't changed that much!" Lori said bitterly. When Daniel looked down, Lori said, "You'll go off to college, prosper in a business, and find some well bred young lady from a fine family to marry!

"Despite you being an abolitionist, seems like all the young ladies in Brunswick County want to make your acquaintance! I saw all kinds of eye batting and fan signaling aimed at you during your aunt's party a few days ago. And that Evelyn Thorne even tripped another girl and spilled punch all over her just to keep her away from you!"

"But Lori, you were the most beautiful girl at the party."

Lori rolled her eyes. "Oh, while I served punch in that ugly calico dress?"

"Remember how much punch I drank? I kept drinking it—just to be near you! And Lori—I know my life hasn't changed much—but not being able to talk to you, or see you whenever I want…" She looked at him, feeling the familiar pounding of her heart, a sensation that always commenced when near him. "Lori—what I'm trying to say—is I miss you."

Tears welled in her eyes, but Daniel couldn't see them in the darkness.

"Just listen." He moved the lamp closer, then pulled a piece of paper from his pocket. "Lori," he held her hand, "I'm here for you. I know things are difficult now but—"

Lori yanked her hand from his. "You don't know just *how* difficult things are gonna get for me!"

"Lori—what are you talking about?"

"It's nothing you can fix! Your uncle wouldn't free me, and now your aunt's—" she shook her head, exasperated, "you might as well forget about me!"

"Forget about you. Lori—I can't do that!" He unfolded the paper he'd taken from his pocket moments ago. "I wrote this, I want you to hear it." He paused for a moment, then began:

The dream we live, our hearts desire
The path we find, will change our lives
God brought us together, and there was never a doubt
The faithful love we have will never run out
In faith we live for God above
As He gives freely His abounding love
In patience we wait for a life together
And as one, we will spend our lives forever

Lori sat silently for a moment. "That's nice. Who's it for? Evelyn Thorne?"

"No!"

"Well, she's mighty pretty."

"I don't care about her! I wrote it for you, Lori! I love you!"

At this Lori burst into tears. "You can't love me! And it's stupid to think you can!"

"No it's not—because you love me too! If you didn't—you—you wouldn't be out here with me—and you wouldn't be crying like this!"

"How — how can we love each other if there's no future for us!" Lori sobbed.

"There may not be a future for us here, but we're not staying here. I promised I'd take you away from all this!"

"Well you haven't yet!"

"I've tried," Daniel exclaimed, "and now I — "

"And now it's too late, because I'm being sent to the fields!"

"What?" Daniel clutched her firmly by the arm.

"You heard me!"

"No, Lori, that can't be!"

"Well, it is! Fanny overheard your Aunt Lucinda and Miss Annabelle talking today. Miss Annabelle saw us together last night. She thinks we're doing more than just talking!"

"How dare she jump to that conclusion!"

"So Miss Lucinda's sending me to the fields tomorrow to keep us apart."

"Lori, don't worry. I won't let that happen. I'll set this matter straight."

"'Don't worry?'" She pulled from his grasp. "You can't do anything about it. If you tell them you love me, they'll think you've gone mad — and then they *will* sell me!"

"Lori, trust me. I'll discuss it with Uncle Elijah in the morning."

"I *have* trusted you!" Lori's tone was biting. "So what are you going to say to him this time?"

Daniel was silent for a moment, his eyes distressed, as he looked into hers. "I don't know yet, but I'll think of something."

"You don't know?" Lori shot up quickly and began to walk away.

Daniel caught up to her in seconds, and grabbed her shoulder. "Lori, look at me," he said, turning her to face him. "I'm sorry for all this, but I promise I'll make it right! But—you—you do love me, don't you?"

"Oh...of course I do," she huffed.

"Lori, I swear, I won't let anything happen to you—you're priceless to me."

Lori remained silent, then said, "Every slave has a price."

"You *won't* be a slave forever." Placing both of his hands on her shoulders, Daniel said, "Lori—I need you to listen to me, and listen very closely. I've been planning an escape for you. I've been working on it for a while—but it's dangerous. I didn't want to tell you about it and worry you, unnecessarily.

"Quite frankly, I was hoping I wouldn't have to resort to this. I kept thinking Uncle Elijah would change his mind—but he hasn't." Daniel hesitated for a moment. "Lori—we'll be escaping together."

She eyed him strangely. "*We'll* be escaping? Escaping together? That doesn't make sense."

"When I went into Wilmington for a few days

last week," Daniel said, "I met with some of Mother's Quaker friends, the Wrights. They're the ones that own an oyster sloop down on the coast." Lori nodded. "They're helping me. But I told them your escape might involve two people, because there's a young man who loves you, and wants to run away with you. And the young man will make the escape easier, because he looks white.

"I just neglected to tell them that—I'm the young man." Daniel smiled. "When I met with them, I wasn't sure if you felt the same way for me as I do for you. But now that I know, I'm going with you.

"With me being white," he continued," we can travel in broad daylight by locomotive, provided we wear disguises. So, if my aunt and uncle try to track us down, they'll start searching in all the wrong places, because they'll assume we've escaped by sea."

Lori only looked at Daniel, as he waited expectantly for her to respond.

"So—what's wrong?" He asked.

Lori shrugged from his grasp, then put her hands on her hips. After blowing out a deep breath, she said, "What you're planning is too dangerous—we could both end up dead! What if it doesn't work? What if we get caught?" Then she added snidely, "You haven't had any luck so far trying to free me."

"Dang blasted, Lori!" Daniel said angrily. "This is a far better plan than either of my parents could've devised! I'm doing all I can for you! You could at least show a little appreciation and have some faith in me! "

"The whole thing's too risky — and besides, it's *crazy* for a white person to escape!"

"But I'll have to. I'll be a fugitive. That's the price I'm willing to pay for you, Lori. I want to be with you — no matter what the cost. And by taking you, I'm stealing Calhoun property. So I'll need to be in hiding, too.

"Martha and Jonas have already started correspondence with their Underground Railroad connections, and I'll be going back to see them in another couple of weeks. By then, they should have all the details worked out. But Lori," he again grasped her shoulders, "before we escape — I want to marry you."

Lori stared at him dumbfounded. For a few seconds she felt almost faint. "Marry me?"

"Marry you." Daniel embraced her. "Will you marry me?"

"Oh, Daniel — yes!" Lori relished the feel of his strong arms around her, feeling safe and secure in his embrace. Pulling away slightly, she gazed up into his eyes. When Daniel leaned down to kiss her, Lori's body tingled all over. She'd never been kissed. Closing her eyes, she enjoyed the warm sensation of his lips pressed against hers.

She was shocked, however, when he opened his mouth and probed his tongue deeply into hers. Lori's eyes opened wide. She froze, but then fell into the soft rhythm of passionate kissing with him, and again closed her eyes.

When Daniel pulled his lips from hers, Lori said, "But—but how can we get married?"

"Martha and Jonas can do it. They've arranged lots of weddings for runaway slaves."

Daniel embraced her tightly again, kissing her hungrily, but after a few moments Lori gently pushed him away. "But—you're not a slave—and you're white."

"Lori, we'll cross that bridge when we come to it."

Daniel reached to kiss her again, but she stopped him. "All right. Let's us say we do get married at the Wright's, then what?" Lori didn't wait for an answer, but instead pulled Daniel back to her lips for more.

When they finally stopped kissing, both were breathless and breathing hard. With his forehead softly pressed against Lori's, Daniel said, "I told them that our destination is Oberlin. We can stay with Sarah and James. That was the original plan we'd decided on anyway, after Mother died."

"Yes," Lori said slowly, "only then we'd believed that your uncle would have legally freed me—and we wouldn't have been married. Daniel, this plan is far too different.

"We'll both be fugitives—and married. Sarah and James will think it admirable that you helped me to escape. But they won't understand us—loving each other." Lori stepped away from him. "We can't tell them."

"They'll have to accept it sooner or later."

"But Daniel—what about the Fugitive Law? Sarah and James could be fined, thrown in jail—or even worse!"

"Lori, we'll be well protected in Oberlin. Plenty of fugitive slaves live there because it's safe. The folks up there *ignore* that 'kidnap law.'"

"But—what if your aunt and uncle send slave catchers after me?"

"They won't get to you because they'll have to kill me first."

Large tears pooled in Lori's eyes, then streamed down her cheeks. "Daniel—I couldn't bear to lose you—you're all I have..."

"Lori," he looked deeply into her eyes, now lit by moonlight, "I'm not planning on dying, but I'll do whatever it takes to protect you." Daniel kissed away her tears, then smiled. "Oberlin's rather inhospitable to slave catchers. And I reckon, once we're gone, Uncle Elijah will convince Aunt Lucinda that trying to catch us isn't worth it. Besides, she'll be so involved with Annabelle's wedding she probably won't even care about us any more."

"Daniel, I hope you're right."

"I am," Daniel said confidently. "I'll see to it that you won't have to stay here much longer. When I go back to the Wright's, I'll know more. Then shortly after that, we can start our escape."

Lori looked at him, amazed. "Daniel, aren't you the least bit afraid — not only about the escape but — you'd be giving up everything you have — or at least life as you know it — for me."

Daniel appeared serious as he said, "Lori, I want you to be free and I want to be with you. Giving up all I have is nothing compared to not having you. And — I suppose I am scared. I wouldn't be human if I weren't. But God will protect us."

Lori was silent as she continued to gaze into his eyes, then said, "He can do anything, no matter how big or how small."

"Keep remembering that," Daniel said, leading her back to the pond. "I'm as eager to leave this place as you are. Folks are getting more hostile by the day about the slavery issue and abolitionists."

As they sat by the water again, Lori thought about Daniel's brother. Handsome and charismatic, Jonathan had been a lawyer. Known as a firebrand in defending the rights of Negroes, he was an outspoken advocate for the enslaved, and viewed as a threat to the local political machine.

Lori remembered the night Daniel had found his brother's body, beaten bloody beyond recognition. Lori drew her knees to her chest, then hugged herself at the thought of the same thing happening to Daniel.

After the tragedy, she remembered Miss Rebecca repeating, "God's mercies are new each morning." But Lori wondered if God would give her enough strength to go on if Daniel were taken from her.

"I've got my share of money from Mother's estate," Daniel said, pulling Lori from her thoughts. "Uncle Elijah thinks Sarah and I will have enough to last us for a lifetime, provided we're wise in our financial decisions. The bank in Wilmington's already arranged a bill of exchange with Sarah's bank in Oberlin, and my account's already set up there."

"Daniel, not *all* your money's in Ohio, is it?"

"No. I still have plenty here for traveling expenses, and I have enough to take care of everything after we leave this stinking place. Now, we'd best be heading back. You need your rest and I need to think about talking to Uncle Elijah in the morning." Daniel stood up, then extended his hand to Lori.

While they slowly walked to the big house, Lori's gaze dropped as she thought about her first day in the fields.

Noticing her downcast eyes, Daniel stopped. Raising her chin with his fingertips, he said, "Lori, I promise, everything will be fine. You

won't have to go to the fields if I can help it.
And before long we'll be in Ohio."

Chapter 7

The next morning, asleep in her attic room, Lori was awakened by a bright lamp shining in her face.

She sat up to see Miss Lucinda standing over her. "It's four-thirty. I need you to get up now!" Lori didn't question her, although the servants rose at five. "Put this on," Miss Lucinda thrust something at her, "and meet Fanny at the back door. You'll be living in the cabins from now on, and working as a field hand. Fanny's going to show you to your new home. Don't bring anything but the clothes on your back!"

When Miss Lucinda left, Lori lit a candle. She shook out what looked like a long gray cotton smock, sleeveless and gathered at the waist.

She knew this would happen, but despite knowing, a lump in her throat continued to grow larger and larger. Lori tried to hold back the sobs welling there, but couldn't.

Her crying awoke Violet. "So," Violet stretched and yawned, "you're going to the fields now?"

Lori continued to sob and ignored the girl.

"Hope you don't get bit out there," Violet smirked. "But a snake bite's better than bein' eatin alive by a gator." Violet then rolled over for a few more minutes of rest.

****

"I have a few minutes to talk before Jenkins comes to see me with the morning report," Elijah said, as he and Daniel walked to his office. After breakfast, Daniel had asked to speak to him in private.

Once in his office, Elijah shut the door, saying, "I figured you'd want to talk to me about what's happened." He settled into a large black swivel chair behind an expansive flat top desk. After closing a copy of *The Southern Agriculturist* and pushing it aside, Elijah motioned Daniel to have a seat in a black leather chair that faced his desk.

As Daniel sat down he said, "Uncle Elijah, there's been a misunderstanding about Lori and me. What Annabelle said isn't true. We did meet, but we only went off to talk."

"Sure you did, son." Elijah said, the skepticism clear in his voice. "And we just want to make sure that nothing *more* than talking happens." Crossing his arms on his desk, Elijah leaned forward. "I don't like what clandestine meetings could lead to. I don't approve of that behavior and neither did your folks."

"I'd *never* behave inappropriately with Lori," Daniel declared.

"Boy, you say that, but one thing can lead to another! It's human nature, and a young, red blooded man that's alive can't help but take advantage of a situation that presents itself. Now, a healthy young buck like you could go stirring up all kinds of trouble carrying on with that—"

"But I wouldn't sully Lori as much as I care for her!" Daniel realized too late that what he'd said all but sealed Lori's fate to working in the fields.

Elijah immediately rose to his feet. With his large frame looming over Daniel, he said, "As much as you care for her? What the hell's wrong with you, boy? Sounding all emotional over some darkie!"

Daniel stood quickly to face his uncle. "What I meant was that I—I care for her like a sister."

Pressing his meaty hands on the desk between them, Elijah leaned toward Daniel so that he was only a few inches away from him. "No—I understood what you meant, and you can't go covering it up now. Her going to the fields is the best thing possible for you. And if you go sneakin' off to see her again, I'll have no choice but to sell her South."

"But, Uncle Elijah—"

"There are no buts about anything this serious, Daniel."

Elijah sat down and tipped back in his chair. Steepling his fingers over his girth, he said,

"She's nothing. You'll forget all about her."

At this, Daniel's face burned. "You don't know Lori at all! How dare you—"

"Don't back talk me, boy!" Elijah said firmly. "What you told me—about you caring for her—that stays between us, but you go near her again—she's gone!"

****

Lizzie, the only other slave in Lori's cabin, was asleep. Using the dim light of a candle to see, Lori pulled the letter from beneath her pallet. She wanted to read it one last time before destroying it. The letter was from Daniel. Fanny had brought it to her yesterday. She'd also brought a small pocket Bible that Daniel wanted Lori to have, so she could read it for encouragement.

From the letter, Lori had learned that if Daniel spoke to her again she'd be sold. Daniel had also written that when the time was right for their escape, he'd have Fanny send another message telling Lori the designated time and place to meet him.

Although that information was important, she just wanted to read the ending again. The part *after* his profuse apologies.

Dearest, always know that I love you more than I can ever express, and I pray that God will bless us with a long and happy life together. Know that not a moment goes by when I am not preoccupied with thoughts of you. Know that I am counting the days until you are my cherished wife. My undying love, Daniel.

Lori told herself that she could manage working in the fields, but only with God's grace. However, she'd hoped Daniel could prevent this. He hadn't. Instead, he'd failed her once more. Reading his words allowed Lori to forget her anger and resentment toward him — though only for a few seconds at a time.

Daniel wasn't stuck doing backbreaking work in a marshy swamp amongst dangerous insects and reptiles. Lori sighed, as she reread his letter, treasuring his words for what must have been the hundredth time. Then, glancing at Lizzie, who still slept soundly, Lori burned the letter in the candle's flame.

Chapter 8

Daniel waited outside the spacious guestroom on the first floor of the big house. He watched for a few moments from the open door as his sister stood on the far side of the room, packing a large trunk for her and her husband James's, upcoming departure.

Upon hearing him knock, Sarah looked toward her brother and smiled. For a split second, Daniel saw his mother in her face. Sarah was just as beautiful and bore a striking resemblance to Rebecca. Her face was pretty, with her mother's pleasant smile, apple cheeks and warm brown eyes. Honey blond hair, styled in thick sausage curls, tumbled past her shoulders.

"Sarah," Daniel shut the door. "I need to speak with you alone. Where's James?" he asked, striding toward a window at the side of the room.

"He's in the library going through those books from Mother's estate. Uncle Elijah pleaded with us to take as many as we can. Aunt Lucinda's been complaining about the amount of space they'll use up."

Daniel hardly paid attention to her. Pushing aside the white lace curtain puddled decoratively on the floor, he gazed through the long panes of glass.

Sarah must have sensed his distraction. "You're concerned about Lori, aren't you?"

"Yes." Daniel turned from the window, then leaned against the wall, crossing his arms.

"Well," Sarah said, packing a shirt she'd just folded, "you needn't worry. Everything will be fine. Jonas and Martha will provide a safe escape and our home is open to her." As Sarah spoke, Daniel looked down, contemplating how to tell her of his plans.

"She'll be in good hands and she'll be safe." Daniel's gaze remained downcast. "Daniel," Sarah said, "is something wrong with Lori? I didn't see her yesterday or today. Is she all right?"

Daniel hesitated. "She's — been sent to the fields."

"The fields!" Sarah gasped. "Whatever for? Lori's shown no insolence or disobedience of any kind, and she's certainly not equipped to do that kind of work! We've got to get her out of here."

Daniel's eyes met Sarah's. "The sooner the better. Sarah — I need to talk to you — about me being in Oberlin, too. I'll be arriving sooner than planned.

"I'm leaving at the same time that Lori is, and

I'm hoping the original plan we discussed after Mother's death is still permissible to you. Both of us can live with you. We can assist with expenses and do whatever you need to help in your household."

"Daniel — that's fine. You know our home is open to you. I'm glad you've made that decision. It's safer for you to leave the South all together, rather than stay for a year as Uncle Elijah suggested.

"If it were up to him, he'd want you to remain here permanently. You're a marvel in mathematics and mechanically inclined. You'd be an asset to him in running this place, or that cotton plantation he wants to buy. And you'd be married off in no time.

"Aunt Lucinda must have invited every unmarried girl in the county to her party, and they all wanted to meet you. Your dashing good looks made them forget that you're an abolitionist.

"But just wait until you get to Oberlin." Sarah smiled. "I've told several young ladies about you there, as well, and I have a particular one in mind that I'd very much like you to meet. Her name is Emma Spencer. She's quite beautiful and very nice.

"She teaches reading with me at The Liberty School, the school for the runaway fugitives. The two of you would make a beautiful couple, and Mother's locket will make a splendid wedding present for her — or whomever your future wife will be. I don't know why I didn't think to give it to you in the first place. I must agree with Uncle Elijah, Annabelle is spoiled, and she probably wouldn't appreciate the heirloom. So I think it's fitting that — "

"Sarah," Daniel interrupted his sister's rambling, "there's more that I haven't told you." He hesitated. "I'm leaving — because I'm helping Lori escape. I'll be providing her with all the assistance she needs."

"Well, since you are here, making sure she gets to the Wright's safely would be the chivalrous thing to do. Then Lori can travel with the others Martha and Jonas are helping. How soon after that will you tell Uncle Elijah you're leaving?"

"Sarah, you don't understand. I'm going to help Lori with her entire escape. From here to Oberlin." Sarah looked at him in surprise. After a few seconds she tried to speak, but couldn't. Reading the silent protest in her frightened eyes, Daniel said, "Sarah, don't try to stop me."

Swiftly walking toward him, the tiered white ruffles of her dress moved like wings. "Daniel — you can't!" Sarah placed a hand on her forehead, then grabbed one of the black walnut posts of the four poster bed. Sitting down, she said, "I — I feel faint! Darling, you could get yourself killed!"

"Sarah, I have to." Daniel sat next to her. "I feel responsible for Lori's safety."

"Jonas and Martha will see that she's safe! So there's absolutely no reason for you to put *yourself* in harm's way!" Tears welled in her eyes as she grasped his hands. "Daniel, I have yet to recover from losing Jonathan and Mother so closely together. I can't face another loss. I do *care* about Lori's well being, but blood is thicker than water. I know you feel like an older brother protecting your little sister, but — but she's not Mary!"

"Sarah, I want to help Lori. I've made my decision."

"Darling, unless you're insane — I — I don't understand why you want to do such a thing."

Daniel squeezed her hands gently, then stood to leave. "Expect us soon. I'll send correspondence when I know a more exact time."

Chapter 9

Less than a week had passed since Lori's placement in the fields, but she felt like she'd been there for months. The stares had finally subsided, but she knew the gossip hadn't.

Bent over with the hot sun beating down on her back, Lori trudged through the tepid marsh up to her knees pulling weeds. This was a difficult adjustment to which she hadn't yet adapted. Her back ached, her thighs throbbed, and she'd never been so filthy and smelly.

The tedious work couldn't dull the feel of the unbearable heat, the squishy mud between her toes, or the itchy mosquito bites up and down her arms. In addition, she was on constant guard against water moccasins and gators.

All the hands knew that working on a rice plantation meant you could die any time because of all the hazards lurking in the paddies.

Several women were scattered among what seemed like a never-ending maze of rice fields. Lizzie worked alongside Lori, moving faster, even though she must've been four times Lori's age.

"Hurry up, Lori," Lizzie whispered. "I showed you how to move fast, now move, 'cause Jenkins is a comin'."

Lori picked up her pace and grabbed at the weeds rapidly. She heard swift hoof beats as Jenkins approached the grassy bank. His horse whinnied, then sighed with flapping lips. Jenkins said nothing. From the corner of her eye, Lori could see him observing her on his sleek black horse. Slowly he rode along the bank, paying special attention to her.

When Jenkins stopped, Lori hesitantly began to glance up.

"You don't need to look up here at me," Jenkins said sternly, fingering his lash. Lori immediately dropped her gaze. "You just keep working hard — and fast — so I don't have to use this." From her peripheral vision, Lori saw Jenkins pat the whip. "Mrs. Calhoun told me to keep an eye on you, to make sure you keep up." Jenkins watched Lori for a few seconds more, then rode away.

"You doin' fine," Lizzie said. "He don't use the lash much — and I ain't never seen him use it on a woman."

****

Using the back of her hand, Lori wiped sweat from her brow as she headed toward the bank with Lizzie.

With their tasks completed, they slowly

walked to their cabin. A young girl named Juno grabbed Lori's arm. Juno lived in the cabin next to Lori's. She was probably about thirteen and had taken a liking to Lori.

While Lizzie walked ahead, Juno whispered something in Lori's ears. "Be careful," Juno said. "That cabin you livin' in—it cursed." With that, the girl ran off.

Lori shook her head at the superstitions believed by ignorant Negroes, but at the same time, was curious to know why Juno thought that.

Once inside her cabin with Lizzie, Lori sighed, looking down at her mud-caked dress. "I never knew I could be so sore or so tired." After a long stretch, Lori rubbed the small of her back, then settled down on her stiff pallet.

"You young and healthy," Lizzie said, sitting on the other pallet. "You'll get used to it."

Lizzie had told Lori she'd been at Dancing Oaks for what she guessed to be about thirty years, and she put her age at around sixty. But to Lori, she appeared much older. Deep wrinkles embedded Lizzie's face, as though sculpted by a potter's hands. Her hair was white like cotton, and her skin as dark as black strap molasses. She wasn't very tall, and her stooped spine made her appear even shorter.

Lizzie slapped her thighs and rubbed them. "But you sure is lucky you missed out on that double hoein' time. You'd be a lot more tired, hurtin' all over, and your hands would be bloody from usin' that hoe. You'd feel like your back was broke."

Lori looked at Lizzie astonished. "Did you do that?"

"Sure did. My body growed accustom to it, I guess. I still got some life in me yet, praise the Lawd. Once I gets too old to work, Cap'n Cindy'll want to cut off my rations. If you ain't doin' work, she don't see no reason to feed you. She cut off rations before, but Master Elijah too big hearted to let anybody starve. He make sure the overseer give all the hands food. But that Cap'n Cindy — she a mean woman!"

"I know she's mean," Lori said coldly.

Lizzie didn't say anything as she eyed Lori keenly for a few seconds. "I know *you* know how mean she is. Bein' she's why you out here."

Lizzie had no doubt heard the rumors, Lori thought.

"On account of you and her nephew."

"Despite what you've heard," Lori said defensively, "Master Daniel is a gentleman. He never once touched me — in a way he shouldn't."

"Well, if he ain't poked you yet, that's what he's aiming for."

Lori's mouth dropped open at Lizzie's crudeness. "Master Daniel is a decent man *and* an abolitionist!"

"Master Daniel is a white man! And I ain't

never known no white man to treat a Negro woman no better than dirt!"

"Lizzie, you're wrong about Daniel! He—" Lori stopped abruptly.

"He what? Don't let him be fillin' your head with lies, 'cause he a white man first! And I only known of a few white men that didn't think a slave woman was something to use any way they pleased. Master Elijah's one—and Jenkins. Master Elijah got rid of the last overseer. He couldn't keep his pants buttoned up round the women out here in the quarters, and Master Elijah don't approve of that. Now Jenkins—he keeps to hisself, and his bottle on the weekends."

Eager to change the subject, Lori said, "Juno—told me something. She says this cabin's cursed."

"Humph," Lizzie snorted.

"Why did she say that?"

"It ain't cursed. But the nigguhs is so afraid, none of 'em want to live in it with me. Just 'cause a bunch of bad things happened here, they think the cabin's got a hex on it."

"So—what—bad things happened?" Lori asked.

Lizzie's eyes welled. She grabbed a wadded rag from her pallet and wiped them. "I used to live with my son and his wife. They had three babies. But last Christmas, all three of the youngins took sick with fever and died."

"Lizzie—I'm so sorry. That must've been terrible."

"Oh, chile—it was." Lizzie leaned back against the wall, then gazed up at the split log beams above. "Not long after that, my son got a snake bite. He ended up dead from infection."

"Lizzie—no," Lori said sadly.

Lizzie's eyes met Lori's. "Then his wife—she come down with the melancholy. She wasn't herself, just walked 'round in circles mumbling. Master Elijah wanted to keep her. He thought he give her enough time, she'd heal—but that mean ol' Cap'n Cindy—she sold her off!"

"Lizzie, how horrible."

"It's all right, chile." Lizzie smiled slightly through her tears. "The good Lawd give me strength. One day, freedom gonna come. And all the white folks that's been mean to they nigguhs be seein' some bad time ahead. You reap what you sow."

They sat silently for a few moments, then Lizze said, "The first thing I'm gonna do when I's free, is learn me to read. I wanna read God's word like it really is.

"Used to be a hand here that read it to us. His name was Zeke—but he gone now—years ago." Lizzie's eyes dropped to the rag in her wrinkled hands. "I can still remember the truth of what he read. The truth the white folks don't practice. But—I wish I could read it myself."

Perhaps, Lori thought, as they sat quietly, this was why God had placed her here. For all the pain and suffering Lizzie had experienced, Lori could be a blessing to her. She moved from her pallet and reached underneath it, pulling out her pocket Bible.

"What you got there?" Lizzie asked.

"It's a Bible. After you've fallen asleep every night, I read it. But now I'll read it for both of us."

"You can read?" Lizzie asked in disbelief. Lori nodded. "Now, chile, don't go gettin' yourself in trouble readin' 'round here!"

"But I want you to hear the Word like it really is. I'll even teach you the alphabet so you can learn how to read." Lori smiled. "That'll be our secret. No one will ever know."

Lizzie's eyes looked scared and uncertain. "You too trustin', chile, and you don't—"

"Lizzie, I want to teach you. You've taught me how to survive out in the fields; this is the least I can do for you."

****

Jason, Juno's older brother from the neighboring cabin, went out after dark one evening to relieve himself. As he passed by Lizzie's cabin, he noticed a dim light. The shuttered window flew open from a gust of wind, enabling him to see inside. Filled with excitement, Jason saw Lori *reading*! At last, a slave at Dancing Oaks who could!

This would be kept a closely guarded secret from the white folks, but it would travel fast along the slave grapevine.

Chapter 10

Evelyn Thorne sat daintily stirring a cup of tea in the parlor of Dancing Oaks with her best friend, Annabelle, and Miss Lucinda. Evelyn heard them prattling on and on about Annabelle's wedding, but she was much too distracted to listen.

Although today was perfect for a visit, Daniel wasn't around—and that was the main reason she'd come by to call. The other bucks in the county seemed doltish and silly compared to Daniel. Evelyn could have any one of them for a husband.

All she'd have to do was snap her fingers. However, she refused to settle for doltish and silly. Evelyn wanted Daniel.

She grimaced slightly, still trying to figure out why Daniel hadn't noticed her at the party. He'd seemed aloof and detached; perhaps preoccupied by his mother's sudden death.

He'd also lost his father and brother not that long ago. So many losses, Evelyn thought, but she could help him. Evelyn believed she could easily make any man forget his troubles.

She was one of the most beautiful, if not *the* most beautiful girl in Brunswick County. A woman's hair was her glory, and Evelyn had been blessed with an abundance of raven locks, and as for her figure, she had the smallest waist and the largest bosom of any girl of marrying age.

To entice a man, all she had to do was bat her large blue violet eyes, or smile her charming pixie smile, or crinkle her tiny, slightly upturned nose. From just a glance, men were driven mad by her. But why hadn't Daniel been? Evelyn was determined to find out! She stirred her tea so vigorously, the spoon clanked against the cup.

"Evelyn," Miss Lucinda said, "is something wrong?"

Evelyn stopped stirring and gazed up from the amber whirlpool she'd created in her teacup. "Oh, no, Miss Lucinda." A bright smile lit her face, displacing the grimace. "I was just thinking about your poor, dear nephew, Daniel. Is he—all right? I assume—something's bothering him; he seems rather melancholy. But, I suppose he's still mourning his mother's passing."

Miss Lucinda took a sip of tea from her pink and white luster teacup. "Yes, dear. He and his mother were very close. We all—miss her," she said with a small, tight smile.

Making an effort not to sound forward, Evelyn asked in feigned innocence, "Is Daniel here — today — right now?"

Annabelle shot Evelyn a piercing stiletto glare. "Why?" she asked sharply.

"I — I just want to offer him a listening ear — if he'd like to talk."

"Evelyn, I think that's a splendid idea!" Miss Lucinda sat up tall, clasping her hands. She sounded almost gleeful. "You could be just the tonic Daniel needs to get his mind off his mother, and — and other things. He's at the mill with Mr. Elijah right now, but, Evelyn, dear, why don't you plan on staying with us for supper?" Miss Lucinda patted the sides of her dull brown hair, then adjusted her chignon. "Perhaps you can walk in the rose garden with Daniel afterward."

"Oh, Miss Lucinda, that would be lovely! I can't think of anything I'd rather do," Evelyn said excitedly. Then glancing at Annabelle's frigid glare, she added somberly, "So I can ease his mind from sorrow."

"Well," Miss Lucinda stood quickly, "Excuse me for a moment while I tell Fanny to set another place at the table. I'll have her put you right next to Daniel."

Miss Lucinda grabbed the skirt of her manure colored dress and giddily scuttled from the room.

After Miss Lucinda was gone, Evelyn pounced on Annabelle. "Just what is the meaning of those looks you've been giving me each time I inquire of your poor, dear cousin? Your eyes nearly cut me to the heart!" she exclaimed dramatically, placing a delicate hand over her ample bosom.

Annabelle slowly put her teacup and saucer on the mahogany tiptop table in front of them. "It's clear that my 'poor, dear cousin' isn't the least bit interested in you!" She said, with her frozen gaze on Evelyn. "I don't see why you're intent upon pursuing him like a wild animal when you're only making a fool out of yourself."

Evelyn clicked her tongue. "How do *you* know he doesn't fancy me?"

"Just because most men are drawn to you like—"

"Like moths to flame!" Evelyn smiled.

"No," Annabelle raised a brow, "like dogs to a freshly butchered bone." As Evelyn gasped, Annabelle continued, "That doesn't mean every man is. From what I recall at the party, you failed to wile Daniel with your charms. He looked right past you."

"He did not!"

"Oh, I forgot. He *did* look at you—when you tripped poor Amanda and mussed her dress with your punch so she couldn't beat you to him!"

"Oh, that Amanda." Evelyn nonchalantly smoothed the folds of her pink and white dress. "Bless her heart. She's just a clumsy girl because of those dreadfully large feet. I couldn't help it if she bumped into me and made me spill my punch. Now, back to your cousin. In my opinion, Daniel's just shy. That's why he hasn't made any obvious overtures toward me. But I know he'd like to."

Annabelle snorted a half laugh. "You wouldn't want him."

Evelyn raised her chin. "What do you mean I wouldn't want him? Every girl in the county wants him. But only one's going to get him, and it's going to be me!"

"He's different." Annabelle smirked.

"Different?" Evelyn's eyes widened. "Different how?" She lowered her voice to a whisper. "He likes women, doesn't he?"

"Of course he does!" Annabelle said, then added softly, "*No* Calhoun men are Nancy-boys."

"So—are you referring to his family's abolitionist leanings?"

Annabelle pursed her lips. "Well—that's—that's part of it." She paused briefly. "Besides, he'll be leaving to go to school in Ohio. Then he'll probably *stay* there, and keep company with all those other *deranged* abolitionists.

"So—he couldn't possibly make you happy.

You wouldn't want to live in Ohio. Why—that very thought chills me to the bone."

"It doesn't bother me," Evelyn sighed, smiling. "Where he'd go, I'd go. Even to the brutal cold of Ohio. I'd make the sacrifice of living in freezing temperatures surrounded by a bunch of Yankee abolitionists just to be with him."

"What about your livelihood?" Annabelle asked. "I don't know what kind of money he'll make. But it won't be what you're used to! Daniel won't prosper like a wealthy planter, because he'll be too busy being an abolitionist!"

"Oh, Annabelle!" Evelyn tipped her head, "Daniel will do just fine, because—because he'll outgrow his abolitionist tendencies and come to his senses. My father says that abolitionists are just misguided souls. That's what Daniel is right now, and he needs me to help him—see the light!

"Whatever Daniel decides to do," Evelyn continued, "he'll do well, and prosper—in Ohio. He'll pursue a well paying profession, worthy of his talent—and when we marry, we'll be wealthy. He *does* have the fortune his mother left him."

"My father believes his inheritance will last a lifetime," Annabelle said, "but fortunes can be lost *easily* by foolish decisions."

"I'd hardly think Daniel a fool."

Annabelle looked coolly at her friend. "Evelyn, stop wasting your time *dwelling* on my cousin."

Evelyn's eyes narrowed. "What aren't you telling me?"

Annabelle hesitated. "There's nothing more," she said tightly.

"You *are* hiding something about him, aren't you!" Evelyn smiled slyly.

"The fact that he's an abolitionist bound for Ohio should be enough to disinterest you."

"I don't believe you," Evelyn laughed. "But I do know this! You're harboring some ill will against your cousin Daniel. You're still mad about your father giving *him* that locket instead of you!"

"Hush up about that!"

"Well, goosy, when Daniel and I marry, and it's given to me as a wedding present — I'll let you borrow it!"

Chapter 11

Violet was glad she no longer shared her attic room with Lori, and she'd been happy to see her sent off to the fields. However, it was just as Violet had suspected.

Word spread fast among the slaves at the Calhoun place that Lori could read. If Cap'n Cindy knew that, she'd have Lori's hide whipped good! As Violet dusted the dining room, she smiled, envisioning Lori strung up by the wrists as Jenkins flogged her. No more prancing around on a high horse after that.

While moving her feather duster along the sideboard, Violet wondered just how Miss Lucinda could find out. Violet couldn't tell her. All the other servants liked Lori, and they'd never forgive Violet if she told on her. Sighing, Violet decided that sooner or later, she'd figure out a way for Miss Lucinda to know that Lori could read.

"Oh, Violet."

Upon hearing her name, Violet turned to see Miss Evelyn standing at the dining room entrance.

"Yes, Miss, Evelyn," Violet smiled. "It's a surprise seeing you here again today."

Evelyn raised a brow. "Not that it's any of *your* concern, but I forgot my handbag yesterday."

That excuse couldn't hold water, Violet thought. Miss Evelyn probably left her bag on purpose, just so she could come back today and visit with *Daniel* again.

Miss Annabelle wasn't around right now to keep Miss Evelyn entertained. She was out back at the kitchen cabin attending to a minor crisis, in place of her mother. Miss Lucinda was resting on account of another sick headache. So Miss Evelyn was left alone, and to her own devices.

"Now, Violet," Miss Evelyn said, "if anybody *knows* anything, it'll be you. So perhaps you can help me. I'm not satisfied with what I've been told about Master Daniel."

So, Miss Evelyn wanted to ask questions, and Violet knew why. Yesterday after dinner, as she'd trudged back and forth to the kitchen carrying dishes and food, Evelyn had seen what happened in the rose garden, while Miss Evelyn and Master Daniel went for a stroll.

Miss Evelyn's bare shouldered lavender dress was so low, her bosom was just about spillin' out of it.

Master Daniel couldn't help but notice,

although he'd tried not to look. And each time she'd thrust her teats in his direction, he backed away, like he was afraid they'd start spewing snake venom.

Miss Evelyn tossed her heavy curls from side to side, moved her hips to make her hoopskirt sway, and batted her eyes until she looked dizzy. But despite all that, Master Daniel hadn't seemed the least bit interested.

"What can *you* tell me about Master Daniel?" Evelyn asked, as she sidled toward Violet like a viper.

"Well, Miss Evelyn, he's a right fine gentleman," Violet replied, knowing full well what Evelyn was trying to pry out of her. Miss Evelyn could trap any man just as easy as a rattler could catch a rat, but Daniel hadn't given her the time of day because his heart belonged to another.

Violet wasn't stupid. She'd figured Daniel's "closeness" to Lori was more than brotherly. The very night she and Fanny had talked about Lori going to the fields, Violet had seen for herself why Lori was being sent there. From her little window on the third floor, she'd seen Lori and Daniel go off together. When Lori had risen around midnight, Violet had pretended to be asleep. And Lori hadn't come back for over an hour.

"Yes, Violet, I'm aware of that," Miss Evelyn

said, sounding slightly exasperated. "But is there anything else you can tell me?"

"Just what do you want to know, Miss Evelyn?"

"First of all," she dropped her voice to a whisper, "does he fancy women?"

Violet gasped, feigning astonishment. "Of *course*, Miss Evelyn. Why would you think he wouldn't?" She blinked wide blue violet eyes, similar to Evelyn's. They shared the same father.

"Hmm...well," Evelyn knitted her brows. "It's just that—that Master Daniel seems woeful—and rather—preoccupied. I realize he's distraught over his mother's death, but life must go on." Evelyn grasped Violet's arm tightly and leaned close to her. "Tell me," she lowered her voice, "is Master Daniel ill?"

Violet smiled. "Oh, no'm. He's just as healthy as a ox!" Then she bit her lower lip, attempting to look innocent. "That is," she said softly, "'ceptin'—for his heart."

Evelyn released Violet's arm. "His heart?" She asked alarmed. "What ails his heart?"

"Affections," Violet paused a long moment, "for a girl."

Evelyn's ivory face reddened. "Tell me more."

"Now, Miss Evelyn, I don't know much, but he came here with a slave girl from his mama's place who's owned by Master Elijah and Miss Lucinda," Violet prattled quickly. "Her name is Lori, and she and Master Daniel grew up together. She was workin' in the house after they came here, but she musta done somethin' bad 'cause she got sent to the fields. I don't know what she did, but Master Daniel acts like he's broken hearted 'bout her bein' put out there."

Evelyn crossed her arms and clicked her tongue. "Is that all? A little Negro *slave girl*? I hardly think Master Daniel would be concerned about that. Although...he is an abolitionist...and they *do* see things differently." Evelyn thought about this for a few seconds then said, "Perhaps he's somewhat concerned about the girl's well being, but as long a she's careful, she won't *die* from working in the fields."

"But I can tell you something else about her that you—"

"Violet," Evelyn took a deep breath, "I don't care to hear another thing about that *slave*. Let's us get back to Daniel. I want you to think—and think *hard*," she commanded, as though reprimanding a child. "Is there something else that could possibly be bothering him?"

"Well, Miss Evelyn," Violet began slowly, "I think—maybe *you* should ask Master Daniel about Lori."

****

Evelyn considered this for a moment. No, it certainly wouldn't hurt to ask. She did remember seeing a new servant girl at Miss Lucinda's last party, and Daniel seemed familiar with her. "Maybe I will."

Violet looked around cautiously, then lowered her voice. "Rumor is, she can read. But don't tell anyone you heard it from me. You *know* how Miss Lucinda would feel about that. Um, um, um." Violet shook her head. "I don't know what would be worse. Lori havin' her hide whipped — 'cause sometimes Miss Lucinda has a body beat near to death for reading — or her being sold South.

"I hope, for Lori's sake, that she really can't read and it's just an ugly rumor. But livin' with abolitionists all those years, you know how they feel about book learnin' for all."

Violet stepped closer to Evelyn and dropped her voice to a whisper. "You've seen Lori, Miss Evelyn, I know you have. She was serving punch at Miss Lucinda's last party — the *dark* girl.

"You remember seeing Master Daniel talking to her — and laughing with her, don't you? He tried to do it on the sly, when he didn't think anybody was lookin'. But he was around her so much you couldn't help but notice. And when he wasn't right next to her, he was gazin' in her direction — and she was gazin' right back."

Evelyn's mind reeled back to the party. She

did recall how Daniel had seemed particularly animated upon each brief encounter with that black girl, the new servant Evelyn had never seen. Although other servants had offered the same refreshment, he'd only sought her. Could what Violet said, actually be true?

Before Evelyn could ask any more questions, she heard the front door of the mansion open. Quickly moving to the dining room entrance, she saw Daniel in the foyer on his way to the stairs.

"Oh, Daniel," she called. Seeing her, he stopped. Evelyn eagerly grabbed her skirts and charged toward him.

"Evelyn," Daniel said, "how nice to see you again." He backed away from her predatory advance, inching closer to the stairs. "How beautiful you look in that dress."

The compliment he tossed stopped Evelyn dead in her tracks. Standing still for a moment, she gazed down, admiring her green muslin dress, then ran a hand through her jet-black curls. "Why, thank you, Daniel. Do you really like it?"

"It's lovely on you." He put a foot on the bottom step.

"Oh, aren't you the charmer?"

Daniel looked up the staircase as though distracted. "What brings you to Dancing Oaks today?"

"Oh—I left my handbag here yesterday—so I—came by to fetch it—and—to visit with Annabelle for a little while." She moved toward Daniel, stopping only mere inches away from him. "Also, my father's looking to buy a new maid for me. He's selling my Chrissie to the Crawley place because he's letting her marry one of the bucks over there."

Evelyn paused for a moment, then said, "So—I uh—hear you came here with a girl—a *Lori* from your mother's estate?" As close as she was to Daniel, for a split second she saw his eyes widen and his face blanch.

"Lori is *not* for sale! Now, if you'll excuse me, Evelyn, good day." Daniel abruptly turned away from her and headed up the stairs.

Taking in a deep, tight breath, Evelyn balled her fists. That look, and that curt response, told her all she needed to know. Seething, Evelyn pursed her lips hard. Miss Lucinda would be waking soon.

****

In the library, Lucinda sat at her desk and opened her journal. More than two weeks had passed since Evelyn had informed her of Lori's ability to read. But Lucinda had had to wait patiently for the right time to punish her. Tomorrow would be the day.

Daniel was off visiting friends in Wilmington. He wouldn't be back until late tomorrow evening.

Elijah, with his soft-hearted self, would be leaving tomorrow morning. He'd be gone all day negotiating a deal for that cotton plantation.

Lucinda had instructed Jenkins to whip Lori close to death. That girl had caused enough trouble leading Daniel down the road to ruin, and acting dignified as royalty when she wasn't anything but a nigger. However, her worst offense was reading! Under no circumstances would a literate slave be tolerated at Dancing Oaks.

Elijah had told Daniel to stay away from her, and he had, so she wouldn't be sold. But Lori could be flogged; and if she died, so what? Slaves died every day.

In her journal Lucinda wrote:

The unspeakable situation has been remedied for good...

Chapter 12

Daniel gazed out through the open window. Fat drops pelted the ground during a light shower, filling the small spare bedroom with the wet smell of fresh rain.

At the Wright's simple cottage in Wilmington, Daniel readied himself for his return to Dancing Oaks. The escape plan was complete. As Daniel packed his things, he thought over every last detail. The disguises were ready and the safe houses secure. The routes for trains, stagecoaches and the final ferry were all mapped out.

On his last visit here, Daniel had said that he was the same size as "the young man" who'd be escaping with Lori. Since "the young man" looked white, it was decided that he could travel as a wealthy planter, with Lori as his young servant boy.

Daniel had provided money and measurements for the outfits to be made by a local Negro seamstress. But Daniel had had to convince Martha that a disguise was actually needed for the "young man."

"Thou has given me money that need not be spent. If the young man is thy size, can he not wear thy clothes?" She'd asked. Daniel had told her he didn't want the young man to look at all like him. "He should be flamboyant," Daniel had said.

Still not convinced, Martha had said, "Flamboyant, and draw attention to himself?" Daniel had had to think fast. "You do understand, Martha, he doesn't want to look like a Quaker." Daniel had laughed, stalling to think of something else to say. "And imagine him as — perhaps, new money."

Martha had finally given in. But the colorful attire designed by the seamstress was beyond anything Daniel could have imagined. Yesterday, Daniel had bought a fake beard and spectacles from a small theater company in town. He hadn't wanted to impose that errand on Martha. No need having her exposed to those disreputable theater people.

Daniel had brought extra garments and additional funds on this visit to be kept at the Wright's for the escape. Again, he'd said these items were for the "young man." He'd also given Martha money and Lori's measurements so she could purchase clothing for her. As a field hand, Lori had only one thing to wear, the gray cotton frock. It was now dirty and ragged, hardly suitable for anything else.

Lori needed male clothing as a disguise for travel, as well as dresses for Ohio. In addition, Daniel had told Martha to instruct the seamstress to make a wedding gown and veil from the finest fabric, sparing no expense.

At the end of the next week, they would escape, stopping first at Martha and Jonas's home. Leaving from Winnabow to get here, they'd travel up the Cape Fear River in a rowboat. During his prior visit in Wilmington, Daniel had purchased one and rowed back to Dancing Oaks. Down river it had taken him less than two hours.

The ride upstream would be more strenuous and take a little longer. However, the Cape Fear was a docile river, so Daniel could easily navigate the boat. And luckily, he and Lori wouldn't be seen on the night of their escape. According to *The Farmer's Almanac*, there'd be no moonlight on account of a new moon.

After rowing to Dancing Oaks, he'd hidden the boat, placing it in a well-marked spot he'd practiced finding in the dark with only the light of a lantern.

The rowboat was in a secluded area not far from the plantation grounds, near the bank of the Cape Fear.

He'd turned it upside down and covered it with pine straw, bunches of wire grass, Spanish moss and scrub oak branches.

As Daniel closed his carpetbag, he thought about another pressing issue he'd need to remedy soon. Martha was downstairs preparing supper. For the past couple of hours, Daniel had smelled chicken baking and collard greens boiling. But he'd lost his appetite because of the matter concerning "the young man." Why had he waited until the last day of his stay to reveal the truth? Surely Martha and Jonas would understand. Or would they? Daniel wondered.

After Martha called him to supper, Daniel slowly walked down the stairs, agonizing over how to tell them. As his boot heels echoed on the pinewood steps, he smelled molasses and ginger. Martha had baked gingerbread for dessert, but the fragrant aroma did nothing to revive his appetite.

Jonas raised the window higher in the small dining room as Daniel strode in. The rain had stopped. "I have noticed that thou are rather quiet today," Jonas said.

"And thou lacks thy usual exuberance," Martha added, as she placed a dish of greens with ham hocks on the simple rectangular table. She wore a soft white cap on her head and a white apron over a light blue dress.

Physically, the Wrights were a mismatched pair. Jonas, tall and lean with jet-black hair, had stern, hardened features deceiving of his kind nature.

But Martha was short and plump with golden hair and a pleasant round face. She possessed a disposition just as sweet as her appearance.

"I was — thinking about the escape…" Daniel said quietly.

"Do not worry about the escape, or Lori." Martha said. "I know of thy concern for her. Thou can rest assured that all is in place for a successful journey. God's hand will guide her — and her young man." Martha smiled.

She went back to the kitchen and moments later returned with a bowl of oyster stuffing. Placing it next to the greens, Martha said, "Daniel, not a day goes by that we do not think of our dear, sweet Rebecca. And we are pleased to see thee continuing with her mission."

"Yes, Daniel," Jonas said, setting down the platter of chicken he'd carved, "thy mother is truly missed, and thou are quite courageous to carry on. For it is thy mission as well, and one of great difficulty.

"Now, Daniel, please sit down," he motioned to a bench alongside the wooden table, "and let us partake of this meal."

Jonas and Martha sat on the bench opposite Daniel, and then all held hands for a moment of silent thanksgiving. Afterwards, the plates were served, but Daniel couldn't eat a thing. He only stared into the light brown gravy covering his chicken and stuffing.

"Daniel, why does thou not eat?" Martha asked. "Are thou ill?"

"Martha, I'm fine. But there's something I need to tell you. I just haven't known — quite how to — explain it." Daniel hesitated, wary of their reaction. "I know that you believe God is revealed to each person through an Inner Light that leads to truth. In — in God's eyes — we're all the same — and — and…" He knew Quaker opposition to slavery had its limits. How would the Wrights accept love between a white man and a Negro woman?

"Go on, Daniel," Jonas prodded after a long silence.

"The young man who'll be escaping with Lori…"

"Yes," Martha said, as she and Jonas waited for him to continue.

Daniel only poked at his greens with a fork, unsure of what to say next. Finally, putting down the utensil, he met their eyes.

"God has led me to an unexpected place — a place that you may not understand."

Martha gazed at her husband. Jonas leaned back on the bench, pulling slightly at his beard.

"To where is God leading thee?" he asked.

Daniel began sweating and mopped his forehead with a cotton napkin. "I'm — I'm the young man," he blurted quickly.

"Lori and I love each other. We want to be together as man and wife." Twisting the napkin tightly with both hands, he waited uneasily for their reaction.

Jonas and Martha glanced at each other uncomfortably for a moment before looking at Daniel.

"Daniel," Martha said, "has thou prayed about this? Has thou meditated upon this decision and given it firm and thoughtful consideration?"

"And does thou truly believe that this is God's leading for thy life," Jonas said, "down a path of difficulty and hardship — with a Negro as thy wife?"

Daniel took a deep breath. "Jonas, Martha, I have prayed. And I have thought — meditated — about it for a long time. This is God's leading for me. I love her. I realize things won't be easy. But I want her with me. And — the Lord provides."

The Wrights gazed again at each other briefly, then Martha said, "So — thou *are* certain that this *is* God's leading — and His will for thee?"

"I am."

After a few seconds of silence, Jonas said, "Well if the good Lord intends for the two of you to love each other, so be it."

Martha smiled. "And it appears that we will have a wedding to plan for thee."

Her eyes watered, but she held back her tears. Because of the choice he'd made, Daniel was uncertain if Martha's tears of were those of joy or grief.

Chapter 13

Luther Jenkins was poor and white, but he'd never considered himself trash. The Negroes considered themselves above such vermin and thought just as meanly of poor white trash as the rich white folks did.

Overseers weren't held in the highest esteem, but Jenkins hadn't planned on keeping this job for any longer than two years. He lived in a spacious cabin and drew a handsome annual salary of nine-hundred dollars. He'd saved just about enough to purchase that farm in Indiana, the one he'd wanted for Ruby. However, she'd died before they married. Coming down South to escape from the pain of losing her, as well as to earn money, had seemed like a good idea at the time.

Jenkins had hoped that while an overseer he wouldn't have to whip someone "near to death," let alone that someone be a woman. Well into his second year, this was only his third flogging. But this one included specific instructions he didn't know if he'd be capable of carrying out. That girl probably wasn't even eighteen.

Jenkins picked up the cowhide whip from his dresser, feeling its sharpness against his calloused fingertips. The lash was new, just a few weeks old, and still smelled like fresh rawhide. Jenkins had seen it made.

It was a strip cut from the whole length of the ox. And the ox used had been the largest one on the plantation. While moist, the cowhide had been twisted until it tapered to a point. When dried and hardened, sharp edges projected from every turn, so that with each stroke, it could cut into the flesh.

Jenkins threw down the lash, then took a long swig of whiskey. Cracking a whip, he supposed, had officially made him into a cracker. Glancing at the bottle, Jenkins realized he'd already swigged half of it to numb himself to the deed he was about to perform.

"Damn it, Ruby! I don't want to do this, but Mrs. Calhoun's gonna have my job if I don't!" Maybe Mr. Calhoun would come back early, Jenkins thought. He'd never stand for this. But if the master didn't come back soon, Jenkins would be stuck doing Cap'n Cindy's dirty work.

Jenkins felt sick. Time was passing, and Mr. Calhoun was unlikely to show up before the scheduled hour. At least, he hoped that, maybe Mrs. Calhoun wouldn't be around to supervise the ordeal. Then he wouldn't have to whip the girl so hard. He could still barely imagine whipping her at all.

Cap'n Cindy'd been at his first flogging, to make sure he'd been effective, but she hadn't been there the second time. But those slaves were men, Jenkins recalled. He'd never whipped a woman and didn't know if different procedures applied.

Jenkins took another deep swig. "What would you think of me, Ruby?" The whiskey burned his throat. "A part of me's glad you're not here to see what I've become...lower than low."

****

"Strip her to the waist!" Lucinda yelled.

"Stop it!" Lori kicked, scratched and screamed as Jenkins and Boyd, the Negro driver, dragged her behind the barn toward "the tree," a large oak with low hanging branches ideal for stringing up wayward chattel.

"Don't!" Lori screamed, as Boyd, a large black Negro, restrained her hands behind her. "No!" She tried to back away, only backing into Boyd's bull like frame, as Jenkins awkwardly unfastened the buttons of her top and forced it past her shoulders. Boyd then maneuvered her arms from the sleeveless openings.

"Get off me!" Lori protested through tears, struggling futilely against the two men. Jenkins yanked her head back and stuffed a handkerchief into her mouth. He probably didn't want to hear her cries, Lucinda thought. But he hadn't heard anything yet.

Once Lori's screams were reduced to whimpers, the chickens could be heard clucking inside the barn. The wind swooshed around them scented by dried grains, hay and manure.

"Now tie her hands and feet and string her up to the tree!" Lucinda ordered. Lori continued kicking, so Jenkins and Boyd had to wrestle her to the ground, muddy from an earlier soaking of rain. Boyd forced her hands over her head and tied them, while Jenkins sat on her legs and bound her feet.

Boyd slung Lori over his massive back like a rice sack and carried her to the tree.

"Her feet should barely touch the ground!" Lucinda instructed. After Boyd had strung Lori by the wrists to a sturdy branch, Lucinda said, "Make sure she's up there good and tight!"

Boyd looked at Lori's hands. "Them ropes is cuttin' into her. Her wrists is bleedin', Miss Lucinda."

"Then your work is done."

As Boyd trudged off, Jenkins pulled the lash from his saddle bag. "Mr. Jenkins," Lucinda crossed her arms over her rust colored dress, "you may commence with punishment. But take that rag out of her mouth, first."

Jenkins took the cloth from the girl's mouth. Breathing hard, Lori began, "The Lord is my shepherd, I shall not —"

But suddenly, the lash cracked hard against her flesh, cutting into it like a hot knife.

Jenkins flinched slightly, as Lori screamed loud enough to be heard clear over to the next plantation.

Jenkins hesitated. "Keep going, Mr. Jenkins!" Lucinda demanded. "And crack that lash like a man, not a little girl. If you can't do it any harder, I'll have to do it myself — and *then* find a new overseer!"

Looking down at the ground, then at Lori, Jenkins didn't move.

"I'm waiting, Mr. Jenkins!" Lucinda crowed sharply.

Jenkins took a deep breath, then cracked the whip.

The first few lashes broke Lori's skin, and soon the blood flowed like she'd been ripped open from neck to hips. After about a dozen lashes, her screaming stopped.

"She might be quiet, Mr. Jenkins, but she's not near dead yet."

Chapter 14

When Lori's eyes opened slightly, it was dusk, but her pain was so excruciating she wanted to die. As she lay on the cool wet ground behind the barn, she saw the dim reflection of salt crystals scattered around her. Perhaps she was expected to live. Salt was used to lessen the scarring and stop the bleeding, as well as intensify the pain.

Death, however, would bring peace — and that's all Lori wanted. It felt like her back was on fire, with a million tiny needles driving themselves through her torn flesh over and over again. Lori wanted to scream, but she was too weak.

"Dear Lord," she prayed silently, "take me…take me now…" Closing her eyes, Lori drifted back into unconsciousness.

****

After the steamer docked at Winnabow, Daniel made his way to the livery stable. He'd arranged for a horse from the plantation to be waiting for him.

Around nightfall, he approached the Dancing Oaks stables, only to find Fanny running to him crying and calling his name.

"Master Daniel, Master Daniel!"

"Fanny, what's wrong? Why are you out here?"

"It's Lori." Fanny gasped, gulping air. "Master Daniel, she's hurt—she's hurt bad."

"Hurt?" Daniel's heart raced. He immediately thought she'd been bitten by a snake. "Where is she?"

"In her cabin with Lizzie tendin' to her."

Pulling on the reins, Daniel turned his dappled gray horse in the direction of the quarters. "What happened?"

"Miss Lucinda found out she could read and had her whipped near to death!"

Daniel rode off, swatting the horse's rump with a crop. The animal moved swiftly, leaving moist bits of earth in its wake.

Cool wind pressed hard against Daniel's face, forcing tears that nearly blinded him from the corners of his eyes. The ride took only minutes, although it seemed like hours.

Daniel saw a group of slave women on their knees crying and praying outside Lori's cabin as he rode toward it. But upon hearing him, they scattered, running to hide behind nearby trees.

When he dismounted, one of the women peeked from behind an oak. Recognizing him she whispered loudly, "He come to see if she dead."

With his heart tight and still beating rapidly, Daniel tried to open the cabin door, but it was latched, so he began banging loudly. After a moment, Lizzie opened it.

Near the wall, Daniel saw Lori, unconscious, on her pallet. The iron smell of blood was in the air. The same smell he remembered when he'd found Jonathan, beaten, bloody — and dead.

"Has the doctor seen her?" Daniel asked as he walked quickly past Lizzie, but after a few steps more, he stopped. The flickering candlelight revealed the damage of the lash. Daniel almost vomited as he absorbed the full impact of Lori's wounds.

She lay limp on her stomach facing him with closed eyes. A scratchy coverlet was draped just below her back where the injuries stopped. What he saw resembled something from a butcher's cutting board. Lori's skin, once a deep beautiful brown, was now swollen and bloody, with pink flesh exposed, torn open by deep angry slashes.

"Miss Lucinda didn't send for no doctor," Lizzie said, passing Daniel with a slow shuffling gate. "She just left her out there to die. Wouldn't let nobody near her. But after a while, she got Boyd to bring her back here.

"Then Miss Lucinda told me to clean her up. She brung me some butter to put on her, and a cloth to cover the wounds. "Hmph," Lizzie snorted as she knelt next to Lori.

"Acted all high and mighty after she had the chile tore up like this." Rubbing butter onto Lori's back Lizzie muttered, "It's a sad, sad day."

Daniel still couldn't move. What he was seeing had to be a nightmare, it couldn't possibly be real. After a few seconds, Daniel gathered his wits and walked to Lori. However, seeing her mutilated and near death was too much for him to bear.

He'd failed her, and now she was almost dead because he hadn't been here to protect her. Daniel knelt beside her and wept, consumed by guilt—and rage.

How could Aunt Lucinda do this? He thought angrily, as gut wrenching sobs wracked his body. Daniel never suspected she'd go this far. He'd choke her to death right now if he could!

Through tears, Daniel said softly, "God, Lori can't die...it wouldn't be fair. I—I've lost so much. You can't take her too..."

Holding Lori's hand, Daniel began praying silently. "God—she's mine. Take anything else—but not her—I won't let you have her..." But Lori lay listless, barely breathing.

"Massa," Lizzie said, "I don't think she gonna make it."

"She's—*not*—going to die." Daniel forced the words.

"But she might've lost the will to live." Lizzie mopped her eyes with a dirty rag. "She can either be here in pain or be in glory with Jesus. If I was her—I'd be wantin' to die."

Daniel looked into Lizzie's face. Her red eyes were defeated and hopeless. "But she can't die," he said softly, "she's my life." Lightly touching Lori's cheek, he whispered closely to her ear, "Lori...don't die...don't leave me..."

"It ain't no use," Lizzie said.

"Lizzie—pray with me that she'll live! Please!"

Lizzie frowned at Daniel, as though sizing him up. For a long time she said nothing, as she continued rubbing butter onto Lori's back. "Now, sir," she finally said, "I know you's an abolitionist and Miss Rebecca's boy, and she was a good woman. But you's a white man!

"You don't need to be playin' with this chile, makin' her miserable! When you marry a white woman and toss her aside—she'll be wishin' she had died! So, you just—move along—leave the chile be in peace. She better off without you here playin' with her heart."

"Lizzie," Daniel said firmly, "you're wrong about me! I love Lori—I want her for my wife—and I'd never dishonor her in any way—never!"

Lizzie sat dumbfounded, her wrinkled face creased in disbelief. The whites of her eyes expanded against her dark brown skin, and she eased away from Daniel like he was a feral dog.

Lizzie looked at him like he'd gone mad, but Daniel didn't care. Saving Lori was his main concern. When he grabbed her thin wrist, she gasped, startled. "Lizzie, You have to believe me!"

Realizing he'd frightened the old woman, Daniel dropped her arm. "I'm sorry." He looked at Lori. Her breathing hadn't improved. His tone calmer now, Daniel said with a shaky voice, "Lizzie, I'm — I'm begging you to pray with me." As Daniel began to pray again, he wept.

Lizzie was quiet at first, while she watched Daniel. However, after a few moments she said, "I guess you couldn't be more woeful if the girl was white."

Lizzie joined Daniel in prayer, yet after several minutes had passed, Lori barely appeared to be breathing. Through his tears, Daniel remembered his mother weeping over Jonathan. "He was yours, Lord, not mine..." She'd cried in prayer over and over.

Slowly, Daniel realized that Lori belonged to God — not him. But does it have to be this way, Lord? Daniel wondered. Why? It isn't fair. Despite his doubt and pain, Daniel tried to understand that he had to let Lori go.

He struggled silently for several moments, not wanting to pray any more, at least not like his mother had.

But then, cradling his head in his hands, Daniel cried softly, "She's yours Lord, not mine. I—I don't need her—but I do need You. I know that You will always be with me. Thy will be done…"

A short while later, Lori took in a deep breath, then slightly opened her eyes. Seeing Daniel, she whispered his name.

"Lori, I'm here." He held her hand and squeezed it tight. Although her breathing was stronger, she fell back into unconsciousness.

"Thank God!" Daniel exclaimed. "Lizzie, she'll be all right, I'm sure of it! But—I've got to get her out of here!" Panic filled his voice. Standing up, Daniel raked a hand through his hair. "I've got to take her away—tonight!"

"She can't be goin' nowhere, all tore up like she is!" Lizzie protested.

For the first time, Daniel noticed Lori's dress bunched in a corner on the dirt floor. It was saturated with blood. He started for the door, not looking back. "She won't stay here another day!"

****

Grateful for the light of a full moon, Daniel quickly drove back to the stables on his horse. The first part of his and Lori's escape would have to begin tonight. Waiting for the scheduled time he'd agreed upon with the Wrights wasn't an option now.

However, they'd have to postpone the remainder of their getaway until after Lori healed.

At this point, going back to the Wrights seemed his only alternative. Hopefully, he and Lori could hide there for a while, and Lori could receive a doctor's care. As Daniel approached the stables, he thought fast, trying to devise a way to get Lori from the cabin to the rowboat he'd hidden near the riverbank.

After dismounting, he opened the wide stable door. Using the moonlight, he found a wagon and filled the bed with straw. He hitched his horse to it, then got on and drove for several minutes to the back of the big house. Daniel assumed that all would be asleep.

Quietly, he climbed down from the wagon, then walked to the back door. So as not to make a sound, he removed his boots and left them outside. The heavy door creaked as he opened it, unsettling the silence.

Feeling his way along the wall, Daniel approached the back stairs. The moon's silver glow shining through the unshaded windows helped to guide his steps. Yet once inside the rear stairwell, it was completely dark. Praying not to trip, Daniel grabbed the wooden railing and began his ascent. Elijah's snoring was the only sound he heard.

When he reached the second floor, Daniel touched the wall, using it to lead him. As the floorboards creaked, he passed by the closed doors of Annabelle's room, then Uncle Elijah and Aunt Lucinda's. Feeling the hot rush of blood to his face, Daniel held his breath, fighting the urge to burst in there and tear his aunt from a peaceful sleep. He wanted to pummel her senseless, then kill her with his bare hands, but he moved on.

Once inside his own bedroom, Daniel closed the door, debating whether or not to light a candle. If one of his relatives should wake, light shining from under his door might draw attention to him.

Although most of what he needed was already at the Wright's, he didn't want to leave behind any of the valuables he'd stored in his top dresser drawer. After a couple of seconds, Daniel fumbled for the matchbox in his pocket. Not wanting to miss anything in the dark, he chose to use a candle.

The stillness intensified the rough sound of the match strike. Giving off the hot smell of phosphorous, the flame flared brightly before shrinking to a tiny light. As he hastily lit the chamber candle on his nightstand, Daniel burned a fingertip. For a brief moment, the smell of singed flesh surrounded him.

Moving the candle to the dresser, Daniel opened the drawer and grabbed the remainder of his money, which consisted of a thick stack of bills, his father's pocket watch, and then his mother's locket.

Ignoring the minor irritation of a burned finger, Daniel quickly stuffed everything into his pockets. The last item he took was his pistol. After shoving it into the back of his trousers, he snuffed out the flame.

Daniel left his room, and again used the wall to guide him, but this time to the formal front stairway. Holding tightly to the rail, he quickly descended, but stumbled down the last few steps of the cantilevered elliptical stairs, making a loud noise.

Daniel stood still for several seconds, his heart beating rapidly. He heard nothing, aside from Elijah's snoring. When convinced he'd aroused no one, Daniel moved to the unoccupied guest bedroom on the first floor. Bright moonlight shone through the large windows of the parlor and dining room, helping to lead him.

Once he reached the guest room, enough moonlight was visible through these windows to help Daniel find the large trunk at the foot of the bed.

His mind raced as he removed a spare bedcover and cotton blanket.

He'd made it this far. If he were to get caught, he would say he was suffering from chills and fever.

His last stop was Lucinda's medicine chest near the back door. The pinewood cabinet stood about four feet high. Inside were four deep shelves. Daniel had seen the small amber colored laudanum bottle on the top shelf, near the far left end when Lucinda had gotten him a bandage one time. Now he needed the opiate for Lori's pain.

Daniel panicked upon remembering that Aunt Lucinda kept the chest locked. Still holding the cumbersome bedcovers with one arm, he threw them to the floor. He felt for the metal knob and turned it, hoping that by chance, the cabinet had been left unlocked. It hadn't. Time was rapidly slipping away. Daniel needed to get Lori out of here, but he didn't want her to suffer.

Digging quickly into his pocket, beneath the stack of bills, Daniel pulled out a pocketknife, then found its small, narrow blade. Feeling once more for the knob, he located the keyhole below it with his finger and jammed the blade inside. With shaking hands, Daniel tried to jimmy the lock.

The knife made a scraping sound as he maneuvered it around the keyhole. He tried to work stealthily, but the longer it took, the more his hands trembled. The scraping became louder. The lock would be ruined, and so would his knife. That was of no concern, but time was.

About to give up, Daniel made a last firm twist to the right. An uncomfortable click reverberated with a sharp echo. Daniel tried the door. It opened. He reached in the chest, moving his hand all the way to the left. Feeling the smooth glass of the laudanum bottle, he snatched it, then crammed it into his pocket.

Without shutting the medicine chest, Daniel picked up the bedcovers. He turned to open the back door. But suddenly, the glimmer of candlelight shone behind him, and a firm hand gripped his shoulder.

Daniel shot around, ready to strike, forgetting his story about chills and fever.

"Master Daniel," Fanny whispered, her eyes red and swollen, "is Lori all right?"

Relieved, Daniel let out a deep breath. "She'll live—but I'm taking her away from here tonight." Fanny gasped, but before she could say anything, Daniel stopped her. "Fanny, you haven't seen me." The woman was silent. "Do you understand? I don't want to get you in trouble."

Fanny nodded. "I haven't seen you."

"I have to go," Daniel whispered urgently, as he slipped through the back door. "Thank you, Fanny—and goodbye."

****

Daniel tried to drive the wagon as fast as he could over the uneven ground to the slave quarters without making too much noise. But as he passed Jenkins cabin on the way, he heard a door squeak open, then bang against the split logs.

"Who's out there—what're you doing?" The voice was loud and the words slurred.

Daniel pulled on the reins stopping the wagon. The full moon revealed Jenkins, and the reflection of a glass bottle held in his hand. The sight of the overseer made Daniel's blood boil. Jumping from the wagon, he strode forcefully toward the man.

"What're—"

Before Jenkins could finish, Daniel grabbed him by the neck of his nightshirt and threw him to the ground.

"Hey!" Jenkins protested, as Daniel yanked the bottle from his hand and crashed it against the cabin steps, splattering strong smelling whiskey everywhere. "Damn! Why'd you do that? Jenkins whined. When the overseer tried to struggle to his feet, Daniel forced him back to the ground, holding the jagged bottle neck to his throat.

"I'm gonna make a bloody mess out of you just like you made out of Lori's back," Daniel said through clenched teeth. He pressed the broken glass into Jenkins clammy skin.

"I'm gonna slit your throat."

"Then go ahead." Jenkins didn't fight back.

He reeked of whiskey. Dropping his head back, he began to cry. "I was just doin' a job...I was just doin' a job..."

Daniel pressed the bottleneck into Jenkin's skin, but stopped. He threw the piece of glass aside. Cutting his throat would be too quick. He wanted to hurt the man and cause him an excruciating death. Straddling Jenkins, Daniel gripped the man's neck tightly with both hands.

When the overseer tried to fight him off, Daniel squeezed harder. The man gasped for air, kicking wildly. When Jenkins ceased moving and almost lost consciousness, Daniel realized what he was doing was wrong. He removed his hands from the man's neck.

As Jenkins coughed and gasped, Daniel, still straddling him, took several deep breaths. After a few seconds, he rose to his feet. Looking down at the pathetic wretch, Daniel said, "Vengeance is mine, sayeth the Lord."

It wasn't his place to punish the overseer, yet when he'd escape with Lori only moments later, Daniel couldn't chance Jenkins causing a drunken display of humiliation.

Watching the man weep and writhe like a worm in the dirt, Daniel reached for his pistol. With it, he struck Jenkins hard against the side of the head, knocking him out instantly.

****

When Daniel opened Lori's cabin door with the blanket slung over his shoulder, he saw the women who'd been praying outside earlier. They were crowded around Lori, but quickly rushed out upon his arrival.

Lori was awake now. Lizzie had placed the cloth on her back to act as a dressing over her wounds. Seeing Daniel, Lori reached weakly toward him with one arm.

"Daniel...don't...don't leave me again..." Her voice was barely above a whisper.

Daniel quickly moved to her and knelt down. Holding her hand, he said, "Darling, I won't—I promise. I'm taking you away from here."

"To your mama's?"

Daniel started to say something, but the words caught in his throat.

Lizzie sat by Lori on the floor. Shaking her head, she muttered, "The whippin'll cause her to be outta her mind for a few days."

"Lori," Daniel said, "I'm taking you to a place where you'll be safe—and cared for." In the candlelight, he saw that the cloth on her back had absorbed a pinkish ooze.

Moving her to the wagon would be painful; so would the ride over the bumpy ground to the riverbank. Daniel pulled the laudanum bottle from his pocket and uncorked it, releasing a mild alcohol smell. Putting the medicine to her lips, he said, "Drink this. It'll make the pain go away for a while."

Without hesitation, Lori sipped the clear liquid and soon lost consciousness. After wrapping her in the blanket, Daniel gently lifted her from the pallet and carried her to the wagon. Lizzie followed behind him.

Now Lori was totally dependent on him, Daniel reflected, carrying her fragile frame. Her life was completely in his hands. With a fully loaded pistol, he'd kill anyone who came near her, or who'd try to stop him.

After Daniel placed her on the soft bedcover he'd put over of the straw, he noticed the slave women peeking from the trees and whispering.

"He come to take her away..."

"But what they gonna do if..."

"The white folks..."

"When Cap'n Cindy..."

"Where they go..."

"What 'bout Jenkins..."

Only hearing snippets of their astonished murmurs, Daniel turned to Lizzie. Holding her rough, wrinkled hand in his, he said, "Thank you, Lizzie. Thanks for all you've done for Lori, and thank you for praying with me."

"Take good care of her," Lizzie said, watching Daniel hurry to climb on the wagon.

"You have my word," he whispered loudly. Daniel grabbed the reins and departed from Dancing Oaks for the last time.

Chapter 15

In the dark secret room of her home, Martha Wright finished cleaning Lori's wounds with warm water. She swatted away the flies, then applied a new covering of Tatum's Medicinal Ointment. The strong smell of grain alcohol and aloe vera would keep the insects away.

The room, used to hide runaway slaves, was narrow and windowless, with one side sloped along the roof pitch. Martha worked by the light of an oil lamp.

She sat on a low stool next to Lori, who lay asleep on a small feather mattress pushed against the wall. A good friend and abolitionist doctor had treated Lori's back shortly after she'd arrived, and then instructed Martha on how to care for her.

While Lori slept soundly on her stomach, Martha studied the deep wounds, pitying Lori the scars she'd carry for the rest of her life. Martha sighed. Although disfiguring, scarring was preferable to death.

When Martha placed a clean linen cloth over Lori's back to absorb the pus that still oozed from the lacerations, Lori took a deep breath.

Martha leaned down to look into her face. Seeing her eyes open, Martha said, gently, "Lori, does thou know where thou are?" Lori only blinked groggily, but instead of closing her eyes again, kept them open. She was fully awake for first time.

"You're safe," Martha said reassuringly. "Does thou remember me? I'm Martha Wright." Martha had met Lori more than once when she'd attended abolitionist meetings in Rebecca's home.

Lori nodded slightly. "How long..." Her voice, just above a whisper, sounded parched and scratchy.

"You've been here less than a week." When Martha applied a slight bit of pressure to the cloth on Lori's back, Lori moaned. "I'm sorry, dear," Martha said. "I have been trying to wean thee from laudanum, but perhaps—"

"No—I want Daniel. And I—I need water."

Martha turned toward the table where the oil lamp sat. Next to it was a glass and pitcher of water.

Lori propped herself on both elbows, wincing a little, then drank slowly, draining the glass Martha held to her lips.

Taking the glass away, Martha said, "Daniel will be happy that thou are awake and finally asking for him. He's come to sit with thee and pray for a while each day."

Lori inched her body back down, gasping with each little movement. "He's safe?" she asked, once settled on the mattress.

"Of course," Martha smiled.

Hiding an escaped slave wasn't anything Martha and Jonas hadn't done. As Quakers, they condemned slavery as ethically and religiously wrong. But their current situation was a little different, because now they were hiding a fugitive white man, as well as a runaway.

The Wrights hadn't expected Lori and Daniel so early, and neither had they planned to hide them for an extended period of time. Fortunately, their secret room was available because Lori would need to stay here as she recuperated.

Originally intended for storage, the room had transformed into a secret hideaway. It had hidden numerous runaway slaves, yet had never been discovered. A small entry door was behind one of the bedsteads in an upstairs bedroom. Although the doorway was no more than three feet high, it led to a long room under the eaves, big enough for six people. From the street no one would ever suspect that a room existed here.

Martha had sent new letters to the safe houses outlining the current state of affairs. She'd set a new date of departure, approximating that Lori would be able to travel within a few weeks.

After securely covering Lori with a sheet, Martha bent down to pick up the porcelain wash basin from the floor. The white rag in it was now pink, and the water rose colored from Lori's wounds. "I will send Daniel in to see thee," she said, standing to leave.

"Martha, wait," Lori said weakly, "my back...how does it..."

Gazing at Lori grimly, she said, "Lori, thy back is healing. That is what is most important, but—it will be scarred, and deeply, I'm afraid. However," Martha smiled, "outer scarring does not diminish thy inner beauty."

Lori lay motionless for a few seconds, then nodded, pursing her lips.

****

Daniel bounded up the stairs two at a time after Martha told him Lori had asked for him. He quickly walked down the narrow hall to the sleeping chamber which hid the secret room, then stooped through the low doorway into the hideaway.

Daniel was enveloped by a sweltering heat. The tiny space was cramped and when he rose, his head nearly grazed the ceiling.

The only ventilation was a narrow set of slats near the ceiling.

Over the mustiness, Daniel smelled the medicinal ointment. Walking softly toward Lori, he said her name.

Dim lamp-light and a bit of natural light from the small doorway allowed him to see her face. His heart sank. She appeared to be sleeping again. Daniel sat on the floor next to her.

"Lori," he said once more, leaning against the mattress.

When he reclined with his face toward her, Lori's eyes opened. She exhaled and smiled when she saw him. "Daniel," she whispered, and reached a thin arm from beneath the sheet to hold his hand.

"Lori, I love you." He kissed her hand. "The doctor said you'd be fine—but I was afraid you'd never wake up." Daniel's eyes welled, but he held back the tears.

"I'm awake now." Her voice was louder, but hoarse.

"And I thank God for that," Daniel said, his voice soft, yet urgent with excitement. "Lori, I've missed you—I've missed you so much. I've sat in here every day, praying over you—and now you're finally awake—it's an answered prayer. Each day you're better—means we're closer to getting married, and to leaving all of this behind."

Lori looked into Daniel's eyes for a long moment, then said, "Daniel—we—we can't—"

"Darling, I know we can't escape any time soon. We'll stay here until you're healed."

"No. Not that...We can't..." Lori's eyes closed, but she opened them again.

"What is it Lori? What can't we do?"

Lori said nothing for a few seconds as she gazed tiredly into Daniel's eyes. Then, pulling her hand from his she said, "Daniel — I'd rather die — than marry you…"

Daniel felt the blood rush from his face. "Lori — what — what are you talking about?"

Lori's eyes closed, and she said nothing.

"Lori!" Daniel gently touched her shoulder through the sheet, but when she flinched, he quickly removed his hand. "Lori, I'm sorry," he blurted, "but — but what you said — you can't mean that…"

Lori still didn't respond. Daniel pushed himself away from the bed. With raised knees, he draped his arms over his legs. The tears he'd held back, now flowed freely as he dropped his head in despair. Because he hadn't been there to stop the flogging, she'd never forgive him.

In moments, however, his tears turned from sadness to rage. He'd risked his life for her, yet now she wanted to cast him aside! Daniel pulled a handkerchief from his pocket and wiped the tears and sweat from his face. He stopped crying, then rose to his feet and gazed at Lori.

The sheet tucked around her delicate form revealed that she was thinner, almost emaciated since she hadn't been eating. He'd always protect her, and he'd always love her. She needed him.

Daniel tried to convince himself that Lori still wasn't in her right mind. Why else would she have said that she didn't want to marry him? For a long time Daniel looked down at Lori, hoping she'd wake again soon.

****

It wasn't until the next morning that Martha called Daniel to see Lori. Walking boldly down the hall, Daniel held on to what Martha had told him only moments earlier, "Lori appears more alert today." And perhaps now, Daniel thought clenching his fists, she'd be in her right mind.

A part of him felt that Lori owed him. He wanted to be with her at all costs, and she'd better feel the same! However, he was prepared to beg and plead his way back into her heart.

Inside the secret room, she still lay on her stomach. He could see the whites of her eyes sparkling in the dimness. She smiled, as though glad to see him. Could she have forgotten what she'd said the day before?

"Lori," Daniel said, kneeling beside her, "how are you feeling?"

"Better — today," she said slowly.

"Do you — do you remember what you said to me — yesterday?" As Lori nodded, he felt a shard of pain slash through his heart. "Lori — why did you say that? I'm — I'm sorry — please forgive me! I wish it had been me instead of you! I'll do anything to make this up to you — but don't — don't stop loving me."

141

"Daniel—I could never stop loving you—I said what I said—because of how much I *do* love you."

Exasperated, Daniel blew out a breath. "Lori—you're either not making sense—or you're toying with me!"

Lori shook her head sadly. "I'm not—I don't want you to think that. But I'd rather die—than ruin your life."

"Not having you in my life would ruin it!"

"Daniel—you don't know what you're saying."

"I'm not the one who's been delirious and out of my head!"

"Daniel—I—I was out of my head—but I'm not anymore. And I've been selfish. I've blamed you for not helping me to escape. But—you've done so much—and I haven't appreciated it. Now you're in hiding, putting your life in jeopardy—and breaking the law—all for me."

"And I'd do it all over again!"

"No, Daniel—you have everything—without me. But with me, a successful future for you is impossible. Marrying me isn't realistic—for either of us."

"Loving you isn't unrealistic—and neither is marrying you! It'll be difficult—but—we'll manage. I don't care about being accepted by the finest families and all that rigmarole. You're more important to me than that!"

"But you'd be better off if we didn't—"

"Confound it, Lori!"

"Daniel," Lori said softly, "it would be best if we — go our separate ways. I don't want you to feel — obligated to me."

"Lori, I — "

"And I don't want your pity. Once I'm healed, I can take care of myself. Now, Daniel — go." She blinked heavy eyes. "I'm tired — I can't talk any more... but think about what I've said." Lori closed her eyes and drifted off, leaving him in limbo once more.

Daniel rose from Lori's bedside and walked to the wall. Leaning his back against it, he slid to the floor. He wouldn't leave. He'd wait for her to stir again.

****

Daniel awoke suddenly, drenched in sweat. Using his shirt sleeve, he wiped his face and forehead.

He wasn't surprised that he'd dozed off. He'd hardly slept the night before, agonizing over what Lori had said. Indeed, since Daniel had been at the Wright's, a good night's sleep had eluded him, because he'd been so concerned about Lori's condition.

Daniel pulled out his father's pocket watch. Two hours had passed. He snapped the time piece shut, then gave it a wind and placed it back in his pocket. Before he'd nodded off, he'd rehearsed what he'd say to Lori when she awoke, to convince her that she was wrong.

Moments later, she moaned, rolling stiffly to her side. The bed linen slipped, revealing the tops of her breasts. The lamp-light reflected sweat glistening against her skin. Although tempted to stare, Daniel was quickly at Lori's side, pulling up the sheet to cover her completely.

When he sat down next to her on the floor, she opened her eyes and gazed tiredly into his. After a deep breath, she said his name.

"Lori—I'm here. Are you all right? Do you need anything?" She shook her head. "Lori—I need you." Her eyes widened as he spoke. "If I didn't love you so much, I'd leave. If I didn't need you to make my life complete, I'd leave.

"If I didn't want to have children with you, and grow old with you, I'd leave. I'm not going anywhere without you.

"You'll just have to tolerate me, and how much I love you. So—I hope that won't be too difficult."

"Daniel—you—you really love me—that much?"

"I thought you already knew how much I loved you."

"But—"

"There's nothing I—we can't handle. The Bible says, 'I can do all things through Christ which strengtheneth me.'"

Lori nodded.

"So," Daniel said, "marry me?"

For several seconds, Lori said nothing. Her brow furrowed. It appeared as though she wanted to argue, but didn't have the strength.

"Don't hesitate, Lori," Daniel pleaded, "don't leave me hanging."

"I'll—I'll marry you," she said as tears welled in her eyes.

Daniel's face creased uneasily. "You don't—look—or sound too sure."

"But I am, Daniel," her voice broke as she nodded slowly, "I am..."

Daniel kissed her forehead. "I'll never let anything bad like this ever happen to you again, I promise."

"I believe you," she whispered.

We're going to be fine, Lori." He hesitated, then said, "Blasted," his tone defiant, "I know we'll be fine!"

Gently cupping Lori's face in his hands, Daniel spoke almost in whisper. "You'll never know—how sorry I am for what happened." A stream of tears stained his face. "It's my fault. If I'd been there—"

"Daniel, don't say any more," Lori said, wiping his cheeks with her fingertips. "It's not your fault. We didn't know what your aunt would do."

Daniel turned away from Lori, propping his back against the mattress. "As much as I've tried—I can't forgive her," he said bitterly.

Lori squeezed his shoulder. "But, Daniel—I

have."

Turning quickly to meet her eyes, he said, "But, Lori—how could you?"

"Because your mother always said, 'hate the sin, love the sinner.' She didn't know who killed Jonathan, yet she told me she'd forgiven the killer—whoever it was—because that's what God would have wanted her to do."

Daniel dropped his gaze for a moment, then let out a deep sigh. "I—I can't forgive Aunt Lucinda—not now. Maybe one day—but not at this point. I haven't arrived at that place yet."

As Lori nodded with understanding, Daniel wouldn't mention that he'd almost killed Jenkins. Then looking deeply into her eyes, he said, "Lori, what can I do? What can I do to make all this up to you?"

"Daniel—you don't have to do anything. You're here with me. Loving me is enough."

"But Lori—I want to make everything up to you—somehow. I never want to see you hurt this badly—ever again. And I want to give you everything."

Lori smiled. "I don't need everything."

"I'd give you the world if I could." He kissed her hand and held it to his cheek. "Sometimes I wonder why God let this happen. But then I remember what Mother said—after Jonathan—that our pain has a purpose in God's plan, and through suffering—we should glorify God."

"Yes," Lori agreed softly. "God's plan is greater than our pain. And to all those who believe, He brings good out of difficulty."

Chapter 16

Martha closed the gingham curtains in her little parlor, which now seemed even smaller than usual. Two large high back chairs sat in the middle of the room, while the long benches from the dining area faced them to accommodate the guests for the evening's quiet festivities.

Night had fallen, but despite this, Martha kept the oil lamps low. Over the soft conversation of the few guests gathered in her home, she heard footsteps upstairs as she hurried to the kitchen. Glancing toward the top of the stairwell, she caught a glimpse of black boots and the hem of white satin draped over a crinoline.

In moments, Jonas would tell Lori and Daniel to come down and take their places. Martha wouldn't wait to see the young couple make their way to the parlor. Instead, she tended to the task at hand, finishing preparations for the small wedding celebration.

With Lori's wounds healed and her strength regained, the time had come for her and Daniel to leave.

But before their life threatening escape the next morning, they'd marry in secret tonight.

Once in the kitchen, Martha took a deep breath, inhaling the precious aroma of cinnamon, nutmeg and cloves. Then, after greeting the last two guests to arrive inconspicuously through the back door, she carried a freshly baked spice cake to the dining room and set it on the table next to a bowl of punch.

A simple glass vase filled with pink roses from Martha's garden, flanked by two burning candles, served as the centerpiece. For tonight's gathering, Jonas and Martha had carefully handpicked a small assembly of guests and sworn them to secrecy.

Martha hurried to the parlor. Sitting next to Jonas, she glanced toward the opposite bench where Dr. Zachary Hayden sat with Charlotte and Nigel Carver.

The old doctor, a quiet widower, had treated Lori's back. He fidgeted, cleaning his spectacles. Being cross-eyed and a man of few words had always set him apart from the community. In addition, his acceptance of marriage between the races contributed to his eccentricities.

Charlotte Carver simply beamed, admiring Lori's dress. She was the Negro seamstress who'd made it. She'd also created the escape disguises, as well as a little something for Lori to wear on her wedding night.

Charlotte sat with her husband, Nigel, a freeman and carpenter. Their four year old daughter, Abigail, sat between them, occupying herself with a peg wood doll in a frilly green dress.

For free Negroes, the Carvers had means. Charlotte was her master's child. She'd been granted her freedom by him, and when Nigel, also owned by her father, wanted to marry Charlotte, Nigel was given his manumission, as well. Charlotte's father had provided them with land for a house, and each month continued to supply them with a tidy sum of money.

Martha's gaze moved from the Carvers to Curtis and Lacey Burns, who shared the same bench with her and Jonas.

The Burnses, a middle aged colored couple, had worked for over twenty years as paid house servants in Rebecca Taylor's home. They'd known Daniel since birth, and remembered the day Lori came to live at the Taylor place.

Since moving to Wilmington, the Burnses had been employed by a wealthy banker. At night, they assisted in helping runaway slaves escape through Wilmington's maritime Underground Railroad network.

A miracle had surely occurred the evening Daniel had arrived in a rowboat with an injured Lori.

Curtis had just completed an assignment as

lookout for a group of runaways when he'd seen Daniel wandering the riverbank, looking for help. That night, Curtis had taken them to the Wright's home in his wagon.

The parlor remained silent, as the assembled guests faced the large high back chairs where Daniel and Lori took their seats.

No minister was present. Martha smiled at this, because it had taken her a while to convince Lori that Quakers conducted their wedding ceremonies without them. Martha had explained that only God can join a couple in marriage.

Now, however, Lori seemed not to care about the lack of a minister. Martha watched as the bride and groom slowly rose together. Lori glowed as she looked at Daniel, who was handsomely attired in a black suit. After several moments passed, Daniel began to recite his vows.

"In the presence of the Lord," Daniel said, "I take Lori to be my wife, promising with divine assistance, to be unto her a loving and faithful husband, until death shall separate us."

As Lori continued to gaze adoringly at Daniel, Martha marveled at her transformation. Once her appetite had returned, Lori had gained weight. Now she resembled royalty in a white satin dress with a scoop neck and capped sleeves.

Martha had commissioned Charlotte to sew a wedding gown, with money Daniel had provided along with Lori's measurements, as well as with instructions by him to make his beloved look like a princess.

The v-shaped bodice accentuated Lori's tiny waist, all twenty inches of it. The long floral veil, with satin flowers adorning the headpiece, hid any visible scars on Lori's back, because Charlotte had utilized an abundance of lace and tulle.

"In the presence of the Lord," Lori repeated, "I take Daniel to be my husband, promising with divine assistance, to be unto him a loving and faithful wife, until death shall separate us."

Silence followed for a few moments more, and then Dr. Hayden rose to speak. Uncomfortable standing before a crowd, even a small one, he cleared his throat while plowing a hand through his disheveled gray hair. "May God bless this couple—with safe travels and good health."

After Dr. Hayden sat down, Charlotte Carver stood up. High yellow in complexion, her long curling tresses covered the bare shoulders of her lavender gown. "I ask the good Lord to clothe them in safety and cover them with His strong hand of protection."

Little Abigail stood next. Her knee length dress, worn over a petticoat, was lavender just like her mother's.

As Charlotte sat down, Martha heard her whisper in her daughter's ear, "Say it just like we practiced."

Accentuated by a strong lisp, Abigail said, "Lord, please clothe them in safety and protect them." The little girl giggled, covering her mouth, pleased by her achievement.

More comments followed from among the assembly. The last to speak was Curtis Burns, a tall brown skinned man. "May God's blessing be upon you always, and may both of you carry on the work that Miss Rebecca and Master William started."

When Curtis finished speaking, Martha noticed that Daniel stood just a little taller, and smiled proudly at the mention of his parents' names.

For a long while the silence lingered. Gazing around her, Martha saw that all eyes rested upon her. Too overcome with emotion, Martha couldn't say a word. Instead, she only dropped her eyes to her lap, and after a few seconds more, Jonas concluded the ceremony by nodding toward the bride and groom.

****

With the wedding festivities over, Lori was alone with Daniel in the bedroom he used at the Wrights. Since no slave catchers had come looking for her, it was deemed safe enough for her not to spend every waking hour cloistered away in the secret room.

Lori sat at a little vanity table wearing a white cotton night-gown trimmed with eyelet lace, as she perused the Quaker marriage certificate that she and Daniel had signed after the ceremony. The oil lamp on the dressing table cast an amber hue over the document. Though written in Martha's beautiful calligraphy, it was only a ceremonial piece of paper, not at all legally binding.

Silently, Lori read the document over and over, as if trying to convince herself that their marriage was real. From behind her, she heard Daniel's footsteps approach.

"What are you thinking?" he asked.

Lori felt the warmth of his lips against her neck as he kissed her. With one hand, she adjusted the gown to cover the slash marks visible at the base of her neck. Although Daniel didn't care about her scarring, Lori was still self-conscious.

She met his gaze in the vanity's oval mirror. He wore a white cotton nightshirt that fell below his knees.

"I can't read your mind," he smiled.

Lori sighed. "What I'm thinking seems silly but — a part of me feels like we're not really married. Even though Martha said that only God can unite a couple in matrimony — our marriage isn't legal."

Daniel gazed down, saying nothing for a moment. Then, "I have something for you — a wedding present, to show you that we really *are* married."

Lori put the document down suddenly, turning to look at him. "Daniel, you shouldn't have—you've already spent a fortune on my wedding gown and—"

"Shhh...just close your eyes...and face the mirror."

Lori did as she was told, and seconds later felt a coolness against her skin.

"Open your eyes."

Lori gasped. "Your—your mother's locket!" she said in a breathy whisper. "Daniel—it's—it's beautiful." For several seconds Lori sat speechless, gazing at her image adorned by the Calhoun heirloom. The gold heart shone brightly against her skin, with its diamonds and rubies glistening. "It's really mine?" Lori grasped the locket as though it might be taken from her.

"Uncle Elijah said to give it to the fine young lady I'd surely marry one day," Daniel said as Lori began to laugh, "and here you are."

Lori rose from the dresser, throwing her arms tightly around Daniel's neck.

Embracing her, he said quietly, "No matter what, you're my wife, and I'll always take care of you."

Lori kissed him softly on the lips. Then gazing into his eyes for a long moment, she turned down the lamp. "We'll take care of each other."

Chapter 17
Petersburg, Virginia
September, 1856

Approaching the station in Petersburg, the steam locomotive roared, then gave way to a loud, lazy yawn. Heavy couplings clanged, while thick metal wheels screeched to a slow halt.

Daniel reached to open his window. The heat onboard was stifling, but with the train moving rapidly, he could only stand so many cinders from the outside hitting his face.   He assumed, that with the train coming to a stop, less ash would be circulating through the air. However, once he opened the window, a puff of cinders stung his eyes and hot soot triggered a cough.

Huffing out a deep breath, Daniel shut the window. He needed fresh air and a long drink of water. He could only imagine Lori's ride in the second-class car, the mandatory place for Negroes. She'd had to put up with all this, as well as the smoking allowed there. Daniel had wanted to ride with her, but she'd insisted he ride in first class to draw less attention to them.

Unfortunately, Daniel believed his clothes did a fine job of attracting unwanted attention all by themselves. He glanced down at his bright yellow trousers. After that long drink of water, a change of clothes would be in order. Daniel was more than ready to discard his disguise.

Miss Charlotte, Martha's seamstress, had outdone herself designing what she imagined a rich planter's son of new money would wear, and she'd described the ensemble as bright and fanciful.

Daniel sighed. His vividly colored trousers did compliment his dark green waistcoat and lavender cravat quite well, but he wasn't a woman! This creation was a bit too dandified, and he felt rather silly wearing it.

As of yet, he and Lori hadn't encountered anyone they knew, and now out of North Carolina, he believed the chance of that happening unlikely.

Using a handkerchief, Daniel wiped sweat and cinders from his brow. Then he removed his soot covered spectacles and cleaned them, too. Once he put them on again, a greenish cast enveloped everything.

The fake beard was another annoying part of Daniel's disguise. It was hot, a little scratchy, and the spirit gum used to adhere it now felt less than secure since he'd perspired so much during the train ride.

Although trains were faster than stagecoaches, and lacked the bumps and jolts along the way, the hefty price of thirst, half suffocation and temporary blindness was paid for their convenience.

But because of two intolerable passengers, today's excursion had seemed more horrendous than any other Daniel had experienced during the escape. The toothy, freckled redheads wore identical dusty rose dresses along with matching dusty rose bonnets. They'd talked and giggled their way loudly through the entire trip, seemingly oblivious to the heat and cinders.

They sat directly in front of Daniel. Their backs faced him, but they'd looked over their shoulders and smiled several times after first boarding the train. However, the looking had transformed into shameless flirting once the train had begun to move.

They'd tried to rope Daniel into their conversation, but he'd resisted. Although cordial, Daniel had ignored them by reading a copy of *The Weldon Patriot* and Herman Melville's *Israel Potter*. And when they'd introduced themselves, he'd feigned partial deafness on account of an ear infection. This ploy had prevented further attempts at conversation from the girls, but it hadn't prevented them from gazing in his direction throughout most of the trip.

Now, as the train came to a complete stop, jerking the passengers forward, Daniel felt relief knowing he wouldn't have to endure the girls' foolishness a moment longer. Standing to leave, they turned to him and said goodbye in unison.

"It was so nice talking with you," one of them yelled loudly, on account of his ear problem.

Daniel stood and nodded politely. "It was a pleasure."

The girls didn't respond as they eagerly assessed his physique from head to foot. As though undressing him with their eyes, they burst into a fit of the twitters. Shaking their fans open simultaneously, the girls fluttered them coyly in front of their faces, then waved to Daniel as they departed from the train.

Daniel decided he'd stay put for a while. Once he got off the locomotive to find Lori, he wanted those girls as far away as possible. When he felt enough time had lapsed, Daniel stood up. After grabbing his suitcase and gray top hat, he made a hasty retreat for the exit.

Sneezing black cinders, he stepped from the train. But after his sneezing stopped, Daniel heard an annoying, yet familiar cackle off in the distance.

As the sound came nearer, it intensified in annoyance and familiarity. He froze, praying he'd been mistaken.

Turning slightly in the direction of the

cackling, Daniel was just in time to see Priscilla and his cousin Jesse greeting the freckled redheads.

He whipped back around, hastily putting on his top hat, at last thankful for one part of his disguise, despite it's bright purple hat band. Through the smoke, noise and people bustling about, Daniel searched frantically for Lori, finally spotting her near the second-class car.

She wore loose fitting jeans and a dark jacket made of kersey fabric over a white cotton shirt. A snug cap hid her hair and stiff wooden soled shoes with coarse leather uppers were on her feet. Wishing he looked half as manly, Daniel quickly approached her.

"Lori," he said urgently, "we have a problem. Walk with me, and walk fast. Lori grabbed her carpet bag and began walking with him. "Under the circumstances, we need go in separate directions for a while. Wait for me behind that hotel." He pointed to a three story red brick building adjacent to the station. "I'll make my way to you as quickly as I can."

"What's the problem?" Lori asked.

"Daaaaanny!" a loud voice called.

At that, Daniel didn't need to explain things further. Lori lowered her head and briskly walked to the hotel.

Priscilla, Jesse and the redheads were still a good distance away and Daniel continued to walk fast. If he ignored them, perhaps Priscilla would assume she'd been mistaken.

Or, Daniel hoped, maybe he could lose them. He saw a train starting its slow, torturous departure. It huffed loudly, hesitated, as if to take a breath, then jerked forward, pulling its gargantuan weight.

When the train exhaled thick white puffs of steam, Daniel glanced over his shoulder. His pursuers had vanished in the mist, but in seconds, reemerged, like the phoenix from the ashes.

Losing them would be impossible. They couldn't have recognized Lori—but how could he explain away his disguise? Daniel's mind raced. He'd have to think of something to tell them.

****

"Daaaaaanny!" Priscilla yelled. She was on a mission; no one knew what had happened to Daniel, yet she'd found him! Wearing a red plaid dress and bonnet to match, Priscilla yelled again, "I know that's you up there! Yoohoo!!"

"Come on, girls," she said to her twin cousins, Cammie and Pansie Stevens.

All three picked up their heavy skirts, revealing ivory kid boots that laced up the sides, and they started to run.

When the girls had pointed out the handsome gentleman they'd met on the train, Priscilla knew him instantly, even from a distance. She'd recognized his walk, and then explained who he was, eliciting trills of excitement from her cousins.

"Priscilla, come back here!" Jesse passed the twins, as he walked fast to catch up with his wife.

One long legged stride of his was equivalent to four of theirs when they ran, and six when they walked. Grabbing Priscilla's arm, Jesse prevented her from going any further. When she stopped, so did Cammie and Pansie.

"Just why are you restrainin' me like an animal?" Priscilla frowned.

"Yeah, Jesse," Cammie said, "why are you stoppin' her when she says that's your cousin, up yonder?"

"He's mighty handsome," Pansie added, "and we want a proper introduction!"

Jesse ran a hand through his soft brown curls. "Would ya'll look at the man!" Exasperated, he pointed in Daniel's direction, then lowered his voice. "Look at his clothes."

"Oh, Jesse," Pansie laughed, "there's nothing wrong with colorful, stylish travel attire—you ought to wear something like that next time you ride the train!"

"I was thinking the same thing!" Cammie snickered.

Keeping his voice low, Jesse said, "Daniel wouldn't want to look that kind of stylish, and neither would I. There's no reason on God's green earth he'd prance around looking like a blasted nancy."

"But it's him, I tell you!" Priscilla declared. "I'd know him to pieces anywhere. I can tell a person by the way they walk."

"Putting one foot in front of another doesn't differ that much between individuals," Jesse argued.

"Yes it does!" Breaking free of Jesse's arm, Priscilla hurried away with the twins skittering behind her. "And besides, I'm extremely observant—I don't miss a thing!"

In moments, Jesse apprehended Priscilla again, but this time used more force when he clutched her arm.

"What's wrong now, Jesse," the girls asked simultaneously.

"You're hurting me!" Priscilla exclaimed.

Jesse loosened his grip. Smoothing his moustache, he said, "Priscilla, have you forgotten about what Mother wrote?" Jesse spoke slowly while nodding his head exaggeratedly. "That Daniel *left* Dancing Oaks under—somewhat *trying* circumstances?"

"Trying circumstances," the twins exclaimed, "what did he do?"

Jesse paused, looking from the twins to Priscilla. "We don't exactly know the whole story, do we, darlin'?"

Priscilla pursed her lips. "No," she said finally.

As the twins giggled, whispering their insights to each other on a situation they knew nothing about, Priscilla mulled over this possible quandary.

Mama Cindy had written about a so-called scandal involving a slave girl who'd turned up missing at the same time as Daniel, but Priscilla had chosen to believe that no scandal existed at all.

She'd thought that maybe it was a coincidence that the two had disappeared simultaneously. Priscilla didn't know any details about the girl, Mama Cindy hadn't provided any. So as far as Priscilla was concerned, the girl had escaped, plain and simple.

However, it did seem strange that Daniel would just up and leave with no explanation, and not even tell anyone where he was going. He certainly wouldn't do anything illegal. But as an abolitionist, could he be helping the girl escape?

Priscilla wondered further. She'd never seen Daniel in clothes like those. They were fancier than anything she'd ever seen him wear.

He couldn't be a nancy — but could he be in disguise? Then she remembered the colored fellow she'd seen him with earlier — was that…

Priscilla struggled with her emotions for a moment. There wasn't anything really wrong with the abolitionists wanting the slaves to be treated well, and she didn't disagree with all the things she'd learned about abolitionism—but she couldn't condone the illegal aspects of it.

Now Priscilla felt uncomfortable looking in Daniel's direction. She knew if it was him, keeping distant and uninvolved would be best. Priscilla clicked her tongue and sighed at what could be a very disgraceful situation. "Oh, I suppose it's not him," she said. "He wouldn't really wear something like that. I just don't know what I was thinking."

****

Turning his head slightly, Daniel saw Jesse, Priscilla and the girls from the corner of his eye. They'd apparently abandoned their pursuit and now stood several yards behind him in what looked like a deep discussion.

Keeping a quick pace, Daniel exhaled and relaxed a little, although he'd never feel completely at ease until he and Lori had arrived safely in Ohio. But that would take another several days.

****

The afternoon was dreary and overcast and the temperature cool, when Lori stepped from the ferry dock onto free soil. As she followed

Daniel away from the departing passengers, that thought amazed her. They'd crossed the Ohio River from Parkersburg, Virginia into Marietta, Ohio. Smiling, with her heart pounding, Lori savored the bitter smell of soot in the air, because this air was free!

"I think I see our contact," Daniel whispered over his shoulder. While he walked toward a white man smoking a pipe, waiting near a buckboard wagon hitched to one horse, Lori, still dressed in her male disguise, stopped.

Over the sounds of the sloshing river and the blowing of the ferry's smoke stacks, Lori reflected that at last, she was really free. However, she could hardly grasp what that meant. Not to be bought or sold, not to be owned as property, not to lose her children in a business transaction, free to learn, free to go wherever and whenever she pleased. To have a life that belonged to her alone — and no one else.

The concept of true freedom was so overwhelming, Lori almost cried. Indeed she would have, if Daniel hadn't called to her.

"Come along, boy!" He motioned with his hand.

Longer hair and the scraggly natural beard of a young male were the only vestiges of a disguise for Daniel now. He'd discarded the fake beard and his clothes were no longer those of a dandy.

When she caught up to him, he said under his breath, "We're in Ohio now. You are free. The worst is behind us."

Chapter 18
Oberlin, Ohio,
October 1856

"This place ain't nothin' but a nigger lovin' town, and all y'alls gonna burn in hell," the slave catcher yelled angrily. His voice reverberated through the large church, bouncing off the walls and high ceiling.

Lori knew who he was. Talk had circulated throughout Oberlin after his arrival from Virginia a few days earlier. His name was Augustus Slade, and now he stood in the doorway of First Congregational Church during Sunday morning service. Many turned to look at him, shocked and appalled by his presence.

Lori heard several close to her, Negroes and whites, murmuring their disapproval of the man's very existence. Had she been anywhere else, Lori would have felt compelled to hide. But here among a white majority that supported Negroes, Lori felt somewhat safe, although this intruder had now shaken her security.

Timidly, she peered over her shoulder. Slade appeared not to have shaved for several days.

He wore a floppy hat, tattered around the edges. From the looks of the dirt on his ragged coat and the dingy shirt that stretched over his protruding belly, he probably hadn't bathed in weeks. His scowling visage would only add to the nightmares that had plagued Lori since the flogging.

Not separated by race, white and Negro parishioners sat side by side here at First Church. Lori, seated between Daniel and his sister Sarah, shrank in her seat. As she pressed close to Daniel, he reached for her hand, then held it discreetly, tucked beneath her skirts, so Sarah, sitting with her husband James beside her, couldn't see. As of yet, Daniel and Lori had not revealed their marriage to them.

"Brother," Preacher Charles Finney said, his face stern and bearded, "come in and repent of your sins!"

Slade held up a beefy fist. "Y'all's is the ones that's the damn sinners, congregating together here and depriving a white man of his legal property! I don't know where that nigger's hid, but when he's found, y'alls gonna pay!" He trudged from the church, his spurs and boot heels echoing loudly.

****

Lori pulled her black woolen cloak tightly around her. While leaving the church with Daniel, Sarah and James, the chilly breeze wasn't the only thing that made her tremble.

Towering oaks and sycamores, dressed in red and gold, surrounded them. The fall leaves filled the air with a crisp brittle scent. At first Lori had thought the turning trees in Oberlin were just as beautiful as those in North Carolina. But now, beneath their beauty, and the seeming tranquility of the town, Lori realized that she'd never really be free. She might just as well be back in North Carolina with those beautiful trees, and no false illusions.

Lori said nothing, nor did anyone else as they walked toward their two-seater buggy. They were still uncomfortable from the unexpected interruption at the church service.

"I don't think I'll ever get used to the cooler weather here," Sarah said, in what seemed an attempt to break the uneasy silence. "The chill will only worsen in the winter since there aren't any barriers to block those deadly gusts from Lake Erie." She raised the hood of her gray cloak, covering her long golden curls.

For a few moments more, they walked quietly, as Lori reflected on the two weeks she'd lived in Ohio. "I thought the weather was the only negative thing about Oberlin — until today," she said slowly.

The college here, founded by two missionary preachers, exuded a religious fervor, and that atmosphere influenced the town. Piety was the unspoken motto of Oberlin, and prayer was the single most significant act of devotion that symbolized all that Oberlin College stood for.

There were no saloons in Oberlin, nor billiard parlors, and smoking wasn't allowed in public. Lori and Daniel had been enjoying the feel of this progressive northern town. Here, blacks were regarded as equals, could receive educations, could even own businesses. But today's visitor had shattered Lori's precarious sense of refuge.

"Lori," James said, as they approached the buggy, "not everyone who lives in Oberlin is an abolitionist." Sarah's husband was tall and lean, with a handsome rugged face and thick auburn hair. His eyes were a penetrating hazel, but now appeared more serious than usual.

"There are those willing to help the slave catchers," James said, helping Sarah to her seat, "but of course, they're outnumbered. The Negro Mr. Slade was looking for is a Mr. Dawkins. But he was spirited away to Canada three nights ago, right after word spread of Slade's arrival. Dawkins had been living here for two years, but apparently…"

Lori felt a sinking feeling in the pit of her stomach. Daniel held her hand as she stepped up to her seat. "I thought I was free here, but— I'm—I'm really not…"

"Lori," Daniel said, "if Aunt Lucinda and Uncle Elijah didn't send slave catchers to find us in Wilmington, they're not going to come after us here."

"I must agree with Daniel," Sarah said. "You needn't worry, you're safe."

"And we'll make sure you stay that way," James added.

Chapter 19

Two days after the Slade outburst at church, Lori took a walk with Mrs. Carlisle through some of the surrounding neighborhoods close to Sarah's home. Mariah Carlisle, a colored woman, worked for Sarah as a paid housekeeper and cook.

As they strolled down College Street, Lori stopped upon hearing what Mrs. Carlisle had just told her. "Mrs. Carlisle," she pointed to the large house they were about to pass, "you said a Negro lives there?"

"Yes, Lori." Mrs. Carlisle sounded annoyed. She kept walking, leaving Lori behind. "And he's not just any Negro. He's a lawyer, just like Mr. Cartwright, and Mr. Cartwright knows him quite well."

"James knows him? What's his name?" Lori asked, still gazing at the two story white frame home.

"John Mercer Langston. Come along, Lori," she called.

Lori trailed quickly after Mrs. Carlisle's long graceful strides.

Catching up to her she said, "I still can't believe what life is like here. What I've seen today and yesterday almost makes me forget about…"

"The incident…at church?" Mrs. Carlisle asked. Lori nodded without a word. "Put that behind you."

"As long as I see more of what I've seen today, I think I'll be able to," Lori said softly. "Sometimes—I—I feel a little out of place here. This town—this place—still seems so strange. Yesterday you take me to your husband's blacksmith shop—a shop he owns! Then we go to a grocery store *owned* by a Negro, and today, that house back there." She glanced over her shoulder taking one last look.

"I suppose it is all rather strange, considering where you come from—and what you were," Mrs. Carlilse said coolly.

Lori frowned and sighed, thinking about Lizzie, Fanny and Juno. She missed them. Sometimes she even felt a little guilty about escaping and leaving them behind.

But here, aside from the slave catcher, the only other unpleasant person she'd encountered was Mrs. Carlisle. Lori had assumed that as a Negro, Mrs. Carlisle would show some warmth and kindness toward her. There really was such a thing as "southern hospitality," but Mrs. Carlisle, born in Ohio, knew nothing of it.

A tall, queenly woman in her late forties, Mrs. Carlisle had the straightest back Lori had ever seen. Her ebony skin reminded Lori of black velvet, and her height and carriage, combined with her high cheekbones and slightly slanted eyes, gave the impression that she looked down on everyone.

"Now, Lori," Mrs. Carlisle increased her pace, "we must make haste. I've lots to do before Mrs. Cartwright's company comes tonight."

"There's plenty I can do to help you."

"I'm *sure* there is." Her acrid tone implied condescension regarding Lori's former slave status.

"Besides chopping vegetables," Lori said. That's usually all Mrs. Carlisle allowed her to do. "I can bake the cake. Sarah wants a pound cake for dessert and mine is superb." Embarrassed by her boasting, Lori added, "At least—that's what I've been told."

"*I'll* bake the cake."

"But, Mrs. Carlisle, I'm quite capable!"

"Mr. Cartwright is especially fond of my cakes, especially my pound cake."

"I wasn't a common field hand," Lori snapped, "and while I lived with Daniel's mother, I wasn't treated like a slave at all! I learned to bake from her cook because I enjoyed it, and Miss Rebecca was never disappointed with anything I made!"

Mrs. Carlisle's brows raised in surprise at Lori's tone. "Alright then, you may. But just this once."

****

Sarah's cozy home was a simple, two story wood frame painted white with a gable roof. Once Lori and Mrs. Carlisle had returned, they began preparing dinner.

In the kitchen, Lori stood on one side of the cutting board, mixing cake batter with a wooden spoon, while Mrs. Carlisle was on the other, unwrapping a pork roast from brown paper.

"May I ask, Mrs. Carlisle, how your daughters find Oberlin College?" Lori was still in awe that this black woman was sending both of her children to college, and paying for their educations with money she and her husband earned all by themselves.

"Both find it quite to their liking. My oldest will be graduating this year. She plans to teach."

"That's what I want to do. So, do the Negro students and the white students learn in the same classrooms?"

"Yes Lori. Remember where you are. They even eat alongside each other."

"That's so unbelievable to me! I'm still not even used to *not* sitting in the balcony at church. Do you know how many Negro students attend the college?"

"I believe my daughters have said about

thirty. That's out of perhaps twelve hundred students. A small percentage—"

"But the doors of education are open to us! Sarah's taking me on a tour of the campus tomorrow. I can't wait to see it all for myself."

A few moments of silence passed, then Lori said, "I think you'll be pleased when Daniel and I aren't here to interfere with your work." Mrs. Carlisle said nothing as she seasoned the pork roast with salt and pepper. "We won't be attending Oberlin until next year, of course, but did Sarah tell you that starting next week, I'll be teaching with her at The Liberty School? I'm looking forward to being a blessing to those former slaves by teaching them to read and write."

"Remember, not all of them are *former* slaves." Mrs. Carlisle set the roast in a large Dutch oven made of cast iron. "Some are fugitives, just like…" Mrs. Carlisle stopped, changing the subject. "Will Daniel be doing that, too?"

"Oh, no. He's meeting with Mr. Westmore at his bank today. Since Mr. Westmore is a friend of James's family, he's agreed to let Daniel work at his bank."

"Good," Mrs. Carlisle said. "What will he be doing?"

"I don't know yet," Lori said, "but James mentioned that Mr. Westmore would decide after talking to Daniel. However, Mr. Westmore can rest assured that Daniel can do anything. He's quite intelligent, *and* resourceful. I'm sure that any position he provides, Daniel will be more than capable of performing."

Mrs. Carlisle gave Lori a sharp look. "You certainly *enjoy* talking about *Daniel*." Lori felt a hot rush of blood sting her cheeks. "I hope he isn't filling your head with a bunch of foolishness."

Lori's jaw dropped slightly. "Why, Daniel would do nothing of the kind."

"And," Mrs. Carlisle continued, "if he's given you any indication that living here, the two of you—"

The back door to the kitchen opened. It was Daniel, just arriving home from the bank. Dressed in a brown suit, he was now clean shaven, with his hair a bit shorter since the escape. "Mrs. Carlisle." Daniel nodded in her direction, receiving nothing but a look of disdain in return. "I hope you're having a fine day."

Mrs. Carlisle snorted, then pricked the pork roast with a knife several times and began inserting garlic cloves.

With no response forthcoming from her, Daniel turned toward Lori. With a wink, unseen by Mrs. Carlisle, he said, "Perhaps I could talk to you about something—out on the front porch, when you've finished with what you're doing."

"Of course," Lori beamed.

When Daniel left the kitchen, Mrs. Carlisle leaned close to Lori. "Now if a white man shows any interest in a Negro girl, besides sleeping with her, there's something wrong with him for thinking he can't do any better. You remember that, you hear! You'd best stick with your own kind."

****

Lori grabbed a thick woolen shawl from the walnut cloak rack near the front door, and then walked outside to meet Daniel on the front porch.

When she opened the door, she found him sitting on the white wooden balustrade, gazing through the trees in Sarah's yard to the muddy street beyond. He stood.

"How was your meeting with Mr. Westmore?" Lori asked.

"Marvelous — and you'll enjoy meeting him when he comes to dinner this evening. But the bank's not what I wanted to talk to you about." He hesitated for a moment. "I believe that it's — that it's time to tell Sarah and James."

"Time to tell them what?" Lori asked innocently.

Daniel crossed his arms. "I believe you know what I'm referring to."

Lori's dark almond eyes widened. "You think," she lowered her voice to a whisper, "you think we should tell them we're — married?"

"Yes." Daniel nodded with authority.

"But Daniel — we can't — not yet! If they know — that'll ruin everything!"

"Lori, you underestimate Sarah — and James."

"Do I? I'm not sure about James, but Sarah's likely to have a conniption fit!"

"Lori, she has to know! I'm not going to continue living a lie in front of her! It was bad enough at Dancing Oaks when Annabelle wanted to stir up a scandal between us. Now that we *are* married, I don't want to sneak behind my sister's back just to be with my wife. I'm not willing to stay apart much longer. Remember our last time together — at the safe house in Marietta — that was weeks ago!"

"Daniel," Lori dropped her tone to a whisper, "lower your voice, Mrs. Carlisle might overhear you. She's not too fond of either of us to begin with, and she's already implied that you're a lunatic."

Daniel laughed. "I don't want to disappoint the old biddy, so I don't care if she hears us or not! So come here," he said, grabbing Lori tightly around the waist. "It's high time we started *acting* like Mr. and Mrs. Taylor again!"

After kissing her firmly on the mouth, Lori pushed him away.

"Daniel, stop! Someone might see us." Her eyes darted cautiously from the porch to the street.

"You're right." Grasping her hand, Daniel led her into the house and up the stairs.

She laughed, as he dragged her to his bedroom. After shoving her inside, he closed the door and locked it. When Daniel quickly removed his jacket, Lori said, "This isn't a good idea." But while she talked, he moved close to her and kissed her neck.

"Not here, not now. We shouldn't—" she persisted. Soon, however, his lips met hers to quiet any further protest. After removing her shawl, he unbuttoned the top of her dress and pushed it from her shoulders.

Lori's lips held fast to his as she pulled her arms from the dress sleeves, then discarded the garment to the floor. When Daniel kissed her shoulders, Lori slipped her arms behind her back to unbutton her skirt and untie her petticoats.

Stepping from her clothes, she wore only a thin chemise, pantalets and stockings. Daniel carried her to the bed, then gently placed her on the feather mattress.

In his haste to remove his cravat and shirt, Daniel knocked over a stack of books from his nightstand. They crashed loudly to the hardwood floor.

"Daniel!" Mrs. Carlisle called from downstairs. Lori sat up startled. "Is that you up there?" the housekeeper asked in a brittle tone. "And just where did *Lori* go?"

Daniel unlocked the door and opened it a

crack. "That—uh—was me, and Lori—went for a walk."

"Another walk?" Mrs. Carlisle asked suspiciously. "And just what are *you* doing?"

Looking at Lori, barely dressed and disheveled, he replied, "I'm just—rearranging something."

"Well, don't break anything!"

When Daniel closed the door and locked it, Lori relaxed and smiled. As he came toward her, she reclined. Sitting on the bed, Daniel placed one arm on each side of her. "So," he said, looking deeply in her eyes, "I assume I've convinced you that there's no reason we shouldn't continue?"

Lori nodded while gazing into his strong chiseled face. His muscular arms were like the strong trees of a forest, and the contours of his chest, a canopy of protection. She felt an uncontrollable longing as her passion increased from a slow burn into an inferno.

"I've missed you." Lori sat up slowly, then grabbed Daniel hungrily around the neck, kissing him with an almost desperate urgency. But her fiery thrust of passion pushed Daniel from the bed.

He fell off, pulling Lori with him. Laughing, they hit the floor with a thud. Seconds later, however, they heard footsteps near the bottom of the stairs.

"Daniel! Be careful! I don't want Mrs. Cartwright fretting over something breaking! You hear? And just when do you expect *Lori* back?"

Daniel rushed to the door, again opening it slightly. "Mrs. Carlisle, I assure you, I won't break anything. And I'm not sure—how long Lori will be gone."

After closing the door, Daniel and Lori quickly finished undressing each other, then fell gently on to the bed in a warm embrace, and enjoyed the pleasure of their marriage.

****

After falling asleep, entwined in each other's arms, they were awakened by a knock at the door. Daniel eased himself up against the black walnut headboard.

"Daniel," Sarah said, "are you in there?"

Upon hearing Sarah's voice, Lori began burrowing beneath the abundance of bed covers.

"We should tell her now," Daniel whispered as Lori covered her head. She quickly flipped the covers back and mouthed a firm NO, before disappearing again.

Daniel cleared his throat. "Uh—yes, Sarah, I'm here."

His sister tried the door. Daniel tensed, realizing he'd forgotten to lock it as Sarah peeked in. Sarah wore a pink and red paisley dress with long puffy sleeves. Sausage curls spilled over her shoulders, and Daniel felt the blood drain from his face.

The side of the bed where he lay was visible from the door. Fortunately, his and Lori's clothes were strewn about the floor on the opposite side.

Surprise crossed Sarah's pretty face. Her gentle brown eyes widened upon seeing her brother in bed with bare shoulders. "Oh, pardon me." She closed the door, leaving it open only a crack to give Daniel privacy. "I certainly didn't mean to disturb you."

"I was—just taking a short rest."

"Without a shirt?"

"I was feeling a little—warm."

"But now you're under all those covers?" Suddenly, Sarah pushed open the door. "Chills and fever!" she exclaimed, throwing up her arms. "Daniel, I must feel your forehead." Grabbing her skirts, she started in the room.

"No!" Daniel stopped her before she'd barely taken two steps. "I'm fine. As a matter of fact, I was just getting up to dress."

"Oh, then," she backed out and disappeared from view, closing the door almost completely, "go ahead, I won't keep you. But—"

"Sarah—I do need to talk to you about something. It concerns my journey here—mine and Lori's. Actually something that happened before we—" Daniel stopped, when he felt Lori's fingernails dig deeply into his thigh.

"Daniel, I know it was a long, trying journey for both of you. I thank God every day that you and Lori made it here alive. I so admire you for protecting her as you did. A blood relative couldn't have done more. Daniel, you truly are like a brother to her."

"But I feel like more—"

"Oh, Daniel! You feel that you could've done more? What more could you have done for her? She's here, she's safe, and she has her whole life ahead of her—as do you. Which is why I've invited Emma Spencer to dinner next week."

Daniel started to speak, but said nothing. "Oh?" was the only sound he managed to produce.

"She's the beautiful teacher I told you about at the Liberty School."

"Oh?" He said again, feeling Lori's arms possessively encircle his waist.

"You don't remember, do you? Well never you mind about that now. I'm actually looking for Lori. I need her to help Mrs. Carlisle and me with dinner. The Westmores will be here soon. They're both active in the Oberlin Anti-Slavery Society.

"I thought they'd be interested in hearing about the escape and Lori's experience as a slave. Mrs. Westmore is also on the Ladies Board of Managers at the college, so I thought it would be good for Lori to know her."

"When I—see Lori again," Daniel said, feeling her pressed closely against him, "I'll tell her you need her help."

"Mrs. Carlisle said she went for a walk. Do you know *where* she went?"

Daniel hesitated. "Don't worry, Sarah. I'll find her. Sometimes she just likes to go off by herself and read."

"Oh, I see. Well, our guests will be here in a short while. So please find her quickly."

"I will."

After Sarah left, Daniel and Lori didn't say anything until after Lori emerged from beneath the blankets and comforter.

"Daniel," she whispered, her brows knit, "I don't want to lie anymore. When you lie, you're not trusting that God can handle all things. But He can, because He's in control, not us. So you're right, Daniel, we *do* need to tell Sarah and James." She paused for a moment, pouting. "Especially before she starts introducing you to all those young ladies she'd like you to meet."

Daniel smiled, whispering back, "I knew you'd see it my way sooner or later. Of course, now's not the best time with company coming. But later this evening, after they've gone, we'll tell them." He paused. "Perhaps it would be best for me to speak to Sarah and James alone."

At first Lori said nothing, then, "I won't argue with that. I'd rather be spared their reactions. But—what if they don't accept us as married?"

Daniel was quiet for a few seconds. "God's brought us this far—so, if necessary, He'll provide us with some other arrangement."

Chapter 20

Gazing at Lori, Sarah wondered where she'd been earlier in the afternoon. When the girl had turned up to assist with dinner, she'd been evasive about her whereabouts. But that was of no matter now, Sarah reflected. With Lori's help, everything had been ready and in place by six o'clock when the Westmores had arrived.

Sarah sat in the dining room with her guests at a sturdy round table, covered by a pale gray cloth. The table's matching oak chairs were wide with high backs. While Mrs. Carlisle served dinner, a fire burned in the fireplace warming the room. James, seated across from Sarah, heaped potatoes onto his plate, and the Westmores, a couple in their late fifties, sat opposite Lori and Daniel.

Benjamin Westmore, a tall and stately gentleman, had a full beard, generously streaked with gray. His wife Jeanetta, a kind and gracious lady, had green eyes that shimmered and gleaming white hair. Short bunches of curls adorned each side of her face, while her remaining tresses were twirled into a large ball at the nape of her neck.

Mr. and Mrs. Westmore had been good friends with Sarah's in-laws, who were now deceased. Since her own parents had also passed away, Sarah valued her friendship with the Westmores. She could always count on them for advice, as well as a listening ear.

Looking again at Lori, Sarah mused that she did appear refreshed, perhaps even radiant. Her hair, parted in the middle, was styled with a large roll on each side. And the emerald green dress she wore, with its wide ivory stripes and bell sleeves, was quite flattering. Apparently, Daniel must have thought so, too, since he kept stealing glances in her direction.

If Daniel didn't like Emma Spencer, Sarah calculated, surely he'd like Adelaide Grant, the lovely daughter of some friends in the Anti-Slavery Society. Sarah would invite her to dine with them week after next.

"Mrs. Carlisle, you've prepared a delicious meal," Mr. Westmore said, as the housekeeper brought more yeast rolls to the table. "You know I simply adore your pork roast and potatoes." Offering a stiff smile, Mrs. Carlisle thanked him before turning to leave the room.

While they dined, Mrs. Westmore asked Lori question after question about her life in slavery, her family, the flogging and the escape.

"Do consider chronicling your account, my dear," Mrs. Westmore said.

She wore a dark blue dress, its sleeves and collar trimmed in white lace, and a large cameo brooch pinned at her neck. "It's so important for the evils of this stain upon our nation to be revealed."

When Lori looked down for a moment, Daniel asked her if she felt all right. Then, through the flickering flames of the candles on the table, Sarah saw him squeeze her hand. Yet he let it go quickly, as though he'd hoped no one noticed.

Lori gazed at Daniel, smiling warmly. "Yes, I'm fine."

To Sarah, they seemed to look at each other a few seconds longer than necessary.

"I know these are painful topics," Mrs. Westmore said, "but Lori, my dear, we're all so very thankful that you're here now, and safe among us, so you needn't worry about slavery any longer."

"Yes, ma'am. But so many people are still in bondage."

"Yes, my dear, I'm well aware of that. As abolitionists our goal is to end this horror, this disgrace upon our country. Would you be willing to speak at our next Anti-Slavery Society meeting?"

Lori's eyes widened. "Mrs. Westmore—I—I don't know if I could."

"Oh, I understand, my dear. Just think about

it. You're quite bright and articulate, and such a beautiful girl. Our group wants to hear from your people, especially those who have escaped that dreadful institution and have had first-hand experience."

"I will think about it. But I've never spoken before a crowd."

Mrs. Westmore smiled. "That's all right, my dear. Just think of us as a group of friends— *warm* and *welcoming* friends. That's how I look at our community."

She took a sip from her water goblet. "You see, my dear, Mr. Westmore and I came here with the Cartwrights from Massachusetts over a dozen years ago, and we've found Oberlin to be a very special place with a rather fascinating history."

"The community's foundation is rooted in virtue and piety," Mr. Westmore said, "and for abolitionists like us," he chuckled, "this is the perfect place to live.

"In these parts we've earned quite the reputation for self-righteousness and heresy, as well as radicalism. But we're just simple folk with a mutual regard for human rights."

Mrs. Westmore smiled adoringly at her husband, then gazed at Lori and Daniel. "This is an innovative place, my dears. Not only has Oberlin opened its doors to colored students, but it's always admitted women because the intention was to train them to teach and work with their future husbands in spreading the Good News."

"Now, if the school would only allow women to teach," Mr. Westmore patted his wife's hand, "it would be even more progressive."

Lori tipped her head. "I thought you were a teacher, Mrs. Westmore. I must have misunderstood your position."

"No, Lori, my dear, I'm not a teacher. Our Ladies Board of Managers is mainly a disciplinary board. We handle problems related to individual young women. But Sarah tells me teaching is what you plan for your life's work.

"Yes, it is."

"Well, my dear, I'm sure you'll be an excellent teacher. Oberlin will prepare you wonderfully. We've had females go on to accomplish great things. There are some extraordinary young ladies in our student body now." She smiled sweetly at Lori. "And you'll be one soon, my dear."

****

Mr. Westmore had just finished his last bite of cake in the parlor. Sarah had moved her guests there for dessert and coffee. Although considered a vice in Oberlin, Sarah had refused to give up her coffee. The Westmores had no objections to this and enjoyed a cup or two during each visit.

When Mrs. Carlisle walked in to refill the coffee, Mr. Westmore eagerly lifted his cup. "I must say, Mrs. Carlisle, your pound cake is always delicious, but tonight, it has an extra special something to it."

Mrs. Carlisle, dressed in black, said nothing. After she finished filling Mr. Westmore's cup, she stood to her full height and looked down on him. He sat in a burgundy armchair next to his wife, seated in an armless lady's chair. Then Mrs. Carlisle cast an accusatory eye toward Lori, who was nestled on the black lacquered settee with Daniel beside her.

"I made the pound cake, Mr. Westmore. I'm so glad you enjoyed it." Lori sat tall beaming, but under Mrs. Carlisle's icy glare, she shrank slightly and her smile diminished.

"Well then," Mr. Westmore said awkwardly, "that is something, isn't it? Why — both of you make a splendid pound cake. And I'm sure that *you*, Mrs. Carlisle, with all of your expertise, will be teaching Lori a thing or two about baking."

"Perhaps so, Mr. Westmore," Mrs. Carlisle said coolly. Before returning to the kitchen, she addressed Sarah. "Mrs. Cartwright, I'll be leaving now."

"Of course, Mrs. Carlisle. And thank you for staying late this evening."

All were silent as Mrs. Carlisle turned to go. Sarah and James exchanged amused glances as they sat on a rose colored empire sofa.

Once Mrs. Carlisle was out of earshot, Mr.

Westmore said, "The last thing I want to do is offend the poor lady." Then he glanced at Lori. "Or make things intolerable around here for you."

"Thank you for your concern, Mr. Westmore, but I'm used to her." Lori smiled.

"Pay her no mind, Mr. Westmore," Sarah said. "She's rather temperamental, but I couldn't live without her."

James stood up. "Lori, your pound cake is superb. Now, if you ladies will excuse us, I'd like to take the gentlemen with me, so I can show Mr. Westmore my new telescope."

****

"That's quite the contraption there," Mr. Westmore said, after he and Daniel followed James into the small library. He approached the telescope. It sat perched on its stand near a window that was draped with dark green damask curtains, held open by gold-fringed tiebacks.

Mr. Westmore ran his hands over the telescope's cool exterior, feeling the elaborately swirled design etched into the metal. "You've enjoyed looking through this, too?" he asked Daniel.

"I have." Daniel smiled. "But not nearly as much as James."

"Let me dim the light so you can take a look." James reached for the oil lamp on his desk.

With the room darkened, Mr. Westmore bent down to look through the lens. Against a blanket of black sky, he saw a multitude of magnified shining lights. "Stars—so I see— hmm, interesting, very interesting indeed."

After a few moments, Benjamin had seen enough. Not greatly impressed with his enlarged view of the night sky, he said, "I'll leave the stars to you, James."

As James bent to peer through the lens, Mr. Westmore settled into a comfortable wingback chair. "Daniel, you come sit here with me," he motioned to a matching chair, opposite his, "so I can get to know you a little better."

As Daniel sat down, Mr. Westmore asked, "Have you given any thought as to what you'll pursue after Oberlin?"

"Well," Daniel paused, thinking, "I have a taste for adventure, so—I'd like to see the West. Perhaps even settle out there."

"Oh, you would, would you? Well, I have a younger brother, Charlton, a rather adventurous sort, who lives in California. He went out there with one of our cousins back in 1849. Both of them are what the family called wild and untamed. But they've found all the excitement and adventure they could ever want, living in California."

Daniel leaned forward. With elbows on his knees, he smiled. "Did they make a fortune mining gold?"

Mr. Westmore laughed. "They tried, but I don't think their endeavor as miners lasted for more than a day. Right now they're living in the southern part of California, about ten miles out of Los Angeles. They pooled their resources a few years back and purchased two adjoining ranches. They raise sheep, and their land combined equals about fifty-thousand acres."

"Fifty-thousand acres?" Daniel said amazed. "So they've found excitement, adventure *and* success."

"They have indeed. So if you consider going to California, I'll be glad to write you a letter of introduction. I'm sure my brother could help you get a good start out there. You seem quite the capable young man. James and Sarah have spoken highly of you, and I'm impressed with what I've seen so far. Next week I'll see what you're made of when you start working for me." He smiled. "But I'm sure I won't be disappointed."

****

As Sarah and Mrs. Westmore conversed in the parlor, Lori stared at the uneaten cake on the plate in her lap. Rather than joining their discussion, Lori thought about the painful times she'd endured.

Until Mrs. Westmore had asked this evening, Lori seldom thought about her mother. The memories were too painful. And she tried not to dwell on the flogging. The scars were bad enough, but the most vivid memories resurfaced in nightmares.

Feeling drained from the evening's questions, remembering the encounter with Augustus Slade only two days earlier, and thinking about sharing her marriage to the probable dismay of others, had emotionally exhausted her.

"Ladies," Lori put her plate on the coffee table in front of her and stood up, "I hate to be rude, but I must excuse myself. I'm not feeling that well. I—I need to lie down."

"Lori, are you ill?" Sarah asked, concerned.

"No, just tired—and a bit overwhelmed— from our dinner table discussion."

"So sorry, my dear, Lori," Mrs. Westmore said. "You've been through quite a difficult time these past few months. I should have been more sensitive to your state of mind. Forgive me?"

"Of course, Mrs. Westmore."

After saying goodnight to Sarah and Mrs. Westmore, Lori slowly strode from the room.

****

"Sarah," Mrs. Westmore said, after Lori's departure, "she's such a lovely girl, and she sounds well educated."

"My mother had Lori tutored with Daniel. They're just about the same age."

"I see," Mrs. Westmore mused. "Well, my dear, I do believe Lori has taken a fancy to your brother."

Sarah laughed. "They are fond of each other. They were practically raised together. Daniel loves her like a sister. He put his life at risk to help her escape. I begged him not to, but he—"

"Sarah, your brother is taken with her as well."

Sarah pursed her lips, then forced a smile. "As I said, he—uh loves her like a—"

"Like a sister? That's nonsense, Sarah. And I think you know that."

Sarah frowned, perplexed. "Oh, Mrs. Westmore, you can't be serious. Why it's not— it's not possible for him to have those feelings for a…"

"A Negro?"

"Well, yes," Sarah said defensively.

"This is one of those things that can't be helped. We do want equality for the races and— we are all equal in God's eyes."

"But marriage—between the races—that's unspeakable."

"It does happen, though. It's evident by the few mixed marriages we have here in our community. Of course, those unions are disapproved of in general.

"I've asked our James Monroe what he thinks. Although he's quite the advocate for the rights and equality of the colored people, he refers to those marriages as 'distasteful commerce.'"

Mrs. Westmore finished her coffee. After placing her cup and saucer on the small round table by her chair, she said, "Sarah, you handle things as you see fit. But just remember, you can't control another's emotions."

"Perhaps it's just a harmless infatuation," Sarah said, but a tone of desperation laced her voice.

Mrs. Westmore sighed. "Take it from an old woman. I know true love between a man and a woman when I see it." She hesitated for a moment, then moved from her chair to the sofa next to Sarah. "My dear, I feel I must tell you something in the strictest of confidence. Outside of Benjamin and our children, no one knows this — and I'd appreciate you not mentioning it to anyone else."

"Of course, Mrs. Westmore, you have my word."

"As you know, Mr. Westmore and I come from abolitionist families. Aiding and abetting runaway slaves is nothing new to either of us. But long, long ago, when I was but a girl of twelve, my family helped one slave, in particular, who was a rather learned young man.

"From what I remember, he was tall and well built, with skin of a golden brown hue. Even at my young age," she laughed, "I found him quite a pleasure to look at. His name was Silas," she resumed in a serious tone, "and I had an older sister, Emmilene, who was around eighteen at the time. Sarah, I swear to you, in retrospect, I believe it must have been love at first sight between them.

"Father was out in the barn the night Silas first arrived, so Emmilene and I were alone with him for a brief time. My sister couldn't take her eyes from him. And though he tried not to look at her, he couldn't seem to help himself, until my father came back to the house."

With eyes wide Sarah asked, "Did — something happen between them?"

"Well, we assisted the young man for a couple of weeks before he moved on to Canada. He settled there and bought land. But several months later, Emmilene revealed that she'd maintained correspondence with Silas. Her intention, she said, was to move to Canada and marry him."

Sarah gasped.

"Needless to say," Mrs. Westmore continued, "we were appalled, but she refused to listen to reason. My father all but cut her off; never spoke to her or of her again. As far as he was concerned, Emmilene ceased to exist.

"My mother had already died. But I kept in touch with Emmilene until her death three years ago. Silas had passed on the year before that. So you see, Sarah, my sister and her husband, despite the fact that he was a—person of color, had four children and were happily married until he died. They lived in a Negro community, and Emmilene had to—all but become a Negro, but that didn't matter to her. She was with the man she loved."

Sarah's eyes dropped to her lap.

"So — you see what's possible, my dear." Mrs Westmore tilted her head trying to catch Sarah's downcast gaze. "I hope I haven't upset you, but…I assume you've had your…suspicions?"

Sarah nodded silently, then met her good friend's eyes. "Perhaps you're right, Mrs. Westmore."

"It's a matter of the heart, my dear. Emmilene confided to me once that she would have regretted not marrying Silas. He was her one true love."

Silence filled the room for a few moments, and then Mrs. Westmore grasped Sarah's hands. "Worse things could happen," she said softly. "Now, as late as it is, we must be going. Thank you, my dear, for a lovely evening. I just hope I — haven't ruined it for you."

Chapter 21

After the Westmore's departure, James noticed Sarah acting rather agitated.

"Daniel, would you — would you be so kind as to — chop some wood?" She stammered to her brother. After Daniel kindly obliged, Sarah nearly shoved him out the back door before slamming it shut.

"Sarah," James said, "I chopped a rather abundant supply of logs last night, so there's really no need — "

"James, not now!" Grabbing his arm tightly, she ushered him to the library and said, "We must speak immediately."

As she closed the pocket doors, James reached to dim the lamp. "Whatever you wish to see me about, I can listen while stargazing."

Sarah turned to look at him, her face troubled. "*Please* don't look through that blasted contraption of yours now! I need you!"

James left the telescope. Moving toward his beautiful Sarah, he noticed the red flush of her cheeks. Apparently, she was more nervous than he'd realized, and she needed his calming reassurance.

James remained collected in the most difficult situations. He provided a good match for Sarah's nervous disposition, and after careful analysis, he could easily determine the right solution for any problem.

"By the urgency of your tone," James said soothingly, "this sounds serious. And I was so hoping that the rest of our evening would be quiet and romantic, because I, my love, need you too."

When James embraced her, Sarah pulled from his arms. "Darling, I'm sorry, but I can't concentrate on much of anything right now, except Daniel—and the ensuing crisis brewing beneath this roof." Wringing her hands, Sarah walked away from him.

"Daniel—and an ensuing crisis?" James asked. "We've more than enough room in this house, and he's quite helpful to have around. And Lori, I know she's been a help to you, *and* Mrs. Carlisle, although the woman would never admit it. Lori's pound cake is certainly tastier," James laughed, "but don't dare mention I said that to Mrs. Carlisle!"

"James!" Sarah turned to him, raising her fists in the air for a moment. "This isn't about the room, or their help—*or* Lori's blasted pound cake!" She took a deep breath, as though trying to compose herself. "It's about Daniel—and Lori—and the possible—*feelings*—they might have for each other."

James approached his wife with a sly smile. Playfully pulling her close again he said, "Feelings? Dare I say—love?"

Sarah looked gravely into his eyes. "James, I'm afraid this is no time for jesting."

He released her, and for several moments said nothing, then, "Do you mean— you really think they *are* in love?"

"Mrs. Westmore broached the topic. She said something—that made me think it's possible. And I've suspected, though I've tried to deny it. I thought that, perhaps, I was imagining things. But you've seen the way they look at each other. And Daniel—he's quite protective of her."

"Hmm..." James thought for a moment. "Perhaps it's mutual admiration, or familial devotion. You've always said they're like a brother and sister."

"But it has to be more than that, James. Daniel could have sent Lori here alone, but he chose to help her escape the entire way. Facing danger and possibly death for her...that *has* to be love."

"Yes," James said softly. "A young man yearns for adventure. And he especially wants to impress the woman he loves. He's willing to protect and defend her to the death."

"So you see our quandary?"

"Yes," James said, contemplatively. "'Star crossed lovers.'"

"Oh, James, you and your stars! But—but what should we do?"

"Talk to him first, of course. We need to verify our suspicions."

"I suspect we're correct in our thinking," Sarah sighed. "Hopefully, Daniel can get this—this *thing* out of his system. However, we'll need to find different lodging for Lori. We can't have them under the same roof."

"I'd hate to cast Lori out after all she's been through. We are like family to her. So we must first establish, if there is indeed, a problem." They heard Daniel come in through the back door, then he called, looking for them.

"Now is as good a time as any to talk to him," James said, walking to the closed pocket door and opening it. "Daniel, we're in the library!"

Moments later, Daniel walked in, holding a load of firewood. As he carried it to the wrought iron log rack by the fireplace, he said, "I just wanted to say goodnight." He was sweating and slightly out of breath. "And I—also need to—talk to you about something."

"Oh?" Sarah said, as she watched him squat down and put the logs in the rack. After he stood up she said, "Well—as a matter of fact— we uh, we need to discuss something with you, too. So—I guess we should—sit down." Sarah sounded nervous.

She seated herself on the armless chair turned

from James's slant front desk. It allowed her skirts to comfortably overflow the sides. Daniel and James sat in the matching wingbacks.

Before Daniel had chopped wood, he'd removed his suit jacket. Now his shirtsleeves were rolled up and the cuffs of his union suit visible. A slight smattering of wood chips adhered to his clothes.

"What did you want to see me about?" Daniel asked.

"Lori," Sarah said.

For several seconds, an awkward silence filled the room until a burning log in the fireplace popped loudly. It startled Sarah. She jumped slightly, catching her breath. James walked to the hearth and grabbed the poker. After moving the screen, he shoved the offending log, sending up a small cluster of sparks. The room became infused with the smell of a more pungent smokiness as the blackened wood broke into large ashen chunks.

Sarah still hadn't said anything. James waited for her to speak as he slowly strode back to his chair over the creaking hardwood floor. She smiled uneasily at her brother, but then dropped her gaze to her lap and began tracing the design of her paisley print dress with her fingers.

"What about Lori?" Daniel asked.

Finally, Sarah attempted to speak. "Daniel — we — uh — think — she's — and you — "

As Sarah sputtered, James stepped in to smooth the situation. "Daniel," he hesitated, "it's come to our attention that your feelings for Lori appear to be more than, shall we say, brotherly."

As James spoke, Daniel leaned forward, clasping his hands. His eyes moved to the floor. "We need to know the truth," James continued. "We don't want you to ruin your life, or hers, by doing—foolish things."

"Daniel, you're young and intelligent with a bright future ahead of you," Sarah said. "We believe that, under the circumstances, it would be best if Lori found lodging elsewhere, for both of your sakes. We have several friends who would be more than happy to take her in."

Daniel, still gazing downward, appeared lost in thought and paid them no attention.

"Darling," James said to Sarah, "before we jump to any conclusions, we need to verify that there truly is a problem that warrants her removal from this house."

Daniel looked firmly at both of them. "If she's removed, I go with her."

James and Sarah were appalled by Daniel's words, and the tone in which he'd said them. Speechless, they sat wide eyed.

"Daniel, what would make you say such a thing?" Sarah's voice quavered. "What kind of hold does she have on you?"

"She loves me."

"Daniel," James said, trying his best to remain unruffled, "this is—nothing but a—but a passing fancy. White men engage with Negro slave girls because they have power over them. The poor girls are available merely for pleasure. Now, you're *hardly* the type—"

"And I love her," Daniel interrupted before James could analyze things further.

However, James didn't miss a beat and continued, seemingly unfazed by Daniel's admission. "Promises and declarations of love to a Negro girl are so cruel when nothing can happen, as far as marriage or commitment of any kind.

"Then, when a white fellow moves on, the girl is left with nothing—but some yellow bastard children. Daniel—I know you're not that way. And I know you wouldn't toy with the poor girl's emotions—or would you?"

"No," Daniel said firmly, "we're married."

Sarah and James sat silently with jaws agape.

After several moments, Sarah said, "What do you mean, you're married?" She shook her head in adamant denial. "The two of you *can't* be married! That's—that's impossible!"

Sarah stood up, but when she tried to walk, almost fell. Sitting back down, she pulled a handkerchief from the bosom of her dress. Mopping her forehead, Sarah said, "Daniel, I—I can't accept this and I certainly don't condone it!"

"Jonas and Martha provided a Quaker wedding ceremony before we left Wilmington. So whether or not you accept or condone it, we're married with God as our witness."

"I know you must be aware of this," James piped in, "but your marriage isn't legally binding. It's against the law for black and white to marry in North Carolina."

"Yes, James, you're right!" Sarah said, sounding relieved and triumphant. "And thank goodness, Daniel, that what you've done *isn't* legally binding. In time—you'll see what a mistake this has been. You can part ways now with her, and go on with your life.

"I'm sure Lori had no *real* expectations that you'd truly want to spend the rest of your life with her." Sarah blew out a deep breath. "Thank God—there is a way out of this mess."

After a brief silence, Daniel said, "Both of you don't seem to understand. We're committed to each other for life, legally binding or not. We're married in the eyes of God. I love her—and nothing can ever change that."

Chapter 22
Ten Years Later
Little Ways, California
Los Angeles County 1866

Lori watched as Daniel ate the last of a large second helping of everything. The round gate leg table was piled high with pork chops, collards, sweet potatoes and cornbread.

They dined with Avarie and Gussie Chandler, Negro sisters and school-teachers, both brown and plump, like fresh baked yeast rolls from the oven. Each wore spectacles, and hair twirled in a bun on top of their heads. Lori guessed them to be way past fifty, yet their voices were high pitched and sugary sweet.

Since arriving in California three days earlier, Daniel and Lori had been staying with the spinsters in their small, but comfortable, white frame house. They lived in the town of Little Ways, not too far from the Westmore ranches.

Mr. Charlton Westmore had been called out of town on business unexpectedly, right before Daniel and Lori's arrival.

However, he'd be returning to his home later this evening, and would meet with Daniel and

Lori first thing tomorrow morning. Until Daniel found employment and housing, they'd arranged to live at Mr. Westmore's ranch.

Lori's mind wandered. Ever since talking to Mr. Benjamin Westmore, all those years ago in Oberlin, Daniel had had his heart set on moving to California. Now he and Lori were finally here, but they'd experienced quite a journey in the process.

Convincing Sarah and James that they intended to remain husband and wife had been a challenge, but Lori's in-laws had finally accepted Daniel's marriage to her. However, Sarah had expressed her thoughts about them not conceiving children as a blessing in disguise.

Perhaps at one time it was, Lori thought. She and Daniel had graduated from Oberlin, he with a degree in mathematics, and Lori with hers in teaching. And on the heels of that, the War of the Rebellion had come.

Daniel and James had served as officers, while Sarah and Lori volunteered as nurses. The war was a terrible time.

Lori saw things in the hospital she wished she could forget. Bloody war memories resurfaced in her nightmares alongside memories of the flogging.

As soon as the conflict had ended, Daniel began making arrangements to leave Oberlin and move here. Once permanently settled with

Daniel gainfully employed, maybe then children would come, Lori mused. Despite her outwardly indifferent disposition regarding her childlessness, she didn't want to remain a barren woman forever, like Sarah. Sarah had accepted her condition, and she'd tried to make Lori feel better by saying, "God gives us what we can handle."

Sarah was convinced that she'd never be a mother because she worried too much. "So all's well for me," she'd said lightheartedly. "And Lori, with all you've been through, and seeing that your children would be — of different parentage — perhaps not having little ones is for the best."

Lori had smiled and thanked her sister-in-law for her attempt at comfort, but inwardly she'd resented Sarah's opinion. Lori had lost her mother, her freedom. She longed to have children to love and protect — they'd never be taken from her!

Lori gazed adoringly at her husband, thinking what a wonderful father he'd make. God had blessed her by bringing Daniel into her life, but would He ever bless her with a child? Her desire was a constant prayer.

"Daniel," Miss Avarie said, "you eat as much as you want, there's plenty left."

Pulled from her thoughts, Lori glanced at Miss Gussie and Miss Avarie, who were busy assessing Daniel's clean plate. They were kind old ladies, but as sweet as they were, they were hiding something—something about Mr. Charlton Westmore.

Lori had overheard them whispering earlier when she'd walked into the kitchen while they were cooking dinner. Now she felt a little guilty about eavesdropping before she'd made her presence known. Before Lori had cleared her throat and asked if she could help, she'd heard one of the ladies whisper, "He said not to tell them, you know he doesn't want them to know."

But what would *he* not want them to know? The only "he" she and Daniel knew of in California was Mr. Westmore. Lori tried not to be too concerned about this, and if she hadn't been nosy, she wouldn't be in the predicament of fearing the unknown.

She looked down for a moment, ashamed. It served her right. However, with all she and Daniel had gone through, they could handle what Lori assumed to be some sort of disappointment.

When Lori stood up to clear away the dishes, Miss Avarie touched her arm with a soft plump hand. "Sit down, child, I don't believe Daniel's finished yet. A tall, strapping young man like him can probably fit in something else."

"Miss Avarie," Daniel said, "I'm trying to save some room for that chess pie Miss Gussie baked."

"I'm sure you'll like it." Miss Gussie grinned, then gazed at Lori. "And I hope you eat a nice big slice. We need to fatten you up. Married for ten years and no baby yet! A little meat on your bones'll fix that!"

Lori felt her cheeks warm, as she said, "Oh, Miss Gussie, I've had enough. I can't eat another bite. I'll just taste some of Daniel's."

While Lori and Miss Gussie cleared away the dishes, Miss Avarie put out the pie and dessert plates. After resettling her girth at the table, she placed a thick piece of pie in front of Daniel. "You lookin' forward to meeting Mr. Westmore tomorrow?"

"Absolutely," Daniel said. "I have been, ever since his brother Benjamin told me all about him."

Miss Gussie walked from the kitchen with a sugar bowl and pitcher of cream. Lori followed, carrying a tray with cups, saucers and a tall porcelain pot filled with steaming coffee.

The matching set was Chinese, painted in tones of green, white, red and blue. It's design depicted a dragon blowing fire, and mountains could be seen in the background.

As Lori set the tray on the table, Miss Gussie said, "Mr. Westmore was a mite disappointed when he had to go to San Francisco before you all got here. He's been looking forward to meeting you, too."

After Miss Gussie poured coffee, Lori set a cup at each place, then sat next to Daniel and tasted a forkful of his pie.

"There's plenty to go around, sugar." Peering over her spectacles at Lori, Miss Gussie tipped her head. Her first chin buried itself in the second. "You don't have to eat his."

"Honestly, Miss Gussie, I'm quite full. But this is delicious pie. You've fed us well during our visit, and we certainly can't thank you enough for letting us stay with you."

"Why, thank you, sugar," Miss Gussie said. "Mr. Westmore wanted you to feel welcome your first days here. Being a widower, he didn't think staying at his place, with no one around but his cook, would be too hospitable. Mr. Chuck's a good man, but you'll see for yourselves just how wonderful he is when you get to meet him."

Miss Avarie took a sip of coffee, then proudly held up her cup. "This beautiful set was a gift from Mr. Westmore. He brought it back for us from San Francisco."

"It's quite lovely," Lori smiled.

After a few moments of silence, Miss Avarie exclaimed, "I'm not gonna hide it any longer! I know you think we shouldn't tell Daniel, but he'll meet Mr. Chuck in the morning, and it'll do him good to know ahead of time."

"Avarie, Mr. Chuck said not to mention anything. But since you brought it up—in front of them—maybe we should," Gussie said.

Lori looked at Daniel, unsure of what to think.

"Who's Mr. Chuck?" Daniel said.

"That's Mr. Westmore, everybody around here calls him that. Now, Gussie, Mr. Chuck knows we can't keep a secret. That's why he told us in the first place—he *expects* us to tell him, even though he said not to mention it. But if he hadn't wanted us to say anything, he wouldn't have told us at all!"

"Oh, all right, Avarie," Gussie said. "You win, we'll tell them!"

"Would you ladies mind explaining what you're talking about?" Daniel asked.

"Daniel," Gussie said excitedly, "you know you're welcome to stay with Mr. Chuck at his Charlton Place Ranch for as long as you need to, and he's more than willing to help you find a job. But he's prepared to let you live *permanently* at his other ranch, the one called Rolando, if you want the job he'd like to offer you there—the job of *general manager*!"

Daniel's eyes widened. "What?" He looked as though he couldn't believe what he'd just heard.

"Mr. Chuck's cousin, Roland, was killed in a train wreck last year," Miss Gussie said. "He was the owner and managed the place himself up until the tragedy. After that, Mr. Chuck became the owner, but he hired a new fellow to manage things.

"Well, the new man married and moved to San Francisco a few months back. So ever since then, Mr. Chuck's been wearing himself ragged running both places. He was about to start looking for a new man. But once he received word from his brother that you'd be moving out this way, he thought, maybe you'd be interested."

"But he doesn't even know me," Daniel said. "Why would he think—"

"Mr. Chuck says that through the years, his brother's written some very complimentary things about you," Miss Gussie smiled, "and that he thinks quite highly of you."

"Oh," Daniel said, as Lori gently grasped his hand.

"Why, yes," Miss Gussie's eyes twinkled, "and Mr. Chuck knows that in your situation, having Lori as a wife, you'll need a little extra help. He's looking at this opportunity as a head start for you.

"But he doesn't want you to feel obligated. He's an influential man around these parts, and he can get you connected with some of the local businessmen."

"At least the ones that don't have a problem with us Negroes," Miss Avarie quipped.

"I am interested." Daniel frowned, as though uncertain. "But I still can't believe he'd want me for the job. He must know of other qualified men around here, or some that already work for him."

Avarie grinned at Gussie with a knowing glance, then said to Daniel, "Lots of qualified men around alright—but he wants you to have the first crack. Now, we've already spilled the beans about the job, and we have a good idea of why he wants you to have it, but that's his place to tell you."

"Even though we could," Gussie added, "but I suppose that would be gossiping." Then swatting her sister's arm, she said, "But we can at least tell tell him the story about Mr. Chuck's good friend—that Negro that came to visit from Massachusetts."

Avarie burst out laughing. "Mr. Chuck can be a downright scoundrel at times! He took his friend to church with him, then told the man to go to the door alone to see what kind of reception he'd get from the congregation.

"Well, those white folks looked at him like he was crazy, then told him he wasn't welcome, and—"

"And then," Miss Gussie interrupted, "Mr. Chuck walked up behind that Negro and said, 'this gentleman is my guest, and if he's not welcome here, then both of us will worship elsewhere.'"

"Those crackers didn't want to lose Mr. Chuck's big tithe!" Miss Avarie chuckled, "and they begged him to stay—even claimed they'd make a special place of honor for his guest. But Mr. Chuck and his friend didn't stick around. And ever since then, Mr. Chuck's been coming over here to our colored church."

Daniel nodded his head, amazed. "Now I understand the man a little better."

"And I have a feeling you'll get to know him better than most folks," Miss Gussie smiled. "We've been friends with Mr. Chuck since he came here back in 1852. He and his cousin had means. They owned some land up in northern California before they moved down here and bought their ranches from an old, Spanish widow lady.

"Our town's about three miles from the Westmore property. There's a doctor and a post office in Little Ways, so folks that work on the ranches come here quite a bit.

"Well, one day, not long after he and Roland got settled in, Mr. Chuck rode over here to explore. He went beyond where the white folks live and found us by accident," Miss Gussie explained.

"Avarie and I were walking home from the school one day when Mr. Chuck, riding tall on his horse, tipped his hat and introduced himself. Seeing that he'd stumbled into where the colored folks live, he wanted to know how he could help, since he was raised as an abolitionist. Well, finding that out, we invited him to tea that very instant!

"California didn't have any organized abolitionist societies, so we had to fight on our own for any rights we were able to get. And now, even though slavery's over, we're still fighting! But back in the day," Gussie smiled, "we were fortunate when a good hearted abolitionist soul would come along to help us out."

"When we met Mr. Chuck," Avarie said, "our school was in the basement of our church, and we told him that any donation to improve it would be greatly appreciated.

"Not long after that, Mr. Chuck and Roland came to our door and asked if they could build us a new school. They'd been financially blessed and wanted to share what they'd received.

"When the new school was built, we decided to name it The Westmore School. Being humble, Mr. Chuck and Roland didn't want that," Avarie smiled, "but we finally cajoled them into letting us call it that anyway."

"Mr. Chuck's been asking if we need another new schoolhouse, but I think we have enough room, at least for right now. But, we'll probably take him up on that offer in the not too distant future," said Miss Gussie. "More and more colored people are heading out this way.

"Our state was admitted as free, and the colored people that came here, and are still coming, are eager for an education. We have over fifty students in our school now and we thank the Lord everyday for The Westmore School. And," Miss Gussie gazed sweetly at Lori, "we're always looking for teachers!"

"Oh, I'd love to teach!" Lori said.

"Perhaps you could start this fall?"

"Gussie, let the child get settled first," Avarie said. "And after that, she might start having babies."

Lori pursed her lips, feeling embarrassed again. She looked at Daniel. He was trying to suppress a laugh.

Regarding children he'd said, "We'll just have to keep praying," and then added with a sly smile, "and trying."

Now he was probably thinking that their lack of babies certainly wasn't due to a lack of trying.

"Children will come in God's time," Lori said quietly, eager to change the subject from her child bearing capacity. "I'll see what happens with Daniel and Mr. Westmore before I commit myself to teaching," she said.

"That'll be just fine." Miss Gussie leaned over and gave Lori's hand a soft squeeze. She smelled faintly of the pork, sweet potatoes and collards she and her sister had cooked for supper. "And you're right, sugar, the good Lord will give you babies in His time."

Chapter 23

The next morning, Daniel and Lori rode on a two-seater buckboard wagon sent from Charlton Place. Juan, a Mexican man employed by Mr. Chuck, drove them. He almost appeared bronze-like, with brown skin, brown clothes and a wide brimmed brown hat.

Daniel believed southern California, with its mixed population of Spaniards, Indians and Mexicans, to be just right for him and Lori. Being married and of different races perhaps wouldn't matter as much out here. At least that's what he'd been thinking and hoping since he'd married Lori a decade earlier and envisioned moving west.

Daniel gazed at Lori. She returned his gaze, squeezing his arm softly, and then looked beyond him into California's foreign landscape. The terrain appeared different here. He'd read that some called California a mystic land. From the buckboard, Daniel looked across flatlands, treeless except for a few low-growing willows, while far beyond lay deep blue mountains painted against a pale blue sky.

Now with the war over, more whites seemed to be drawn to this place. Some were seeking a new beginning, while others were running from the emotional devastation of war.

Daniel tried not to think about what he'd experienced as a Lieutenant serving his country. Witnessing the inhumanity and brutality of war, seeing men blown to pieces, and encountering Rebel soldiers he'd known from North Carolina were all memories he'd tried to forget.

He'd seen two childhood friends, barefoot in the freezing cold, emaciated and dressed in rags, taken as prisoners. Upon recognizing Daniel, they'd called him traitor and nigger lover. Daniel had fought for Lori, and to abolish slavery, and to preserve the Union.

But fighting against the land he'd called home had conflicted him at times. He'd fought against friends and relatives, and to those loved ones who hadn't died defending their cause, Daniel was dead, because they'd never choose to acknowledge his existence for what he'd done.

Lori squeezed his arm again, as if to bring him back from that dark place. Catching his eye, she smiled, and so did he. Everything he'd done, he'd done for her. And he'd do it all over again. Sharing his life with Lori was what he wanted, and they'd make the best of things. Meeting Mr. Chuck would provide a good start.

For a while they'd ridden on flat land by what appeared to be a shallow river. Now they ascended a hill.

"If you look ahead," Juan said, "you see Mr. Chuck's adobe."

Daniel raised his head as the wagon finished climbing the hill. He saw the adobe through an open gate made of heavy wooden doors.

The house had a two story central portion that was about a hundred feet long, flanked by one story wings on each side. The wings appeared to be fifty feet longer than the central portion, and the roof of the structure was flat.

The outside was whitewashed, while the window frames and balusters of the upper veranda railing were painted green. Daniel noticed bars on the first story windows, and near the top of the outer walls on each wing, funnel shaped holes protruded.

Daniel figured that at one time these had been used to shoot from, while the bars offered protection from attack.

As they rode through the gate, Daniel saw large leafy locust trees scattered about the grounds, and numerous oleander shrubs with bright pink blossoms. Several hitching posts were in what looked like a courtyard, and here, Juan stopped.

As Juan tended to the horses, Daniel stepped from the buckboard onto an elaborate red brick pathway. After helping Lori alight, she tightened the aqua blue bow at her chin. The ribbon of her low-brimmed bonnet matched the blue in her tiered cotton dress, and each tier was trimmed by white lace.

Moving his eyes from Lori, Daniel took in the scenery while inhaling the fresh floral air. However, before he could do too much looking at the surrounding gardens and grassy acreage that stretched beyond the house, a tall white-haired man approached him.

"Nine o'clock sharp," the man said jovially. "I see Juan was right on time, as usual." Juan tipped his hat and smiled at the older gentleman. "Charlton Westmore," the man said, extending his hand to Daniel.

Daniel removed his bowler hat, thinking back to Benjamin Westmore's tall and stately carriage. Mr. Chuck was his younger brother, but even taller, and more rugged.

Broad shouldered with a mountainous chest, Mr. Chuck wore a black shirt, brown vest, and bolo tie knotted at his neck, while brown pants covered his long, sturdy legs. Mr. Chuck must've been in his fifties, but his body was thick and strong, and his keen eyes, gray and determined, like gunmetal.

Although younger than Benjamin by at least ten years, Mr. Chuck's leathery skin was sunburned and lined from the California sun.

As Daniel shook Mr. Chuck's hand, he observed the man's casual attire and weathered face. Can I really do this? Daniel asked himself. Am I cut out to manage a ranch?

Daniel wore a suit. He'd enjoyed working at the bank in Oberlin. That profession would've fit him just fine. But ranching? Daniel suddenly felt unsure of himself. Perhaps he should seek employment at the bank in Little Ways, but then again, perhaps not.

Daniel had executed a daring and successful escape for Lori, and he'd survived the war. If he could do those things, he could certainly manage a ranch. Feeling a little more rugged and confident, a scripture came to his mind, *Lean not on thine own understanding.* He would do this, and he'd let God guide his steps.

"Daniel Taylor, sir. It's a pleasure to meet you."

"It's good to meet you, Daniel. And this young lady," he said to Lori, "must be the beautiful Mrs. Taylor."

Daniel put his arm around Lori's shoulder. As the older gentleman kissed her hand, she smiled, saying, "Yes, I'm Lori Taylor, and it's a pleasure to meet you."

"The pleasure is all mine," Mr. Chuck said. "Now, come in and have a seat with me. My cook, Mr. Ming, is fixing us some tea."

Mr. Chuck led them through the courtyard toward a brick terrace.

They strode into the house from a side entrance, then walked through a wide door that led to a short hall. This opened directly opposite into a garden, so they turned left into a longer hallway.

"Have you ever been in an adobe house?" Mr. Chuck asked as their boot heels echoed on the hardwood floor.

"No. It's different from anything I've ever seen," Daniel said. "It's quite large. How many rooms does this place have?"

"All together, about twenty-six. Some of the men who work for me stay in the wings on either side of the place. Others live down in an old house by the river. And some live in huts around the property. Takes a lot of people to run a ranch this size, but it's nothing like a slave plantation!"

They walked into the parlor through an arched doorway. The large square room smelled of leather and wood.

It had one window facing the courtyard, and another facing the front veranda. A large walnut bookcase filled to capacity, occupied one side of the room, and a fireplace was built into the opposite corner. Surrounding a simple walnut table was a camel back sofa covered in maroon velvet and a set of elk horn chairs.

The horn chairs, covered in worn oxblood leather, were made from a pair of steer horns that framed the upper back and served as arms and legs. The tips of the horns served as feet.

"Make yourselves comfortable," Mr. Chuck said. After Lori and Daniel sat on the sofa, Mr. Chuck settled into a horn chair.

"I've got some good men working for me," Mr. Chuck smiled, "and they come from all over the world. I use Chinese for housekeeping and Mexicans make up a good part of the ranch workers. But I've also got men from New England and Europe. The ranch workers stay around here and sheepherders work away from the house."

Wearing a serious expression, Mr. Chuck leaned close to them. Daniel could smell the cool antiseptic clean of the man's coal tar soap.

"Now, folks will tell you," Mr. Chuck said, "that sheepherders are regarded as one step above social outcasts — not that I agree with that, but if you want to do it, you have to be close to a recluse.

"Sheepherding lets you sever contact with the past, and I've got a lot of broken men here who've taken refuge to escape whatever pain they've experienced in their prior lives. Most of mine are from successful backgrounds — editors, bankers and the like — but they want to live solitary lives because of the war, lost loves, or failures of one kind or another."

Mr. Chuck smiled, "I know that's not the life

for a capable young man like you. So let's talk about your future, but first I must apologize for not being here to meet you when you first arrived in California."

"That's quite all right, Mr. Westmore," Lori smiled. "The Chandler sisters were quite hospitable."

Looking wary for a moment, Mr. Chuck said, "Thank heaven you're both still alive and they didn't *feed* you to death! And please, call me Chuck, or Mr. Chuck, if you prefer. Now Daniel, my brother has spoken in the highest regard for you."

"Thank you; and I don't think I could have worked for a finer man during my stay in Oberlin."

"Benjamin's a good man. But we're like night and day. Maybe he told you as much. Benjamin was the good boy — and I was the hell raiser." Mr. Chuck laughed. "Seems Cousin Roland, who came out here with me, was cut from the same mold.

"We were the two black sheep, so apparently, sheep ranching was the natural thing for us to do. Unfortunately, poor Roland died before his time. I'm sure Gussie or Avarie must've filled you in on that."

"They did, and we're sorry for your loss," Daniel said.

"Thank you." Mr. Chuck gazed down for a

moment, then said, "We both worked hard and enjoyed what we did. And I'm fortunate to still enjoy it and reap the rewards.

"The annual cost of herding, pasturing, shearing and caring for a flock of sheep amounts to only around thirty-five cents a head. When each one yields about six and a half pounds of wool, that brings me anywhere from eighteen to thirty-five cents a pound. I own thirty thousand sheep here at Charlton Place, and thirty thousand more at Rolando. So you can see how profitable that is. Every year up in San Francisco, I market about four hundred thousand pounds of wool from both ranches. Now, with that said, I'd like to offer you an opportunity."

Daniel smiled, crossing an ankle over his knee. "I'd like that very much."

"I'll cut right to the chase because I know Gussie and Avarie told you what I had mind — didn't they?"

Daniel and Lori nodded, laughing.

"My brother was impressed with your potential, Daniel, when he first met you after your — daring departure from North Carolina." Mr. Chuck winked at Lori. "And he's kept me up to speed on your progress — working in his bank and managing it during your winter breaks, graduating near the top of your class, and serving as an officer.

"Benjamin also says that you work well with your hands and have sharp mathematical skills. He was impressed by your attention to detail and your orderliness of mind. And you've certainly demonstrated that you're not foggy headed in the midst of a crisis! Those are all the things I need in a general manager."

When Mr. Ming walked into the room wearing a white apron and cap, they sat silently as he placed white cups and saucers on the table in front of them, and then poured steaming tea from a round white pot. They thanked him, as he quietly left the room.

"Mr. Chuck, I appreciate your confidence in me," Daniel said. "But why me?'

Mr. Chuck hesitated. "So they didn't tell you about Belle?"

When Daniel and Lori gazed at each other questioningly, Mr. Chuck said with a half smile, "That's surprising, as much as Gussie and Avarie like to talk."

He took in a deep breath. "Not long after I moved to California — I married an Indian woman...she was from the Maidi tribe...up north. Belle was dark and beautiful, but some of the folks around here — didn't take too kindly to her."

Mr. Chuck looked down for a moment, rubbing his thighs with the palms of his hands. "Lots of things got back to us, that were said behind our backs — like I was supposed to be crazy for marrying a savage, and that Belle was nothing but a red skinned squaw — and even worse things than that."

Shaking his head slowly, tears clouded his eyes. "Belle died last year. She didn't hold any grudges, but me — I'll never forget. And I know in your situation, with Lori as your wife, you'll face more challenges than most, and have to put up with a lot of — unpleasantries — for lack of a better word. So, the job is yours, if you want it."

"I appreciate that, sir, and I'm more than interested in your offer. I assure you, I can learn anything. I know more than a little about farming from reading and living on my Uncle's rice plantation for a short while, but outside of that, I have no experience in ranching."

"I'm aware of that," Mr. Chuck said, as he reached for a cup of tea, "but I can teach you all you need to know and you'll catch on fast. One day you might even want to own a ranch yourself. And if you are ever interested, I could sell you Rolando. I'm getting too old to deal with both places. Could be a good investment, but that'll be up to you and Mrs. Taylor to decide."

Mr. Chuck finished the last of his tea. "Benjamin also told me all about you, Mrs. Taylor." He smiled, gazing at Lori for a moment, then looked at Daniel and said, "So you decided to thumb your nose at society and go after what you wanted, regardless of the cost. That was a wise decision because you'll never spend the rest of your life trying to forget the happiness you had with her, and wondering what could have been. I admire people who go after what they want, especially when it's risky! That takes grit—and guts.

"And with your grit and guts, Daniel, I want you to seriously consider my offer. Room and board will be provided at Rolando and I'm willing to start you at a salary of fifteen hundred dollars a year. Take your time to think—"

"When can I start?" Daniel interrupted.

Mr. Chuck sat back in his chair and smiled.

"Now's as good a time as any."

Chapter 24
Twenty-two years later
Rolando Rancho, Los Angeles County,
California
Summer, 1888

Perhaps this is something an old woman is supposed to do, Lori thought while sitting at her writing desk in the parlor at the Rolando Ranch house. Now forty-nine, she considered her youth the distant past. Lori pulled her journal from the lap drawer.

Miss Rebecca had never been one to journal, she was always too busy, and not one to sit still, Lori mused, but Miss Lucinda had made time daily. During her brief time as a house servant, Lori remembered the woman scowling at her from that slant top desk in the library at Dancing Oaks. Feeling a chill from that memory, Lori pushed it from her mind.

In the last few years, Lori had discovered that she enjoyed recording her thoughts. After removing the cap from her black fountain pen, she began to write...

June 28, 1888,

Although I have taken to writing in my journal on a somewhat regular basis, I have yet to chronicle a slave narrative. David brought that subject up again last week, as he has for the past several months. However, I would rather forget those days than write about them. But if I were to chronicle something for my son to publish, I would write about how much the Lord has done for me.

Lori paused for a moment thinking about all that had happened since she and Daniel had moved to California. Mr. Chuck had had no children of his own, and he'd treated Daniel like a son. After five years as the Rolando Rancho general manager, Daniel had purchased the place.

Unfortunately, Mr. Chuck had died in 1878, a decade ago, but he'd blessed the Chandler sisters, the Westmore School and the colored church in Little Ways with large amounts of money.

Since Mr. Chuck had had no other living relatives, Daniel inherited Charlton Place, along with the rest of Mr. Chuck's thousands of acres, and what remained of the money from his estate.

However, the material blessings weren't what Lori was most thankful for. She was most thankful for her children.

It had seemed that once she and Daniel were settled here, the children had miraculously arrived, David in 1867, Olivia a year later, and finally Lavinia in 1872.

A shard of pain tore through Lori's heart as she reflected on her youngest daughter. She couldn't help but feel she was partly responsible for how Lavinia was turning out. Thinking back to happier times, Lori remembered that when all of her children were old enough to go to school, she'd gone right along with them to the Westmore School and begun to teach.

How the time had flown by. David had graduated from Howard University. Now married to a lovely girl named Janine, he lived in Little Ways. Olivia was a recent graduate of Oberlin. Lori sighed. Lavinia had refused to go to college. Lavinia had refused to do a lot of things that her mother and father wanted her to do—and her current obsession was scandalous.

Prayer was the only answer for her youngest child. Lori resumed writing...

My children have been my greatest blessing, and I wish happiness for each of them. When David visits today, I hope he refrains from broaching the topic of slave stories again!

Janine is out of town visiting relatives, but David will not be alone when he arrives. He will be bringing a friend, a young man he met at Howard who has just moved to California.

The gentleman is a native of North Carolina, so I like him already. From what David has told me about him, he sounds as though he'd make a fine husband. I am eager to meet him, for Olivia's sake. I do hope she fancies him. I sometimes fear she will be an old maid.

Lori heard boot heels clicking on hardwood before she heard the voice.

"Mother?"

"In here, Olivia."

Lori's oldest daughter stepped into the parlor from the hall. "Just wanted to let you know I'm going riding."

Lori gazed at her daughter's split skirt and cowboy hat. "Make sure you're back in plenty of time to bathe and look like a lady for David's guest."

"Mother, they won't be here for hours."

Before Olivia tuned to go, Lori asked, "Where is your sister?"

"I don't know. Probably talking to herself in the mirror again. I just hope she doesn't embarrass us while we have company." As Olivia strode off, she called over her shoulder, "Don't worry, Mother, I promise to look presentable at dinner!"

Chapter 25
Wilmington, California

David climbed from his buckboard wagon and walked toward the train. The air around the station in Wilmington was filled with soot, steam and dust, but through the throng of people and horse drawn vehicles, he could easily see the disembarking passengers arriving from Los Angeles.

"Josh, over here!" he yelled, waving to the tall, dark Joshua Cummins.

"David Taylor!" Josh quickly made his way to David, carrying a suitcase in one hand and a carpet bag in the other. "Man, it's good to see you!" he said, putting down his bags to greet David.

As they walked to the wagon with David lugging the suitcase and Josh carrying the carpet bag, the easy camaraderie they'd shared years earlier at Howard University returned.

Josh had been in the medical school when David entered the undergraduate program. They'd become friends when David courted Josh's sister, who'd also attended Howard.

The courtship hadn't lasted, but their friendship had. They'd remained in touch.

Through correspondence, David had learned that Josh's parents had died months earlier, and that now Josh wished to set up a medical practice in California.

David put an arm around Josh's shoulder. "So you've come to live in my home state! But now I've got to convince you to leave Los Angeles and live in my hometown!"

"What's wrong with Los Angeles?" Josh had been staying there with a cousin since he'd arrived a few weeks earlier. "My cousin and his wife like it just fine, and from what I've seen, I like it too. But anything's better than the South.

"Those white boys are doing all they can to make life intolerable for any Negro. Los Angeles isn't perfect, but so far, it's looking pretty good," Josh said.

Josh was well over six feet and a behemoth of a man with a rock-like stature, broad and solid. David was a few inches shorter, and his frame lean and wiry. During their college years Josh had joked, "You've got the money, man, but I've got the looks."

Although handsome, with dark brown curls and a copper-toned complexion, David's gangly build couldn't compete with Joshua's well muscled physique.

David took his arm from his friend's shoulder. As they neared the buckboard he said,

"The white boys want to make it hard for a black man anywhere. It may never be perfect between them and us, but at least it's better out here."

They placed the luggage in back, then climbed on the buckboard and left the station. Joshua admired the pale blue mountains peaked in the distance, then gazed toward seagulls flying lazily through the bright blue sky.

He put a hand over his eyes to shield them from the sun as David asked, "Have you definitely decided to live in Los Angeles? Is that really where you want your practice?" He increased the horses' speed as Josh stretched his long legs.

"I think so," Josh replied.

"It's a dangerous place; murders are happening there all the time."

"Then that's where I need to be, so I can save lives." Joshua smiled.

"Well, just wait 'til you see Little Ways. It's a quiet town—safe and beautiful too, and my family's ranches aren't too far away. You're staying with me for a few weeks, right?" David asked.

"Yeah."

"Well, you'll enjoy what you see! There's a lot of growth in the Negro community, and we could use a colored doctor.

"My office is in the Negro business district, and there's a vacant building right next to me.

My father owns it—he can give you a good deal on the rent. And, Josh, you'll like my sister Olivia."

"That's the tomboy sister you told me about. Isn't she getting up there in years? I was looking forward to meeting the younger one, Lavinia."

"Olivia's not that old! She's only twenty and—"

"But I don't want some cowgirl! Now, from what you've said about Lavinia, she sounds like a lady."

"I don't remember saying that much about her, besides that she hates to get her hands dirty. And look, man, Lavinia's not really that—hospitable."

"You know me, David, I like a challenge!"

Joshua's dark and very handsome presence demanded attention. Although he'd never dare look a white woman in the eye, David had seen many an admiring gaze from them in Josh's direction—followed by threatening glares from white men.

David shook his head and rolled his eyes at his friend's arrogance. "Just you wait, Lavinia'll slap you down a notch or two—not that you don't need that with your conceited self! And it's not that she's just inhospitable—she's—she's..." David trailed off.

"She's what?"

David hesitated. "Nothing...you'll see soon

enough when you meet her. You'll be able to figure it out for yourself."

****

David's two story white frame home was situated in one of the newer developments in Little Ways, not too far from Wilmington. After stowing Josh's bags there, they headed to Rolando Rancho to spend the afternoon with David's parents.

****

"Tell me about your paper," Josh said, as they continued riding from Little Ways to the ranch. "It's called *The California Beacon,* right?"

David smiled. "You remembered."

"You stirring up trouble, riling up the white boys with what you write?"

"I try," David laughed. "Gotta have a little fun with the crackers now and then. I publish *The Beacon* Monday through Friday and I concentrate on issues important to Negroes here in California. More and more colored folks are moving out this way. My paper's an asset to the community."

Grinning, Josh inquired, "What do the white folks think of that?"

"It's all about politics. If I publish an article that makes some of 'em angry, they don't retaliate. They know who my father is. His land butts up right against the town. And because of all his land—and..."

"And his money," Josh finished David's sentence.

David shrugged. "I didn't want to sound like a braggart."

"That's okay, man," Josh laughed. "Since your daddy's a powerful white man, folks leave you alone, even if they don't like what you write."

"In a manner of speaking," David agreed.

"Now, what about your father? He doesn't care about you not taking over the family business?"

"No." David shook his head. "Dad knew I wanted to be a writer."

"So he bought you a printing press, and —"

"And the colored community needed a paper. Besides, I don't have a rancher's heart — but Olivia does."

"The manly Olivia," Josh laughed.

"C'mon, Josh, she's not manly!"

"What about her rancher's heart?"

"My Dad's promised Olivia the other ranch on the property. She likes ranching, so Dad told her that, after she gets married, the other ranch is hers to own if she wants it."

"Hmph," Joshua snorted. "That'll be nice for the lucky guy that lands her. She'll be breadwinner and all. But that guy won't be me. Last thing I'd want to be is a rancher. Medicine's my first love. I can't see myself raising sheep."

"Sheep industry's dead."

"I thought you said that's how your father made his money."

"In the beginning, but the drought put an end to that a few years back. Dad leases a lot of his land to small farmers now, and the acres he farms himself just grow a few crops. Another source of income for him is the dairy farm— actually, he's got two, one on each ranch. But lately, Dad's been selling off lots of land to developers. *That's* been making him tons of money."

"Good for him," Josh said. "Well, I'll leave the dairy cows and crops to Olivia. I'm not cut out to be a farmer. I could have stayed in North Carolina and *not* gone to medical school if I'd wanted to do that."

"Don't be so quick to turn up your nose at owning a ranch. Let's say you did like Olivia— and the two of you tied the knot."

Josh laughed. "Not gonna happen."

David ignored him and continued. "You wouldn't have to give up your medical practice. You wouldn't have to be involved with the ranch at all, as long as you have some good men working for you, and a good general manager, they'd run things for you.

"Olivia teaches during the school year, and she doesn't want to give that up, she loves the kids too much. She'd oversee things at the ranch, but she wouldn't exactly be managing the place singlehandedly. So just think, Josh, you'd have your medical practice — and be a gentleman rancher earning a good income on the side."

Josh grinned, looking ahead. "But would the woman by my side be more manly than me?"

****

Nearing Rolando, Josh spotted a young woman on horseback riding toward them from the direction of the ranch.

"So — your father has some female ranch hands working for him?" Josh asked slowly.

"My father doesn't have any female —" David stopped in mid-sentence when he saw the girl. Looking down he grimaced, muttering, "Dang blasted."

"Let me guess," Josh said sarcastically, "Olivia? She's a mess, man, looks like she's covered in mud. What happened to her?"

David shook his head, while pulling on the reins to stop the wagon. "What can I say? You're in California. You're on a ranch. Any woman raised out here is a western woman, and a western woman —"

"Just tell me this," Josh said as he watched the muddy female rapidly approach them, "does she at least know how to bathe?"

Before he could joke any further, Olivia was only a few yards away.

****

"Whoa, Sugar Loaf!" Olivia reigned in her chestnut mare, stopping alongside the buckboard. "Welcome to Rolando!" The horse gave a spirited snort as Olivia extended a muddy gloved hand to Josh.

David's doctor friend eyed the glove but didn't reach to shake it. "Sorry," Olivia retracted her filthy hand and wiped it on her shirt. "I didn't realize it was so muddy."

Now seeing how handsome this Joshua Cummins was, she'd regretted riding out to greet him. She should have gone home an hour ago to "look like a lady" as she'd promised Mother.

But David's friends, at least the ones he'd thought she'd like, were usually highly intellectual—and very strange.

She certainly hadn't thought *Doctor* Cummins would be an exception to the rule, yet this man's physique was powerful. His muscles strained against the confines of his suit, and his face was strong and handsome. With a complexion like chocolate and a self-assured smile, a chipped front tooth didn't take away from his appeal, but only added character.

"I'm—I'm Olivia Taylor," she said awkwardly.

"Joshua Cummins," he nodded politely.

By the look on the man's face, she could tell he'd never seen a female quite like her. His eyes moved from the top of her wide-brimmed hat, then studied her face, splotched with tight drying mud spots.

"I must apologize for—looking this way," Olivia said embarrassed, while she watched Josh's gaze move to her dingy gray shirt. It was originally white; there were a few clean spots where the mud hadn't splattered. Her blue denim split skirt was caked with mud, as were her decoratively stitched cowboy boots, but now the fancy handwork couldn't be seen.

"Just what happened to you?" David said. "I was telling Josh that I wanted him to meet you, but then you turn up looking like this!"

"Blame it on my silly horse!" Olivia rubbed the animal's neck. "Something startled her and she threw me down by the river. Lucky for me, there hasn't been too much rain lately. There was just enough mud—for a soft landing."

"Don't you need to get home and—do something with yourself?" David prodded.

Olivia smiled. She was about a mile from the house. "Yeah, I do," she said, turning her horse around.

****

"We'll take our time and enjoy the scenery while you put yourself back together!" David called after Olivia as she rode away.

Josh watched her ride off and appeared deep in thought. David hesitated and sighed, guessing that Josh had found her disgusting and far from womanly, just as he'd inferred earlier. "Josh, she cleans up nice — really she does. Just forget you ever saw her looking like — "

"David," Josh interrupted him, "why didn't you ever tell me she was so pretty?"

Chapter 26

"Is that fence made from redwood?" Josh asked seeing the high fence David drove through as they entered the ranch.

"Yeah." David steered the buckboard team toward the hitching posts.

"Dang," Joshua exclaimed, "it must've cost a fortune!" When David stopped a few moments later, a stableman met them to tend to the wagon and horses. "So you've got folks for everything?"

David smiled. "I'd better walk you around to the front. Mother hates it when I bring company through the back door."

They strode along a red brick path paved in a herring bone pattern to the front of the house. Josh stopped to stare. The porch was wide and long, covered with rose vines. He inhaled, smelling the sweet fragrance of the red, pink and purple blossoms carried by the salty ocean wind.

"This is quite a place," Josh said. The veranda extended the length of the house with arbors at each end draped with mission grapes. An expansive garden stretched before the front of the house that must've covered two acres. "I didn't know Negroes could live like this!"

Looking at the surrounding garden, Josh saw flowers and blooming shrubs laid out in three tiered raised beds. Pathways edged in red brick separated them. Italian Cypress trees were scattered about the grounds while black locust trees lined the perimeter.

Gazing toward the house again, Josh's eyes traveled to the upper veranda — and stopped. His jaw dropped. Josh pointed, unable to speak.

"Oh," David said, noticing his friend's temporary stupor, "that's Lavinia. She's been waiting for you to notice her."

Standing still, Lavinia gazed away from David and Josh, as if unaware of their presence. She looked off into the sky as though dreaming, while a calm wind tousled her long black hair, raising it behind her like a veil. Remaining silent, Josh took a few steps forward to see if Lavinia was really as beautiful as he thought.

"Don't think she doesn't see us, or *hear* us," David said loudly. "Everything's a production to her." At this, Lavinia shot her brother a nasty look. "Now that you've acknowledged us," David said sarcastically, "this is —"

"I'll meet him when he comes in," Lavinia snapped. She then turned abruptly, went inside, and slammed the door.

****

After enjoying a warm reception by David's parents—one much warmer than he'd received from Lavinia—Josh found himself amazed by Mr. and Mrs. Taylor. Sitting in their parlor with them, he still couldn't quite fathom their story. A respectable white man actually married to a black woman, an act illegal in most places, was something he'd never seen.

Aside from color, the Taylors appeared as an ordinary couple of well-to-do means, even though their circumstances were extraordinary. They'd conquered the odds and were living what seemed an impossible dream.

"So, you've chosen to live in L.A.?" Daniel said.

"I have," replied Joshua, "but David's been trying to convince me to settle in Little Ways."

Light green flowered wallpaper decorated the parlor, and the dark walnut furniture was covered in olive green and floral patterned fabrics. Josh sat in a large armchair, while David sat next to him on a curved back sofa. David's parents sat facing Joshua on a loveseat.

They were an attractive pair, Josh thought. Mr. Taylor's hair was sparsely sprinkled with gray, while Mrs. Taylor's was liberally streaked with it. Her face however, was smooth and unwrinkled.

Mr. Taylor also appeared younger than his years, though his countenance displayed some distinguished looking age lines.

"I think that's a fine idea," Lori said, "and I hope you'll seriously consider it."

"Oh, I just might give it some thought," Joshua said noncommittally, "but, so far, I've—" he stopped in midstream, staring beyond Lori.

She turned to see what had captured his attention. Lavinia stood in the doorway. "Well, come in darling," Lori said, but Lavinia didn't move.

Daniel glanced over his shoulder. "Lavinia," he said sternly, "come in and say hello to our guest."

Josh stood, as though in a trance, while Lavinia approached him. Her strides were queenly, and with high cheekbones and deep green slanted eyes, her face was the most beautiful he'd ever seen.

Lavinia was the lightest of David's siblings and appeared white. Her nose was slim and patrician, and her fair skin could only be described as milk with rose petals. Josh assumed that the look of disdain on her face was caused by his dark complexion. Josh figured that's what David had hesitated to tell him. Lavinia was color struck; *looked* white and probably wanted to *be* white.

Lavinia's dark hair was parted in the middle with a thin braid on each side, pinned away from her face. The braids blended into the rest of her waist length tresses.

The emerald dress she wore accentuated the color of her eyes and complemented her figure. The fullness of her breasts welled beneath the smooth green fabric, beautifully molded against her tiny waist and the alluring curves of her hips.

Lavinia stopped in front of Joshua, lifting her eyes to his. She must have been just a few inches over five feet because his he towered over her.

"I'm Lavinia," she said crisply. "David's told me your name, but I can't seem to remember it."

"I'm Joshua Cummins. It's a pleasure to meet you, Lavinia." When he held out his hand, she hesitated to shake it. David smiled. "It doesn't bite," he teased. At this, Lavinia sneered slightly, then extended her hand to him.

The handshake was the briefest he'd ever experienced. After less than three seconds, she quickly withdrew her dainty white fingers from the clutches of his large black paw.

Saying nothing more to Joshua, Lavinia plopped down insolently in the matching chair next to his.

"Joshua," Lori said, "Lavinia is—is a—uh teacher at the—Westmore School." Falling over her words, Mrs. Taylor sounded embarrassed by her daughter's behavior.

"I have the highest admiration for teachers," Josh said, looking at Lavinia. "And what do you enjoy most about your vocation, Lavinia?"

The girl sighed loudly. "Teaching isn't really what I want to do. My mother's forcing me to do it and—"

"Joshua," Lori interrupted her daughter, "I was about to ask you the same question. What do you enjoy most about medicine?"

Josh felt sorry for Mrs. Taylor. Lavinia seemed a difficult girl. "Mrs. Taylor, I've wanted to be a doctor for as long as I can remember," he said. "If I can help someone or save a life, I'm blessed. And I'm doing what the Lord wants me to do."

"We're all gifted by God in some way," Daniel said, "and God wants us to use our gifts."

"Father," Lavinia leaned toward Daniel, "why won't you let me use *my* gift? There's nothing wrong with what *I* want to do!"

"Lavinia, that subject is closed," Daniel said. "And you can use—*your gift* to entertain the children you teach."

Lavinia sat back and tightly crossed her arms. Joshua witnessed her eyes narrow and a crimson flush crawl from her neck to her cheeks. "So, Lavinia," he ventured to ask, "what is your gift?"

"Acting," she replied coldly, without gazing in his direction.

"Really?" Josh asked. "I enjoy the theater."

Mrs. Taylor pursed her lips. "Joshua, we do too, but it's hardly the vocation of choice for a young lady."

"That's right," Daniel added, "and she's a bright girl, capable of anything." Lavinia glared at her father. "Perhaps," Daniel said to her, "Joshua will hire you as a nurse. Maybe your personality is more suited to medicine. Women are receiving medical degrees these days. You could go to medical school and become a doctor if you wanted to. That's not out of the question."

Daniel moved his gaze to Josh. "The girl's certainly intelligent, but she'd rather…" Mr. Taylor stopped as though remembering himself. "I suppose I've said enough."

Lavinia dug her fingers into her upper arms, making her knuckles turn white.

"Yes, Daniel, I believe you have," Lori said calmly, "and we don't want to spoil Joshua's visit talking about Lavinia's—hobby."

"Mother!" Lavinia shot up angrily from her chair. "My acting is *more* than just a hobby!"

"Darling," Lori said, "sit down, please. There's no need to cause a scene."

"You want a scene?" Lavinia huffed. "I can cause a much worse scene than this!"

"Lavinia!" Daniel said sharply, "watch your tone, and sit down."

Lavinia stood defiantly for a moment, then flopped down hard, sighing in exasperation. Tightly grasping the arms of her chair, she sat tall, as if waiting to spring in attack.

Beauty aside, Josh concluded, Lavinia was mean as the devil, and too hot for him to try to handle.

"Sorry I'm late," Olivia said as she walked into the room.

Josh rose from his seat, marveling at her transformation. She'd been pretty before, even covered in mud, but now she appeared as a goddess.

"Allow me to reintroduce myself," Olivia said, striding toward him with an outstretched hand. "I'm Olivia."

Josh smiled as she approached him. Inhaling the fresh scent of lemon soap, he said, "I'm very pleased to meet you, indeed."

Olivia's skin was honey gold, and her hair, still damp and pulled away from her face, was reddish brown and cascaded in tiny ringlets down her back.

Thick black lashes framed Olivia's large brown eyes, and her nose was soft and rounded. The sensual lips resembled her sister's, but on Olivia's face they were pleasant and smiling, not gnarled in a grimace. Her high cheekbones matched Lavinia's as well, but on Olivia's countenance they appeared sweet and inviting, rather than angry and distant.

From her glowing smile, to the pleasant touch of her hand, Olivia radiated warmth.

Wearing a buttercup yellow dress trimmed

with ivory colored ruffles, she stood taller than Lavinia by a few inches. Her hips were slender, but her breasts were a bit fuller than her sister's, which more than compensated for the lack of curves below her slim waist.

"Shall we have dinner?" Lori asked.

While gazing at Olivia, Josh had forgotten all about eating.

****

The mahogany table was draped with Irish linen and set with Wedgwood china, sterling silver and crystal. Joshua was seated next to Olivia, at Mrs. Taylor's insistence, and she'd placed Lavinia across from him, by David.

Josh flashed Olivia a charming smile, as he heard David grumble to Lavinia, "Try to be nice, okay?"

Dinner was served by a Chinese servant named Mr. Pong. While he set out large serving dishes filled with ham, fried chicken, collards, sweet potatoes and macaroni and cheese, Mrs. Taylor asked Josh to tell a little about himself. "David says you're from Bertie County," she said.

"Yes, ma'am. I'm from Windsor."

"You attended Howard's medical school and then went back to North Carolina to practice for a while?" Daniel asked.

"That's right, Mr. Taylor. But I have a cousin who moved out here a few years back and he's been singing the praises of California ever since. After my parents died, I figured I'd give it a try, too. Nothing for me to lose," he glanced at Olivia for a moment, "but everything to gain."

"I'm trying to convince him to leave L.A. and move over here," David smiled. Looking at his sister he added, "Maybe he needs someone besides me to persuade him."

"Well, in my opinion," Lori said, "Los Angeles is a dreadful place, very violent, and — oh, do forgive me, Joshua, I forgot that's where your people are."

"No offense taken, Mrs. Taylor."

"Joshua," Olivia said, lightly touching his arm for a second, "you *should* consider placing your practice in Little Ways, it's much more beautiful here." She smiled.

"As accident prone as she is," Lavinia sneered, "she'll be your first patient."

Josh kept his eyes on Olivia, while ignoring her younger sister. "Perhaps I will set up my practice in Little Ways. Mr. Taylor," Josh addressed Daniel at the head of the table, "David tells me you own the vacant building next to his."

"That's right. Would you be interested in it for your practice?" Daniel asked. "If you should — move this way, of course."

"Indeed I am," Josh replied, again gazing at Olivia for a moment. "Besides, I'd enjoy working close to David for personal — as well as business reasons. I'd like him to publish some copies of my parents' slave narrative. I'm hoping he'll give me a good rate on printing. Living close by, I wouldn't have to make a special trip each time I need more copies."

Intrigued, Olivia asked, "Your parents wrote a slave narrative?"

Joshua nodded. "Only because I kept on telling them to."

"So," Lori looked at her son, "is that why you've been so insistent upon me writing *my* narrative for a while."

"Yes, ma'am! Ever since Josh told me about his parents writing their story, I figured you should, too. All stories about slavery are important," David insisted.

"But there are so many others that suffered much worse than I did. My story wouldn't contribute much. A long time ago," Lori paused, "someone suggested that I chronicle my account — but I never have." Gazing down she said, "I hardly want to think about it."

"But it's an important way to preserve our family history," David said. "I know slavery is embarrassing, but it's important for future generations to learn about slavery from the people who lived it!

"The white man won't write about slavery like it really was, and it won't be recorded in the history books accurately. So unless it's preserved in narratives, no one will ever know the truth."

****

Lavinia rolled her eyes. Slavery was over, but the shame of it still lingered, along with the indignity of having to be reminded that *it* was a part of her life.

It was like a deep festering wound that, if ever healed, would be dark, raised, and ugly, just like the grisly roadmap of scars carved into her mother's back.

Each time Lavinia was seen with her mother, she could feel the unbreakable bond of slavery linked to her like a heavy, burdensome chain. Because she was Negro, she'd never be good enough.

Life was so unfair! Although she looked white, her blood was tainted, and as long as she lived here, the taint would smell because everyone knew her mother was a Negro!

When her father had taken her on a business trip to San Francisco last year, Lavinia hadn't wanted to come home.

It had been just the two of them, and she had been assumed as white, and treated like royalty during their entire stay!

Being white, and having the privilege whiteness afforded, was the life Lavinia longed for, and she was determined to have it.

However, her mother's very existence had ruined her life. Lavinia hated every drop of Negro blood that coursed through her veins.

Glaring at Lori, Lavinia promised herself that one day she'd escape from here so her mother couldn't damage her life any further.

Lavinia's eyes moved to Joshua. Although the man was black as tar, Olivia seemed quite taken with him. There were certainly lighter skinned Negroes around, but Lavinia had better things to do than waste time thinking about her sister's current infatuation.

Lavinia had had enough! Enough of dark Negroes, enough of slavery and slave narratives! Standing brusquely to leave the room she said, "Excuse me, but I don't have much of an appetite."

Chapter 27

Wearing a white cotton nightgown, Lavinia sat at her vanity while pulling a silver plated brush through her glossy locks.

She'd completed fifty-seven of one hundred strokes when her ritual was disrupted by a knock at the door.

"Come in," she said coolly. Her back faced the bedroom door. In the mirror's reflection, she saw her sister enter her room.

As usual, Olivia was smiling. But tonight the same silly, stupid grin she always wore seemed even broader.

Father claimed that Olivia was the embodiment of honey since she was sweet and amber hued. And because of her grating cheerfulness, Father called her "my sunshine" and "my angel."

Aside from the commonplace endearments of "sweetheart" and "darling," Daniel had no special pet names for Lavinia.

She seethed, glaring at her sister's reflection. As Olivia made herself comfortable on Lavinia's bed, Lavinia thought about how much she hated her, especially when Father praised her for some kind act of selflessness.

Olivia wasn't nearly as beautiful as she was, Lavinia reflected, but she was pretty, in a simple way, and kind. Kind people were weak. Olivia was stupid too, in Lavinia's opinion. Or was she? Were those selfless acts performed to gain Father's attention and approval, and used as a means of manipulating Father to make him love her more?

"Cat got your tongue," Olivia teased.

"No," Lavinia snapped. "You seem rather gay."

"Oh, I am," Olivia smiled. "Joshua and David left a little while ago. Why did you leave the table so suddenly?"

"I said I wasn't very hungry." Lavinia's back still faced her sister as she continued to stroking her hair. "Or don't you remember that?"

"Well, you missed out on a great meal, and some fascinating conversation." Silence fell between them for several moments. "And you didn't get to hear all about Joshua. He's—very nice, don't you think?"

Lavinia said nothing.

"The son of former slaves who went on to study medicine and become a doctor." Olivia paused, as if waiting for a response. With none forthcoming, she said almost timidly, "Wasn't he handsome?"

"Only if you like something that black."

"Lavinia!"

"He looks just like a skillet. In case you didn't notice, he's so black he's almost purple."

"How dare you!" Olivia gasped, as Lavinia swirled from the mirror to look her directly in the eye.

"That — that — *Joshua*," Lavinia said his name like a bad taste was in her mouth, "is just as taken with you, as you are with him. But," she continued smugly, "he didn't give *you* any attention until he realized *I* wouldn't give him the time of day. The darker Negro men are, the lighter they like their women.

"However, Olivia, you should be flattered that any man, even that one, black as he is, finds you in the least attractive, with your long legs and boy hips. And you should be thankful for that large chest of yours, rather than embarrassed by it." Olivia had always been self conscious of her ample bosom. "At least you have one womanly attribute." Lavinia quipped, as she turned back to the looking glass to finish her brushing.

****

Olivia was used to her sister's tongue; its venom rarely shocked her anymore. Why did she think today would be any different? Any good news she'd ever tried to share with Lavinia had only been dashed by her sister's sour disposition.

Be kind and patient with your sister. That's what Mother always said, Olivia recalled. Mother believed that a fever she'd suffered while pregnant with Lavinia had deadened Lavinia's ability to feel compassion. Olivia took in a deep breath. Leave it to Mother to make excuses for her youngest child.

"Just what are you thinking about?" Lavinia's voice cut through the air like a knife.

"Nothing really—just about—about how different we are."

"Oh. Is that all?" Lavinia looked at Olivia's reflection. "Thank goodness I'm not at all like you. I'd slit my wrists if I were!"

Admiring herself in the mirror, Lavinia appeared to reconsider this drastic measure. "Perhaps I wouldn't do that, but I'd live a life of utter misery, because I'd long to be—the younger, smarter, more beautiful sister." She laughed in a lighthearted, ugly way.

Why, do I even try to be a sister to her? Olivia asked herself.

"Now, Olivia," Lavinia turned to face her again, "you're not exactly homely, but you can do better than that Joshua. Marry him and you'll have a bushel full of sooty looking mongrels."

"Lavinia, I'm not interested in what you think about Joshua, and by the way you talk, it's like you forget that *you're* a Negro, too."

"I wish I *could* forget!"

"But that's like saying you wish you could forget Mother!"

Lavinia turned back to the mirror. She resumed brushing, but said nothing.

"Why do you act like she means nothing to you?" Several seconds passed until Olivia couldn't hold back any longer. "You're so cold and hateful! It galls me to think that Mother almost died giving birth to you and—"

"And how many times have I heard that?" Lavinia whipped around viciously, her emerald eyes ablaze. "How Mother almost *died* at my birth, and how little Olivia prayed for Mother to live, and how little Olivia was like an angel in a time of crisis!

"Little Olivia this, little Olivia that! Every time I hear about Saint Little Olivia—I feel like puking! Why doesn't Father ever talk about *me*—the beautiful baby that was born that night, or the blessing *I* was? All he does is talk about you! He's always favored you over me!"

"That's not true, Lavinia! He loves us just the same."

"That's what he claims! But he's done more for you and David than he's ever done for me! He's given David a press. He says the other ranch is yours after you marry. He's constantly making improvements and giving money to that stupid Westmore School you and Mother love so much! But he's never done anything for me!"

"Lavinia, I'm the only one of us who's interested in the ranch and David's paper is needed here! You should go to college, like Mother and Father want you to—so you can become expertly qualified in a real vocation!"

"Acting *is* a real vocation, and I don't need a college education! I'm more intelligent than most, and much more intelligent than you! But Father won't build a theater for me."

"You know why! He thinks acting is a profession for whores!"

"He's misinformed! When he was young, actors might have been considered disreputable—but times have changed. Besides, Father certainly doesn't mind taking us to theater performances in Los Angeles. As I recall, he enjoyed seeing Edwin Booth in *Julius Caesar*. With all the land Father has, and all his money, building a theater for me would be a very small thing. But no, you and David get what you want, but never me!"

"Lavinia, Mother and Father know what's best. They're trying to protect you. The theater world—is an unsavory place!"

"Pooh! Do you know what's unsavory to me? Being *Negro*! I wish Mother *had* died when I was born!"

Too stunned to speak, Olivia only stared at Lavinia aghast. "What did you say?'

"You heard me," Lavinia replied, unfazed.

"You should be ashamed! That's the most hateful thing you've ever said! Take it back!"

"I won't! And I'm not ashamed! If only I were white, life would be so much easier."

"Father owns lots of land around here. He's one of the most powerful men in Los Angeles County. How could things be easier? We've been abundantly blessed!"

"I'd only consider myself blessed if I'd been born white! I don't know why God had to make me black. And I don't even know if I *believe* in God."

"Lavinia! We were raised on that!"

"How do I know that all that—God business wasn't just made up? I read that Darwin fellow's *Origin of Species*. It's fascinating, but beyond your scope of comprehension. Darwin supports the doctrine that all species, including man, are descended from other species. So it made me question if there really is a God."

"How can you say that, Lavinia? Proverbs says 'Trust in the Lord with all thine heart; and lean not unto thine own understanding.'"

"Proverbs this, Proverbs that," Lavinia mimicked. I don't know how many switches Mother wore out on my legs trying to force me to memorize Bible verses before she finally realized those whippings just didn't hurt. All of you seem to spout Scripture as if it's the be all and end all of everything."

"That's because it is!" Olivia said passionately. "The Bible gives us everything we need to know so that we can live safely and productively and be a reflection of Him!"

"Olivia, if you were intelligent, like me, you'd understand why it's important to question things. As for me, I believe in self—self-reliant and self-sufficient. I look out for me. And I'm not depending on anything or anyone else for that."

"But Lavinia, God loves you. He wants you to want Him and need Him, don't you understand that?"

Lavinia didn't say anything immediately. She stroked her hair one last time, then placed the brush on her dressing table. Standing slowly, she turned toward Olivia. "Money is powerful, and tangible. I can see it, feel it, and spend it. It's much too hard for me to believe in something I can't see.

"But I'll tell you something everybody around here *can* see—they can see that we're *Negroes*! We'll always be judged by that. We'll be looked down on and never thought of as good enough. Even if our father is a powerful white man, they know Mother's nothing but an ex-slave, with an ugly scarred up back from a flogging to prove it! And they also know that their marriage isn't legal—and as far as anyone else is concerned, we're nothing but Father's bastards!"

"Lavinia!"

"Don't be so naïve, Olivia! That's the truth and you know it! You may be stupid, but you're not *that* stupid. The life I'm living here isn't good enough. I want more and I'm going to get it. I'm too beautiful and too smart to be chained here as a Negro. I'm destined for *greatness*, not to be some puny schoolteacher to a bunch of little pickaninnies! I don't even like children! And marrying some Negro son of slaves might be good enough for you, but it's not good enough for me, so the sooner I get out of here, the better!"

Olivia stood up, suppressing the urge to throttle her sister. "I can't take anymore of your nonsense!" Leaving the room, she called over her shoulder, "Just let me know when I can help you pack!"

Chapter 28
Los Angeles County, Ten Months Later
Spring 1889

Little Ways was a thriving community, and beyond it lay more thriving communities that flourished on what was once ranch land owned by Daniel Taylor. New shops lined the streets, and new one and two story white frame homes abounded in fresh looking neighborhoods.

Wherever Vernon Hargraves looked he saw people, potential customers—an audience. Why should they have to ride twenty miles into Los Angeles for theatrical entertainment? He could build something out here just as grand as his Hargraves Theater in New York, complete with its double stage and raised orchestra pit.

Vernon inhaled deeply, smelling the fresh spring air. He looked up at the glistening blue sky, then moved his gaze to the snow capped mountains in the distance.

Smiling, he whipped the bay horse's rump to increase its speed. Staying at the inn in Little Ways, he'd rented a horse and buggy and was eager to get to Taylor's ranch.

Vernon had never met Taylor, and he wondered just how easy it would be to do business with him.

Vernon considered himself a premiere businessman. He knew what people wanted, and based on that, he'd accumulated considerable wealth. Some considered him a shady character who'd amassed a shady fortune. Yet his fortune continued to grow through his apartment houses and theater, as well as other establishments throughout New York that featured gambling and booze as the main sources of entertainment. No one really knew too much about Vernon Hargraves, besides his Carrie, and he liked it that way.

One thing that wasn't a secret, though, was his weakness for the deadly W's: whiskey and women. He'd tamed his love for the liquid maiden, at Carrie's insistence, but the fleshly maidens still caused him to stumble.

The theater was a hobby to Vernon, a means of entertainment and escape for the audience, and another way for him to make a buck. He'd been an actor in his youth and always dreamed of owning a theater.

The fortune he'd accumulated through real estate and other endeavors, some shady indeed, had enabled him to pursue this hobby.

His Hargraves Theater in New York City had opened in 1881 on 24th Street near Broadway.

Thinking of it, Vernon smiled proudly. With a seating capacity of five hundred, it was considered one of the most beautiful theater houses in New York, as well as one of the most innovative.

It utilized a double stage, so that as one act was going on, the lower stage was set for the next. During intermission, it was raised to its proper place by pulley cables operated by four men. This saved time between acts. The Hargraves also featured a raised orchestra pit, which was built into the proscenium arch above the stage, providing more room on the lower floor.

To make the name of his theater troupe known throughout the country, his road company toured with his most successful productions and stars. Every spring he took them on a long tour that extended to the Pacific coast.

The theater his players used in L.A. was smaller than The Hargraves. The Los Angeles Theater was an adequate facility, furnished like a palace, with plush silk chairs for the audience. Although comfortable to the paying public, its dressing rooms were dirty, drafty and small, and the actors were forced to dress in grimy spaces no larger than stalls.

Vernon had the idea to build a Hargraves Theater West, something bigger with more seating for the audience, along with dressing rooms suitable for his players. The land he wanted in southern California belonged to Taylor. This area was a good ways from Los Angeles, clean and quaint, but populated enough for a future theater to thrive. Everyone needed an escape.

Through asking the locals in the Los Angeles area, Vernon had found that vast amounts of land south of L.A. had belonged to Taylor, and over the past few years Taylor had been selling off large amounts of acreage to developers.

The theater tour had ended and the Hargraves Players had already left Los Angeles and gone back to New York on the rail cars Vernon had provided them. But Vernon had stayed in California, and come to Little Ways so he could finagle a deal with Daniel Taylor.

****

"Olivia," Lori said, "just a couple more months and you'll be Mrs. Joshua Cummins." Lori sat beside her daughter on a settee in her bedroom doing needlepoint together. Olivia smiled. "So, before you get married," Lori continued, "there's something I want you to have. Perhaps you'll wear it on your wedding day."

Lori put her needlepoint aside, then reached into her pocket and took out a small velvet bag. From it, she pulled the heirloom locket and held it high so Olivia could see the jewel encrusted heart sparkle in the sunlight.

"Oh, Mother!" Olivia gasped, placing her hands over her heart. The needlepoint slipped to the floor, but Olivia failed to notice. Looking at the locket shimmer, her eyes sparkled just as brightly.

"Take it, darling, it's yours."

"But, Mother, it's so beautiful on you, and so special. I almost cry each time I think of Father giving it to you on your wedding night. I couldn't possibly
take it!"

"Olivia, it's an heirloom. I've always promised it to the first of my children to marry. Your grandmother received it as a wedding present, your father gave it to me, now I'm giving it to you. That's at David's insistence. Your brother wanted me to give it to whichever daughter married first.

"At least that's what he told me when I suggested he give it to Janine before their wedding. So," Lori handed her the locket and pouch, "you're the lucky girl."

Thoughtfully gazing at the trinket, Olivia said, "David didn't want to deprive you of it."

Lori clicked her tongue. "No one's depriving me of anything. But you'll deprive me of joy if you *don't* take it and enjoy it as much as I have! You'll see that the most wonderful part of having it, is passing it on to one of your children."

Tears flooded Olivia's eyes. "Mother, thank you." She reached to hug Lori. "Of course, I'll always appreciate the sentiment more than the locket itself."

Lori patted her daughter's back, then pulled free from her embrace. "Olivia, you cry at the drop of a hat. Now stop that before I start!"

As Olivia laughed, dabbing softly at her eyes with a handkerchief, Lori noticed a figure in the doorway. Turning, she saw Mr. Pong.

"Excuse me, Mrs. Taylor," Pong said, in his heavily Mandarin accented English, "there is a Mr. Vernon Hargraves to see you. He ask for Mr. Taylor. When I tell him he is not here, he ask for you."

"Thank you, Mr. Pong. Tell Mr.—Hargraves I'll be right down."

As Mr. Pong turned to leave, Lori glanced at Olivia puzzled. "Vernon Hargraves? Does that name sound familiar to you?"

Thinking, Olivia reached down to pick up her needlepoint. "It does, Mother, but I can't remember where I've heard it."

Lori rose from the settee and started to leave the room. "Well, I'd better not be rude and keep him waiting."

Olivia drew in a deep breath of surprise before Lori reached the bedroom door. "Mother! The Hargraves Theater Players!"

Lori's eyes widened. "My goodness, Olivia! I think you're right. But why on earth would Mr. Hargraves want to see your father?"

****

When Lori walked downstairs, she saw Vernon Hargraves in the foyer. She despised him on sight. Nodding politely, the man raised one eyebrow to a high peak. A sly smile curled his lips, revealing large, gapped yellow teeth. Sporting a thin moustache, he appeared to be in his fifties. Tall and large, Hargraves's frame supported a protruding belly. His receding hairline was combed back with strands of gray glistening in what was left of his pomaded black hair.

Wariness flared inside Lori. That sneaky smile and the leer in the man's gaze made her feel like he was undressing her with his eyes. Self-consciously, she clutched the ruffled collar of her pale green dress, pulling it closer together.

Once near him, she detected the stench of tobacco wafting from his clothes. He reminded her of a stage villain. His brooding, slate gray eyes unnerved her.

As she studied him, the only word that came to mind was shady. But that wasn't surprising; he *was* one of them—a theater person.

Lori tried not to feel bigoted against him. All of her life, she'd felt bigotry from others against her. But in the not so distant past, theater people were known to live dissolute lives and were considered a condemned and despised lot. Their profession was still thought of as disreputable to many, and to think that Lavinia had notions of becoming an actress was a bit more than she or Daniel could tolerate. They hoped it was merely a passing phase and that Lavinia would soon outgrow her foolish dream.

Although the profession of acting was becoming a bit more respectable nowadays, Lori and Daniel preferred not to have an actress in the family. To them, the time when the theater world was considered one of hedonism and violence, and actors were thought of as one step above prostitutes, didn't seem that far away. Many others of strong faith in Lori's age group felt the same way.

Lori couldn't deny, however, that she and Daniel did enjoy the theater performances they'd seen in Los Angeles—yet an actress in the family would be an utter disgrace.

As Lori approached Hargraves with an extended hand, she took a deep breath. Raising her head slightly, she said, "Hello, Mr. Hargraves, I'm Mrs. Daniel Taylor."

****

Vernon wouldn't have believed it unless he'd seen it for himself. Folks said Taylor was married to a Negro woman, and here was the proof. But Vernon hadn't expected her to be this dark. He assumed she'd be a high yalla sort, but this woman was black, although mighty pretty.

Vernon had seen *many* a situation, but he'd never been privy to one quite like this. A wealthy white man married to a Negro?

He knew plenty of white men married to respectable white women, and plenty, come to think of it, married to not so respectable white women, that kept a Negro wench on the side.

But to be "married" to one, living out in the open, and not trying to hide it? That was unheard of. Daniel Taylor was either a crazy fool or just so rich he didn't give a damn.

Shaking Mrs. Taylor's soft hand Vernon said, "It's a pleasure to meet you, ma'am." A layer of charm slathered his tone. "And I must say, I had no idea Mr. Taylor was married to such a beautiful woman."

Mrs. Taylor smiled. "What—what can I—we—do for you," she stammered, as though unnerved by his charm. Her accent was slight, but as a native of Arkansas, Vernon detected a southern lilt.

"Well, ma'am," he cleared his throat, which led to a brief coughing spell, "I want to buy some of your land, and I'm prepared to make you an outstanding offer."

Lori hesitated. "Mr. Hargraves, come have a

seat with me for a moment so we can discuss this further." She walked him to the parlor and took a seat on the sofa. However, when Hargraves joined her there, she immediately fled to the safety of a winged back chair.

"Just — what do you — uh — intend to do with the property you're interested in buying?" Lori asked.

"I want to build a theater. I envision creating a grand showplace that folks will consider *the* theater destination in Southern California! I have a company and — "

"Oh, I'm quite familiar with your company, Mr. Hargraves. We saw your production of *The Ironmaster* a few weeks ago in Los Angeles. And I must say, it was a very fine play with a sound moral.

"It certainly taught my daughters a lesson in how needful it is to study a person's character before marriage, and once married, that a wife should never trifle with her husband's affection. But back to your company, Mr. Hargraves, it has the best scenery and costumes, and your players are the most talented I've seen."

"Thank you, Mrs. Taylor," he smiled, "I'm quite pleased to hear you say that. A compliment from a fine lady, such as yourself, certainly brightens my day." Mrs. Taylor returned his smile, as though enchanted by him.

"But I want something bigger and better than

the theater currently operating in Los Angeles," Hargraves continued. "Something spectacular that'll please the audience, as well as my players. Contented actors, perform more contentedly, of course." He winked. "I'll be heading back to New York soon, but I wanted to talk with Mr. Taylor about my proposal before I leave."

Lori pursed her lips. "I see. Well—Mr. Hargraves, I—I don't think we'd..." When Hargraves looked down defeated, Lori said, "Honestly, Mr. Hargraves—my husband would have to make that decision. He's gone into town to make some bank deposits—so why don't you come back this evening so you can talk with him. As a matter of fact, join us for supper."

****

Lori smiled awkwardly. She couldn't believe what she'd just done. The invitation had slipped from her lips before she'd had a chance to think about it. To socialize with a theater person was an unspeakable act. However, she'd known of many people that were unwilling to socialize with her. Do unto others, she told herself.

Hargraves smiled with gleaming yellow teeth. "Why, I'd be delighted ma'am."

Chapter 29

"Sakes alive, Lori! Why'd you have to invite that low life vagabond back here? You know all those theater people are up to no good!"

Daniel had arrived home about an hour before supper. He'd been relaxing in the parlor with the weekly paper when Lori brought him a cup of tea, and informed him of their expected dinner guest.

"I can tell you right now—"

"But Daniel," Lori interrupted, "it certainly won't hurt us to show—a lost soul—some of our southern hospitality, before he goes back to New York, will it?"

Daniel sighed and relented. "No, darling—I suppose not." He frowned. "At least *Lavinia* will enjoy meeting him."

****

Vernon's eyes met Lavinia's. She sat across from him at the dinner table. Since first seeing the girl, he'd had a hard time keeping his eyes off of her.

It had been after six o'clock when Vernon arrived back at the ranch. Mrs. Taylor had introduced him to the stodgy *Mr. Daniel Taylor*, and then to her strikingly beautiful daughter,

Olivia.

It had been while they sipped lemonade in the parlor when the other Taylor girl appeared. Vernon had stood from the sofa upon seeing her, and sucked in his gut, attempting to look a decade or two younger.

Lavinia was absolutely stunning, and Vernon was convinced he'd never seen a more beautiful female. Standing still for a moment in the doorway, Lavinia had studied Vernon in what looked like amazement.

Her wide-eyed face was flawless, framed by thick dark hair styled in sausage curls that cascaded down her shoulders, and the burgundy satin dress she wore adhered perfectly to her hourglass curves.

"Mr. Hargraves," Mrs. Taylor had said, "This is my younger daughter, La—"

"I'm Lavinia Taylor." The girl interrupted her mother and rushed to greet Vernon. Vigorously shaking his hand, she'd said, "Mr. Hargraves, I can't tell you how excited I am to meet you! When I heard that *the* Vernon Hargraves of *The* Hargraves Theater was actually coming to *my* house for supper, I could hardly believe it!"

"Lavinia, dear," Mrs. Taylor had said, "let go of Mr. Hargraves's hand."

"Oh, I'm sorry." Lavinia had released his hand, then maneuvered herself to his side and sat down on the sofa. When she gazed up to him smiling, Vernon seated himself next to her.

His heart had thumped excitedly and his body sparked hotly from head to foot. He wanted this woman. At least that's what he'd thought initially. But as he spoke to Lavinia and learned of her passion for the theater and her desire to act, his feelings gave way to an even deeper emotion — love.

Daniel Taylor had all but scoffed at his daughter's dream, but Vernon admired the girl's defense of her art — their art, not only a common interest, but a bond between them.

"Father," Lavinia had said, "anything that offers people entertainment and a means of escape should be celebrated!"

Vernon and Lavinia had continued to converse about the theater for several more minutes, but soon, Taylor put an end to this.

"Lavinia," Taylor had said, interrupting them, "you've taken up enough of Mr. Hargraves's time. Let's put the theater to rest for the evening.

"We need to move on to what Mr. Hargraves is here for in the first place — the matter of my selling him real estate."

The real estate conversation had ended a while ago, and now Vernon was at the table with Lavinia, enjoying every moment of being in her presence. When he discreetly winked, she pursed her lips and tried not to giggle.

Everyone had finished eating. Creamed chicken on toast had been served for supper with lettuce on the side, drizzled with vinegar and sugar. A Chinaman cleared away the dirty dishes, and then brought out dessert plates and a platter of fresh fruit. The strawberries, cherries and apricots were some of the nicest looking Vernon had ever seen.

Moving his gaze from Mr. Taylor at the head of the table, to Mrs. Taylor at the foot, Vernon could tell they thought him an unsavory sort. Mrs. Taylor kept fidgeting with her fingers, and throughout the duration of the meal, Mr. Taylor had stared at Hargraves with a stony glare.

Vernon had had a few drinks before he'd returned to the ranch. He'd been warned by the locals that the Taylors didn't drink, and he'd needed a little fix. But he wondered if the Taylors could still smell the booze on him.

Since they didn't drink, he knew they probably wouldn't allow any smoking in their house either, so he'd had a few cigarettes. Now he was paying for those smokes with a hacking cough that sounded a bit worse than usual.

As for the business matter of selling real estate, Vernon had made no headway on that. *Mr. Daniel Taylor* had said, in a most pompous, self-righteous way, that him selling land for a theater would *never* happen under *any* circumstances.

Now the dinner table conversation was strained, consisting mainly of small talk regarding the weather and current developments under construction in California.

Despite the lack of tobacco and whiskey here, along with Taylor's unwillingness to sell him land, and a lackluster boarding house meal, Vernon didn't care—not with Lavinia seated across from him, staring in awe.

And while the older sister Olivia sat next to Vernon trying to be gracious, each time he coughed, she cringed as though preparing for bits of bloody lung to scatter across the white tablecloth.

Again, Vernon cared not. His gaze held fast to Lavinia's as she made "come hither" overtures, batting her eyes and seductively moving her shoulders.

Glancing at Taylor once more, Vernon saw that the man's stony stare had hardened to a grimace. Of course, Taylor, being *"married"* to a nigger, had some nerve looking down on Vernon.

Without a doubt, Vernon knew the Taylor's were ready for him to leave. *Mrs. Daniel Taylor,* the nigger wench, was quite uncomfortable. Looking in her direction now, he saw that she'd begun playing with her napkin, instead of her fingers, and her eyes kept moving nervously from her husband's disgruntled face, to Lavinia's flirtatious gaze.

Vernon relished the situation, but decided he'd best excuse himself rather than stir up more trouble. After finishing his fruit, Vernon stood to leave.

"Well," he addressed Taylor, "I don't want to wear out my welcome with you folks. It's getting late and I need to be moving on." Turning to Lori, he said, "I thank you for your time and hospitality. I've had a lovely evening with ya'll."

From the corner of his eye, Vernon noticed Lavinia's head drop in disappointment. When he gazed toward her and smiled, her eyes met his pleading. "Mr. Hargraves," she began, "perhaps you could stay just a—"

"Lavinia," Daniel said harshly, "Mr. Hargraves, is *leaving—now.*" He stood up brusquely to escort Vernon out.

"Do have a—uh safe journey back to New York," Lori said.

"Thank you, Mrs. Taylor. And it's been a pleasure meeting all of you." He bowed slightly.

"Let me see you to the door," Daniel said. Taller than Hargraves by a couple of inches, Daniel quickly moved him along.

As Vernon stood outside on the front porch, he thanked Daniel again, but hesitated to leave.

Though Taylor had the audacity to be married to a black woman, he knew this proper, southern gentleman would never allow him, Vernon Hargraves of the theater, to court his daughter. But why not have a little fun and shake up this lofty jackass? It would be good for a laugh or two.

Grinning mischievously, Vernon said, "Mr. Taylor, I'd like to make a request."

Taylor appeared taken aback. "And just what might that be, Mr. Hargraves?"

"May I call on your Lavinia before I leave town?"

Mr. Daniel Taylor's face turned bright red, and his brown eyes darkened to black. Beads of sweat popped out of nowhere on his forehead — and it wasn't even that hot! But Vernon had to give the man credit for maintaining his self control.

Sounding cool as a cucumber, *Mr. Genteel Southern Gentleman* said, "I'm sorry, Mr. Hargraves, but *that* is out of the question."

"Well, just thought I'd ask. She's a beauty — can't blame a man for tryin'."

"Goodnight, Mr. Hargraves." Taylor closed the door abruptly.

Vernon strode slowly toward the courtyard, laughing to himself about Taylor's reaction. His buggy waited near the hitching posts, however, before he reached it, someone called to him.

Chapter 30

"Mr. Hargraves!" Turning around, Vernon saw Lavinia quickly running to catch up with him. Again, Vernon sucked in deeply, trying to shrink his protruding girth.

"Miss Taylor?" he said, almost at a loss for words, which seldom, if ever happened. "What are you doing out here?"

She slowed down and walked the last few paces toward his lumbering six-foot frame. Gazing up to him, she smiled, speaking softly, "I snuck out of the back door. No one saw me; then I hid behind some bushes while you spoke to my father. I couldn't help but overhear what you said—you want to call on me!"

Vernon glanced toward the house for a moment concerned that Taylor would see them. He didn't want to get shot.

However, when Vernon looked into Lavinia's emerald eyes, it was as if she'd cast a spell on him. She stood flushed and slightly out of breath; a sultry blush glowed from her cheeks.

With every breath, her breasts rose beneath the lacy neckline of her dress. There *was* such a thing as lust at first sight, and Vernon had indulged in that pursuit numerous times. But he'd never believed in love at first sight, until now—and he wanted Lavinia for his wife.

Shoot—being near her was making him think like a fool! He wasn't a marrying man—at least that's what he'd thought.

"I heard my father say he wouldn't allow that, but *I* want to see you." Lavinia coyly slipped her hand through the crook of his arm, then commanded sweetly, "Walk with me."

He obliged as if hypnotized. They strolled silently through the garden, and the further they walked from the house, the more relaxed Vernon felt. There was less chance of being seen by Taylor.

"Miss Taylor," Vernon finally said, "you're the most beautiful woman I've ever seen—and I want to court you, and be near you, more than anything, but that's the *last* thing your father wants."

Vernon hesitated, breathing in the scent of Lavinia's lavender perfume. "As a matter of fact, I—I think I'm—falling in love with you." Vernon couldn't believe he'd actually spoken those words, but to his surprise, Lavinia didn't even flinch.

Clearing his throat Vernon continued, "Now, you know as well as I do, that you need to listen to what your father says—and—and stay away from the likes of me."

Vernon was trying to do the right thing, which he didn't do very often, and actually preferred not to do at all. Choosing the wrong thing was always more exciting, regardless of the risks. And if you played your cards right, you just might get lucky. Sometimes, life was like a crapshoot, a roll of the dice. You take a chance, and sometimes win big. Vernon glanced toward her house again, which was much further away now. Still no sign of Taylor with a shotgun.

Even though Taylor was a self-righteous SOB, Vernon couldn't fault the man for trying to protect his daughter. And Vernon wouldn't deny that he, himself, was a scoundrel. But if someone like him ever tried to court his precious Carrie, why, he'd —

"Mr. Hargraves," Lavinia interrupted his train of thought, "I don't care what my father says. All *I* care about is being with you. Why, being here with you is like a dream come true."

She batted her thick lashes coquettishly, clutching his arm a bit more tightly against her breast.

"Miss Taylor..." Vernon hesitated, while struggling with feelings of lust and decency, and surprised himself that a decent bone really *did* exist in his body, contrary to popular opinion, including his own. "I've got a daughter myself, a little older than you. Her name's Carrie. She's a quiet girl, and talented — she writes plays. And the thing of it is, Carrie's my heart — and I'd rather die than see her get hurt by some rakish individual."

Lavinia laughed. "Oh, I'd hardly think of you as a 'rakish individual.'"

"The point is Miss Taylor, your father is trying to protect you."

"From you, Mr. Hargraves?" she asked in a sugary tone. "Your intentions toward me aren't dishonorable, are they?"

He stopped walking and looked deeply into her eyes. "Of course not. I'd never do anything to hurt you."

"I'm nearly grown." Lavinia pulled on his arm to keep walking. "I can make my own decisions. So Mr. Hargraves, I want to learn all about you *and* your theater. Mother and Father," she glanced back at the house sneering, "they don't care for theater people."

"I could tell," he chuckled.

"Well, Mr. Hargraves, as I told you before supper, I have aspirations of becoming an actress. Of course, my parents despise the very idea! But they don't understand that my calling is to act."

"Is that so, young lady?"

"Oh, yes. But you see, I don't want to be just any actress, I want to be the greatest actress the world has ever known!"

"You certainly have the beauty for it —
Lavinia." Again, he came to a standstill, gazing
at her. "May I call you, Lavinia?"

"Of course, Mr. —"

"Vernon."

"Of course, Vernon." She tugged on his arm
to resume their stroll. "I have talent too!"

"That's a good thing, because looks wear
out." A beautiful, young stage struck girl,
Vernon thought. Though in some ways, she
seemed more woman than girl. Nevertheless, he
decided to humor her. "So, you say you have
talent?"

"Yes, Mr. — Vernon, I do!"

He pulled from her grasp, stepping slightly
away. Crossing his arms, he looked at her. "Let
me see what you can do. I'll give you an
audition — right here, right now."

"Oh, really!" she exclaimed.

"Go ahead."

"I love Shakespeare!" Lavinia smoothed her
hair and dress. "Here's Juliet's soliloquy from
act two, scene five, from, of course, *Romeo and
Juliet*. I saw your players perform it last year.
Your Juliet was lovely — but I thought I could
perform the role even better! I memorized this
soliloquy and practiced it in front of my mirror a
thousand times."

She took a deep breath. "Please give me a
moment to feel the character." Lavinia walked a

few yards away from Vernon, then paused for a few seconds with her back to him. When she turned to face him, she was Juliet.

The clock strook nine when I did send the nurse,
In half an hour she promised to return.
Perchance she cannot meet him – that's not so.

As she spoke, Vernon saw that her face was transformed, as if by magic. No longer did it possess the bold daring and fearlessness of her personality. Instead, it was serene, gentle and pure, almost like the face of a child. And her green eyes, naturally hard and shrewd, as Juliet's eyes reflected sweet innocence.

Vernon believed Lavinia old beyond her seventeen years. She had a knack for slickness and manipulation, just like he did. But that was part of her excitement and appeal – that, her violent beauty, and the goods packed beneath her dress.

Yet, at this moment, Lavinia's wild beauty was tame, as she appeared a docile, love struck girl, apprehensive, uneasy and only driven by love. She resonated love's pure embodiment as Juliet thinking of her Romeo.

Gone was the sleek, self-assurance in Lavinia's voice. As Juliet, her tone was soft, though riddled with worry, concerning her star crossed beloved.

O, she is lame! Love's heralds should be thoughts,
Which ten times faster glides than the sun's beams,
Driving back shadows over low' ring hills;
Therefore do nimble – pinow'd doves draw Love,
And therefore hath the wind – swift Cupid wings.
Now is the sun upon the highmost hill
Of this day's journey, and from nine to twelve
Is three long hours, yet she is not come.
Had she affections and warm youthful blood,
She would be as swift in motion as a ball.
My words would bandy her to my sweet love,
And his to me...

Vernon stood mesmerized as she concluded her rendition, moved by the tenderness and feeling she'd emoted with her voice, eyes and body.

Her short performance had been filled with passion, invigoration, longing and life. Here stood a girl with talent, stage presence and a passion for her craft.

Running to him, Lavinia said, "Vernon, what did you think?" Smiling broadly, he didn't reply. She blinked her eyes in question. "You *did* think I was wonderful — didn't you?"

Vernon began to clap slowly. "Amazing, completely amazing. Your performance was sheer perfection." Lavinia gasped loudly, raising her hands to her mouth. "Have you appeared onstage before?"

"Oh, heaven's no! My parents would rather die than see me on the stage."

"Have you studied drama?"

"Well, my parents do indulge my passion by taking me to the theater in Los Angeles. I've studied the players—and The Hargraves Players are the best I've ever seen, by the way."

"I thank you."

"Vernon, do I—do I have the talent to be in your company?"

He gazed into her face for a moment. "You have everything. The beauty, the talent..." Vernon then moved his eyes to her ensemble. Cream colored lace adorned the neckline of her burgundy dress. She'd accessorized it with a strand of pearls and matching earrings. "And you know how to dress. I could make you a star."

Lavinia's eyes widened. "A star?"

"A legend." Vernon lightly pinched her cheek. "From my experience," he said authoritatively, "audiences are drawn more to the personalities of the players, not necessarily the content of the plays.

"So the strongest attraction I can give any production is a magnetic, well publicized star. And you, Lavinia, will be my next star!"

Lavinia placed a widely splayed hand over her heart. "Me?"

"Of course, we'd have to uh—hide the fact that—you're a…" When Vernon's gaze dropped to the ground, Lavinia's smile, along with the excitement she'd felt moments earlier, suddenly fled. Turning her back to him, she walked away a few paces. "That you're a Negro," Vernon finished.

Lavinia took in a tight breath. "I want *that* part of my life to disappear completely."

Matter-of-factly Vernon said, "You can easily pass for white. And you being colored," he smiled reassuringly, "that'll be our secret." Turning to face him, Lavinia smiled brilliantly. "You have an exotic look about you," he winked, while creating the new story of her life, "so I'll have my press agent tell the papers that your mother's from Spain."

"Oh!" Lavinia clasped her hands, as though enchanted by the thought of a Spanish mother.

"*That* will add to your mystique."

"Oh, Vernon! Can you really do that for me—and take me away from here?"

He paused. "Is being in the theater what you really want?"

"More than anything!"

"Living a life touring on the road doesn't bother you?"

"It'll be an adventure!"

"Lavinia," Vernon sighed, thinking realistically, "I can't just run off with you."

Lavinia sidled close to him, then seductively caressed his arms. "You can—if you marry me."

"Lavinia—you—you don't know what you're saying."

"*You* said you were falling in love with me."

"But, you're—you're seventeen—I'm fifty four!"

She smiled slyly. "What difference does that make—really?"

Vernon looked deeply into Lavinia's slanted green eyes. They didn't plead, but insisted that he run away with her. Vernon knew what he'd be getting, though. He wasn't a fool, but he *was* acting like one, falling head over heels for this girl/woman temptress. Lavinia didn't love him; she only loved what he could do for her. Yet Vernon wanted her, regardless of the stakes.

She'd reduced him to feelings buried deep within the layers of his roughhewn exterior, the giddy feelings of a teenage boy in love. He felt jaunty around Lavinia, almost like skipping. This longing and yearning for permanence with a woman was something new, and frightening, which made it all the more exciting.

She would be his final conquest. Vernon swore to himself that he'd never look at another woman again. Or, at least he'd try very hard not to look at another woman.

No one could, or ever would, compare with Lavinia. Perhaps, over time, she'd learn to love him.

"I've never given my heart to a woman," Vernon said, losing himself in the powerful eyes that gripped his heart. "But Lavinia—I want to give my heart to you. You make me feel young again." He hesitated. "I've never married...but I want to marry you...so...do you think you could...ever love an old man like me, who's been called a scoundrel and a louse...more than a few times in his life?"

"Can you make me a star?"

Chapter 31

But just think how much trouble and expense--for camel hire is not cheap, and those Bikaneer brutes had to be fed like humans--might have been saved by a properly conducted Matrimonial Department, under the control of the Director General of Education, but corresponding direct with the Viceroy.

.

Lori sat on the loveseat in the parlor reading the last of Rudyard Kipling's short story, *Kidnapped*. It was in the author's anthology *Plain Tales from the Hills*. Daniel had first seen the story in a military newspaper a friend had brought from overseas. He'd mentioned that Lori would enjoy it too, so he'd mail-ordered a copy of the anthology for her.

Now, as she finished the tale, Lori felt thankful that Daniel had never, as Kipling wrote, *"come to his senses and married a pink and white maiden."* Unlike Miss Castries, Lori hadn't successfully been prevented from marrying the man she loved.

Although their marriage wasn't…well, Lori chose not to dwell on the fact that her marriage wasn't legally binding.

Instead, she thought about Olivia and Joshua. At the moment, they were meeting with general manager Tommy Douglas at the Charlton Place Ranch to discuss management of the rented acreage. Joshua had become slightly interested in ranching, but his first love, after Olivia, he'd said, was healing the sick. Although he wanted to know the details of operating a ranch, Joshua was content to let Olivia and Mr. Douglas run things while he practiced medicine.

Lori closed the anthology she held and set it down on the table in front of her. Olivia and Joshua were so in love, and blessed to be living in freedom.

Their marriage would be legally binding, and couldn't be torn apart on a master's whim. The young Negroes nowadays didn't know how good they had it. Gone for good were the days of one person being owned by another.

Lori looked forward to Olivia's wedding day, and also to her first grandchild. David and his wife, Janine, were expecting a baby. Sitting back, Lori closed her eyes. Silently she prayed a prayer of thanksgiving. God had abundantly blessed her life. Without Him, she'd have nothing.

Moments later, she heard Daniel's footsteps. Strong and grounded, they nearly shook the room. He stopped near her, then sat down beside her on the loveseat.

"Another good month," Daniel began, but Lori's eyes remained closed. "I just finished the cash flow statement. And I received correspondence from another developer today..." When Daniel paused, Lori opened her eyes to see him looking at the anthology. His gaze met hers. "So — you finished *Kidnapped*?" Lori nodded. "Is that why you're so quiet?"

"Oh, that, and I was just thanking God for all the good things he's given us. We have each other, our children, good friends, the ranches." She smiled, sighing contentedly. "And Olivia's so in love! I don't think I could have picked a better match for her than Joshua. And David and Janine expecting a baby! I can barely contain my excitement."

"I'm happy, too, darling." Daniel exhaled slowly. "But — it'll take quite a man to tame Lavinia."

"I know," Lori said sadly. "I think — and pray about that — all the time."

"So do I..." Daniel said.

"She's — she's been my cross to bear."

"Both our crosses." Daniel sat back and put his arm around Lori. She leaned against him. For a few moments they remained silent. "If you'd died when Lavinia was born," Daniel said softly, "or at the plantation, I don't know what I would've done."

"Daniel, God would have given you the strength to go on."

"I know, but I'm thankful He didn't put me through that test." When Daniel kissed Lori's temple, she snuggled more closely to him. "I'll let you in on a little secret," he said.

"A secret?"

"Well, it's not really a secret, it's just something I've never shared with you. When you were—hurt at Dancing Oaks, I was angry—with God. I wanted to know why he'd take you from me after I'd already lost Jonathan, Father and Mother so closely together. I'd accepted their deaths—but I couldn't accept yours. I told God, 'Take anything else, but not Lori, she's mine—I need her with me.' But as long as I kept praying that way—you seemed to creep closer to death."

Daniel sat quietly. "But finally God made me see that you aren't mine. You're His—and His to do with as he pleases. And God spoke to my heart, telling me He'd never leave me or forsake me—and that He was—and is—all I need." Lori sat mesmerized listening. "So—when I let you go, and put you in God's hands—you finally took a deep breath, and then—I knew you'd live.

"And when you almost died with Lavinia, I prayed fervently for you to live, but I told God that I knew you were His. As hard as it was, I was prepared to let you go twice, but twice, God gave you back to me."

Lori smiled. "Why didn't you ever tell me that?"

"I don't know. But, perhaps today, we both needed to hear it for some reason."

"Perhaps," Lori said. "We must be prepared to give up all the things we love—no matter how difficult."

Daniel held Lori in a snug embrace and kissed her. Then their youngest daughter swept boldly into the room.

****

"Mother, Father," Lavinia said, "I've come to say goodbye." She appeared dressed and ready to go out wearing a purple satin dress, the top adorned with white lace ruffles. The four tiers of the skirt, along with the three-quarter length bell sleeves, were also trimmed in lace. A tall bonnet sat atop her head decorated with artificial flowers, and she carried a drawstring handbag.

"Goodbye?" Daniel asked. "So just where are you going, my dear?" He released Lori from his embrace, but still kept one arm around her as she sat pressed against him.

"I'm leaving," Lavinia said harshly.

"You are?" Lori smiled.

"I'm escaping! Escaping from this prison!"

"Oh," Lori said calmly. "So, where do you plan on going this time, and for how long?"

"I'm going to New York and I'm not coming back."

Daniel gazed at Lori for a moment. Both tried to suppress their laughter at Lavinia's dramatics.

"Well, just how do you plan on getting to New York and living, once you get there?" Her father asked. "I'm certainly not going to fund your excursion. You can't just pick up and go, for heaven's sake, you're only seventeen. Have you procured some source of employment you've failed to tell us about?"

"I'm leaving—with Vernon Hargraves."

Lori sat up horrified. "Vernon Hargraves?" To Lavinia's satisfaction, her mother no longer found the situation funny. "That despicable character?"

Daniel stood abruptly. Stepping toward Lavinia, he pointed his finger sharply in her face. "Over my dead body will you go alone anywhere, unchaperoned with any man, let alone that filth!"

Lavinia's eyes narrowed. "It's too late. You can't stop me," she said coldly.

Lori rose slowly from the loveseat. Her eyes widened.

"I can't stop you?" Daniel said. A vein bulged from his forehead. Her parents were appalled and Lavinia enjoyed this. "Have you forgotten that I'm your father?"

Shrugging her shoulders dramatically, Lavinia said, "Why, how could I ever forget that?" Sarcasm laced her tone.

Lori put a hand over her heart and Daniel's brow furrowed as he said, "You're an ungrateful, insolent girl!"

"You only say that because you can't control me!" Lavinia snapped.

"How dare you talk back to me!"

"Oh, there's a lot more I haven't said!" Lavinia retorted, emboldened by her father's anger. "You've always favored Olivia over me—and David, your precious first born son!"

"That's nonsense!" Daniel scoffed.

"Lavinia," Lori said, "your father loves all of you the same, you know that."

"And your mother and I have tried to teach you that you can catch more flies with honey than you can with vinegar," Daniel said. "Sweetness begets sweetness, Lavinia. I don't love you any less than Olivia—or David. But your sharp tongue has always worn down my patience, so don't mistake my shortness with you as a lack of love!"

"Even if sugar rolled from my tongue, you'd never give me what I want! Olivia has the ranch, David has the press—I wanted a theater!"

"That's something you'll never get from me!" Daniel said hotly.

"And with good reason," Lori said. "Being an actress is barely one step above being a prostitute."

"Oh, mother, that's hardly the case nowadays! And—regardless—I'm going to New York, and the stage—with Vernon!"

"You're not going anywhere!" Daniel said.

"Darling," Lori placed a hand on her daughter's shoulder, "we love you too much to let you ruin your life."

Pulling away from her mother's touch, Lavinia said, "*You've* ruined my life!"

Shocked, Lori's mouth fell open. "What?"

"*You've* ruined my life—by being a *Negro*!" Lavinia averted her eyes from her mother's. "And I *hate* you for that!"

Lori's voice quavered. "Look at me—and say that."

Lavinia glared into her mother's eyes. They brimmed with tears. "I hate every drop of your Negro blood that courses through my body!"

Lori appeared to shrink. Burying her face in her hands, she began to weep. At this, Daniel slapped Lavinia so hard, her lips split open, bleeding.

"Daniel!" Lori gasped. She moved toward her daughter, but then stopped, as though fearing more rejection.

Daniel, however, backed away from Lavinia, squeezing his stinging hand, as if trying to force away the act of hitting her. He'd never struck any of his children, and now seemed remorseful, yet also angry.

"We took you to church," Daniel drew in a deep breath, "we read you the Bible! We did everything we were supposed to do! You—you as good as made me do that! Saying those things to your mother was worse than her being flogged! Don't you ever speak to her that way again!"

Lavinia cupped her burning cheek with the palm of her hand. Tasting the salty blood on her lips, she cried, "You'd never raise a hand to Olivia! She and David can do no wrong! You give them anything they want, and you've never given me a thing! But Vernon can give me the stage—because we're *married*!" Her parents gasped, then stared at her in disbelief, saying nothing.

"Lavinia," Lori said softly, as though not comprehending what she'd just heard. "Has he—touched you?"

Lavinia ignored this. "The night he came here, I ran after him before he left; no one saw me. He fell in love with me, and we decided to marry right then.

"But you've made a horrible mistake," Lori said. You don't even love—"

"I may not have a ring yet, but he's promised me a huge diamond from Tiffany's once we get to New York. *And, our* marriage is legally binding." Daniel's grimace became more pronounced, and Lori's eyes more distraught. "I have the paper to prove it!"

Lavinia enjoyed the sight of her parents' perplexity. It felt good to hurt them; in a way, it was refreshing. "Vernon has some—some connections in Los Angeles." She pulled the certificate of marriage from her handbag, then hastily handed it to her parents. "One of them knows the Justice of the Peace." After Daniel and Lori had perused the document for what Lavinia deemed long enough to see its authenticity, she quickly snatched it back.

Stuffing the paper back into her handbag, Lavinia said, "Now, after what the two of you did, running off together, do you expect me to actually listen to you? Besides, now I have everything I could possibly want! I'll be on the stage! I'll be a great actress! I'll be a *star*! And I've achieved my dream without your help, or even God's!"

Daniel seethed, his face bright red. "Well, I suppose the stage is right where you belong, because you're acting just like a *whore*! You're no better than a fancy! I've never been more ashamed.

"Running after that man like a common strumpet, then selling yourself to him in a loveless marriage!" Daniel looked at her with disdain. "You disgust me. Marriage is a sacred union, but *you've* made a mockery of it!"

Lavinia swallowed hard, determined not to cry and appear weak. But she'd disgusted her father. Olivia had never disgusted him. Olivia was Father's angel, his sunshine, and the embodiment of honey. He had no pet names for

Lavinia, yet just now he'd called her a strumpet, a fancy, and a whore.

Her emotions welled up inside like a torrent. She couldn't help but give in to them as a broken dam gives way to rushing floodwaters. Hot tears stung her face and bleeding lips.

"*I am Mrs. Vernon Hargraves.* I'm going to New York with *my* husband, and *you can't stop me!*" Gathering the hem of her skirt, Lavinia fled the room.

****

Lori collapsed to the floor on her knees, sobbing uncontrollably. Daniel knelt beside her. Though he tried to console her, he was too distraught to be of much comfort. So instead, they held each other and cried, as though mourning Lavinia's death.

"Daniel," Lori cried, "we can't let her go — we —"

"Lori — she's made her choice — and she'll have to live with it."

"But that Hargraves — he's taking my baby away to a life of depravity — a hell on earth! Daniel, we — we have to do something!"

"We already have. For seventeen years we've loved her — we've given her everything she needs. If she chooses to be a fool, we can't stop her. God gives us our children to raise, and then they're on their own. They're not really ours, are they? They're His. You just said we have to be prepared to give up what we love."

For a while, they held each other silently, then Lori shook her head. "She's always caused me such pain, but this—this is the worst."

"Years ago," Daniel said, "I told you I never wanted to see you hurt badly ever again—little did I know our own child would inflict such pain upon us."

"To keep her from running off with that Hargraves, I'd be flogged all over again if I could." Lori buried her head in Daniel's shoulder. "That pain was nothing compared to this."

"Lori—God doesn't promise that our lives will be easy—or without pain—but His promises are true. He'll never leave us or forsake us. Lavinia is out of our hands now. All we can do is pray that God will keep her safe and under the protection of His wing."

KEEP WATCH FOR
MASQUERADE
BOOK II of the UNCHAINED TRILOGY

Lavinia lives the life of her dreams while sharing her marriage bed with Vernon Hargraves, a man she doesn't love. However, her seduction by actor Kenneth Tyler creates a tumultuous turn of events. Will her life be forever ruined by the tragedy and scandal surrounding her, or will millionaire contractor Andrew Standish provide a way for Lavinia to recapture her lost fame and glory? Will Vernon's daughter, Carrie, try to destroy Lavinia by exposing her as Negro? Find out in *Masquerade, Book II of the Unchained Trilogy,* due out in fall of 2012. Keep reading for a bonus excerpt!

Masquerade
Book II of the Unchained Trilogy
New York City, 1894

They were in Cleopatra's palace. Gauze drapes lined the back of the stage and two huge columns stood on each side with large potted palms in front.

...Here is my space,
Kingdoms are clay; our dungy earth alike
Feeds beast as man; the nobleness of life
Is to do thus...

Kenneth Tyler recited his lines to Lavinia Hargraves as they performed their first dress rehearsal of Shakespeare's *Antony and Cleopatra*. With his dark haired good looks and lanky frame, Kenneth thought himself the perfect Mark Antony. Many actresses had described his smoldering sapphire eyes as deadly, because they'd pierced the hearts of many a woman.

A dagger was strapped to Kenneth's waist and sandals were on his feet. He wore a woolen tunic with decorative body armor and shoulder plates.

The stage directions called for an embrace, yet, as usual, Lavinia stiffened when his arms encircled her. Kenneth continued holding her as he said the rest of his lines.

...when such a mutual pair
And such a twain can do't, in which I bind,
On pain of punishment, the world to weet
We stand up peerless.' "

"I want both of you to walk to center stage while Kenneth is talking," Vernon's voice boomed from the front row. "Stop at center stage when it's time for the embrace." Kenneth and Lavinia nodded in his direction.

Now Lavinia pulled from Kenneth and spoke as Cleopatra. She wore a black braided wig adorned with beads, and a long white muslin sheath, its broad collar decorated in elaborate jewels made of paste.

Excellent falsehood!
Why did he marry Fulvia, and not love her?
I'll seem the fool I am not. Antony
Will be himself.

"Walk away from him some, Lavinia," Vernon directed. Lavinia did as her husband said. "Now, Kenneth, approach her from behind, grab her arm and turn her to face you."

As Antony, Kenneth followed Vernon's instruction, then muttered under his breath, "I'd much rather grab something else."

"Did you say something?" Lavinia whispered.

Kenneth shook his head with a leering smile. "I was merely thinking out loud." From here, Kenneth went straight to his lines and grabbed her arm.

But stirr'd by Cleopatra.
Now for the love of Love, and her soft hours,
Let's not confound the time with conference harsh;
There's not a minute of our lives should stretch
Without some pleasure now. What sport to-night?

Gazing at Lavinia, he raised a brow. "I could think of many," he said only loud enough for her.

Caught off guard, Lavinia forgot her line. Kenneth mouthed the word "hear" to get her started.

"*Hear the ambassadors,*" she said somewhat distracted, and then Kenneth concluded their scene together onstage.

Fie, Wrangling queen!
Whom everything becomes — to chide, to laugh,
To weep, whose every passion fully strives
To make itself in thee fair and admir'd!
No messenger but thine, and all alone,

To-night we'll wander through the streets and note
The qualities of people. Come, my queen,
Last night you did desire it.

Directing his last line to the actor playing the messenger, a young man wearing a simple white tunic, Kenneth said, "*Speak not to us.*"

As he and Lavinia exited the stage, followed by the messenger, Kenneth placed Lavinia's hand on his dagger, then said for her ears alone, "perhaps you can unsheathe my dagger."

"That line's not in the script, Kenneth, and neither was that other line! Performing Shakespeare is certainly *not* the time to adlib," Lavinia admonished sharply, once they were backstage.

Kenneth almost laughed as she sashayed away from him to observe the remainder of Act I, Scene I from the wings.

****

When the rehearsal of the whole play had finished, the entire cast and crew came onto the stage. Kenneth watched as Vernon lumbered toward center stage to join his actors. He'd been observing from the front row.

"Bravo, everyone," Vernon exclaimed enthusiastically, his hog's belly protruding from beneath his vest. "And Lavinia—perfect as always!"

"Mr. Hargraves, what about my Kenneth?"
Jenny Green said, as she bustled behind him, her
cockney accent just as thick as Kenneth's when
he wasn't performing. She'd sat next to Vernon
during the rehearsal. "Wasn't he superb?"
Kenneth listened as his doting fiancé sang his
praises.

Turning to face Jenny, Vernon said, "Of
course, and he and Lavinia are still magic
together, even in a tragedy!" Vernon chuckled,
then yelled toward Kenneth, "Stealing him from
Theodore Johnstone's Players in London was the
best financial move I ever made."

Grasping Jenny's hand in a paternal gesture
Vernon kissed it. "But I saw you first as
Ophelia."

Jenny smiled. "That was a long time ago.
I'm so busy with me two girls, the theater's a
distant memory."

"Never too late to make a comeback."
Vernon winked at Jenny, then clapped to get
his company's attention.

The crew, in modern dress, held conversation
alongside the ancient Egyptians. Male actors
milled about wearing togas and tunics, while the
women cast members were costumed in long
white muslin sheaths with simple beaded collars
and black braided wigs.

Kenneth had overheard Vernon's remark to
Jenny, as he'd spoken to Joel Hancock, the actor

playing Caesar. When he and Hancock had finished their discussion regarding the beginning of Act II Scene II, Kenneth gazed toward Lavinia.

He supposed he should feel at least a little guilty about Jenny giving up her promising stage career for him, but he didn't. Now, too preoccupied with Lavinia, he hardly thought of Jenny at all.

Vernon dismissed the cast and crew after telling them that tomorrow would be a day off, but he expected them the day after for another dress rehearsal. As everyone meandered from the stage, Kenneth watched Vernon as he strode toward Lavinia. Standing in front of her, the old man stood akimbo with his large gut thrust forward.

Hargraves towered over his beautiful, young wife, and Lavinia, as Cleopatra incarnate, gazed up at him, her green eyes rimmed in coal black liner.

They stood at the opposite end of the stage, so Kenneth couldn't hear them. Lavinia looked at him as a pupil would a teacher, not a wife her husband.

Maybe Vernon was telling her to loosen up some and not be so stiff whenever any physicality was required of her.

She was a brilliant actress, but Kenneth was fed up with her tenseness whenever he did more than hold her hand. Only so much affection could be shown on stage, but even a chaste embrace was difficult for Lavinia.

They'd been paired together two years ago in *The Black Pearl*, and that production had been a screaming success, and since then, audiences craved more plays with he and Lavinia together as a romantic couple.

Kenneth's eyes roved over Lavinia's delectable body as he watched her talking with Vernon. While he imagined just what he could do with her body, to bring out her best, Jenny grabbed his arm.

"Kenneth, love, I thought we could dine at the Astor this evening." She smoothed her green satin dress over her expansive hips.

His fiancé's looks certainly couldn't compare with Lavinia's, not now anyway. But at one time Jenny had been a stunning actress, and she was still quite pretty, with thick hair of reddish gold and wide sea green eyes. Yet motherhood had transformed her into a rather frumpish woman whose fashionable clothes tried to, but failed, to conceal a once wispy figure now bordering on fat.

Despite Kenneth's indiscretions, Jenny loved him unconditionally, and was as faithful as a lap dog.

"We might as well enjoy our last few days of freedom while me mum's here to watch the girls," Jenny smiled.

Their chubby daughters, Beatrice and Samantha, were three and five respectively. Jenny's mother, Auralia, had been visiting them in New York so she and Kenneth could enjoy some time without the brats constantly under Jenny's feet. Auralia would be leaving to go home to London in the next few days. Because of Kenneth's womanizing, Jenny had made it a point not to hire a nanny, and their housekeeper didn't live with them.

"Jenny," Kenneth said, distracted, gazing once more at Lavinia, who still listened intently to Vernon, "that sounds fine. Why don't you go home and change, then meet me there?"

"I can wait for you to change from your costume. We can leave together."

"Jenny—I might be a little while. As a matter of fact, before you go to the Astor, stop at Tiffany's. Buy yourself a little bauble."

Jenny sighed, crestfallen.

"That's supposed to make you happy," Kenneth said, lightly pinching her cheek. "Perhaps a ruby to match your lips." He bent to kiss her full pouting lips, something he still enjoyed about her.

"Very well, then," Jenny relented after his brief tokens of affection. "But don't keep me waiting too long."

Kenneth gave her a quick peck on the cheek, then hurried her away.

When Jenny was completely out of sight, he searched for Lavinia. However, now the stage was completely empty and Lavinia was nowhere to be seen.

Kenneth rushed to his dressing room. After shedding his tunic and war gear, he changed into his day clothes, a black suit and vest. Grabbing his bowler hat, he walked down the hall to Lavinia's dressing room.

Lavinia couldn't possibly love Vernon, Kenneth thought. The old bloke was close to sixty and probably only lasted long enough to please himself.

Lavinia, at twenty-one, was young and vibrant. However, she'd never been with a young virile male and experienced the act as it was supposed to be.

Putting his ear to Lavinia's dressing room door, he only heard female voices, Lavinia's, and her maid, Amy's.

Kenneth smiled at the memory of Amy. She'd been a sweet little piece. Quiet and not much to look at, she'd been a tigress in the bedroom.

Kenneth walked to the wings in search of Vernon, but only encountered a few cast and crew members on their way out.

Vernon was nowhere to be found. Good, Kenneth said to himself, as he walked back to Lavinia's door.

She was a lusty, sensual woman; she just didn't know it yet. Her passion hadn't been unleashed because she'd lacked an adequate teacher.

Onstage she'd project warmth in her voice and actions, but any physicality between them, in Kenneth's opinion, seemed forced, stiff and tense. The audience didn't see that or sense it, but he could, and he could make her a better performer, if given the opportunity to ignite the fire within her.

He knocked at her dressing room. "Lavinia, before our first night," he said through the closed door, "I'd like to discuss a way to bring greater depth to our performances."

"Wait just a moment," Lavinia replied. Seconds later, she invited him in as Amy finished buttoning the back of her turquoise dress.

Amy flashed Kenneth a flirtatious smile, which he ignored. No use leading on the poor girl. He had no desire to revive their short lived affair. There were greener pastures to explore.

Amy rolled her eyes, then let out an irreverent snort as she adjusted the fabric over Lavinia's bustle.

Lavinia checked her reflection as she asked Kenneth to have a seat on a satin chair near her dressing table. When she turned from the mirror, Amy brought over a large hat, decorated with white stuffed birds and ostrich plumes.

"So, Kenneth," Lavinia said, "just what do you suggest we do to improve our performances?"

"Lavinia," he glanced at Amy, who was about to assist her with the hat. Amy shot him a nasty glare. "I'd like to speak to you alone, if I may," Kenneth said.

Lavinia hesitated. "Of course." She took the hat from her maid. "Amy, if you wouldn't mind." She motioned her to the door and Amy trudged out, turning her nose up at Kenneth as she passed him, then loudly shut the door behind her.

"I take it Amy doesn't like you," Lavinia said, bending to place the hat on a matching chair opposite Kenneth.

"I'm not here to discuss Amy."

"All right." Lavinia stood tall, placing her hands on her hips. "Tell me what you had in mind."

Before Kenneth began, he took a deep breath. In all his years of philandering, he'd never had the gall to approach a boss's wife.

But if he and Lavinia were to continue to perform as a romantic couple, they needed to do something to enhance the magic of their partnership. "Where's Vernon," he asked cautiously.

"He went home. He was quite exhausted after today's rehearsal."

Kenneth rose from his chair. After tossing his bowler hat to the vacant seat, he swaggered toward Lavinia. "I haven't quite known how to bring this up. Audiences love us together, but our performances lack. We could make them better if ..."

Lavinia raised a brow as she waited for him to finish. "If what?"

He sidled close to her. "If you would unsheathe my dagger," he said slowly.

Confused, Lavinia said, "There's that line again. Just what do you mean by it?"

"I mean—I'd like to slip my key into your lock."

"But I've already let you in here—you don't need a key!"

"I take it you've never heard of a double entendre."

Lavinia blinked her eyes in question. "A double *what*?"

Kenneth laughed. She so wanted to be worldly, yet was still an innocent in many ways.

"What's so funny?" Lavinia asked sharply.

"I won't beat about the bush any longer, Lavinia. I believe that your performance, as well as mine, would vastly improve if—we made love."

Lavinia's eyes widened. Raising her chin she said, "Kenneth! I'm a married woman!"

"Yes, Lavinia, I know. But you're married to an old man—an old man that you don't love."

She backed away from him slightly. "My marriage is none of your business!"

"Your marriage lacks passion, and no, that's none of my business. But improving my performance—and yours, *is* my business. Lavinia, this is the perfect way." He moved nearer to her, all the while gesturing dramatically with his hands. "We can only show but so much of our '*love*' on stage. But if you experience being with me in a way that can't be displayed to the audience, the feeling and depth of emotion we have behind closed doors, can transcend to the stage. Trust me."

This was a ploy he'd used many times with his leading ladies, so many times that he'd actually come to believe it. And it usually worked.

"Has Vernon ever made you scream—in ecstasy?"

Lavinia's face contorted in shock, but then a questioning gaze flickered across it. "How— how dare you ask me such—a—a question! Why, my marriage is a sacred union."

"I've never known you to be so self-righteous," Kenneth smiled. "And you're a much better actress than you're pretending to be now. You're not offended by what I've said, but you are curious, and you never did answer me. Has Vernon ever kissed you—like this?"

Kenneth grabbed Lavinia around the waist, pulling her close. He held her tightly, kissing her with searing passion and pressing his body firmly against hers.

Half-heartedly, she tried to push him away. "Kenneth, please—" Lavinia gasped.

"With pleasure," he replied. Kenneth knew she wanted more, and he kissed her again before she could finish her feigned protest. Finally, her body melted into his, and Kenneth felt victorious as she returned his embrace, *and* his kiss.

When he pulled his lips from hers, Lavinia was breathless.

Disentangling herself from his arms, she said, "That's—that's not what I meant."

"But it is what you wanted," Kenneth said slyly. "I know Vernon's never kissed you like that. And he's never touched you in places that could make you—wildly euphoric, has he?"

Lavinia was silent for a moment. "You think you could?"

Apparently, she'd decided not to fake insult any longer. Kenneth smiled. "Most definitely. Lavinia, I know how to play a woman like a fine instrument. And you, my darling, are no less than a Stradivarius.

"Lavinia, we're magic together now." He observed her mulling things over, then opened his arms in an exaggerated theatrical gesture. "Just think what we'd be if—"

Eyeing him cynically, she crossed her arms. "I'm no fool, Kenneth. You just want to sleep with me, that's all."

Lavinia turned away from him and looked in the mirror. After checking her hair, she picked up the large feathered hat.

"I won't deny that. I'm *dying* to sleep with you. But that's not all." He approached Lavinia from behind, took the hat from her hands and threw it back to the chair. Gently placing one arm around her waist, he said, "I swear, Lavinia, our performances would be even more — explosive," he moved her hair with his other hand and kissed her neck, "volcanic, in fact — if we — made love."

When she leaned against him, Kenneth moved his hands to her breasts. "I have a suite at the Imperial Hotel — where we can — rehearse. Meet me there tomorrow at two."

He pulled a brass key from his pocket. After placing it in her hand, he said, "Dress plainly, so no one will recognize you, and use the side entrance. We wouldn't want to stir up a scandal." He continued to kiss her neck and worked his way toward her ear.

Slowly, Lavinia turned to gaze at him. "I'll take what you've said under advisement."

Kenneth looked at her aghast. "You sound like we've been discussing a business proposal!"

"Haven't we?" Lavinia said. "If I do agree to what you're proposing, *I* have everything to lose — and so do you — if Vernon ever finds out."

"But darling, I won't tell a soul. Discretion is my middle name." Kenneth flashed a sneaky smile. "If Vernon, or anyone else, ever suspects something, just deny it. That's how the game is played," he winked. "You're a great actress, you can be convincing."

Lavinia shook her head, grinning wickedly. "Why on earth does poor, little Jenny put up with you?"

"Forget about 'poor, little Jenny.' Don't give her a second thought, I never do." He laughed.

"Well," Lavinia hesitated, "I may, or I may not show up tomorrow. This is a rather weighty decision for me—so you'll just have to wait and see."

Flabbergasted, Kenneth exclaimed, "But—but if you don't come, you'll never know what you've been missing! And you won't be with just any bloke, you'll be with *me—Kenneth Tyler!*"

Lavinia yawned. "If you've said all you have to say, Kenneth, you may leave now."

14901296R00192

Made in the USA
San Bernardino, CA
07 September 2014